# BETRAYALS

## A **STRANGE ANGELS** NOVEL

# LILI ST. CROW

**razOr bill**

An Imprint of Penguin Group (USA) Inc.

Betrayals, A Strange Angels Novel

RAZORBILL

Published by the Penguin Group
Penguin Young Readers Group
345 Hudson Street, New York, New York 10014, U.S.A.
Penguin Group (USA) Inc., 375 Hudson Street, New York, New York 10014, U.S.A.
Penguin Group (Canada), 90 Eglinton Avenue East, Suite 700, Toronto, Ontario, Canada M4P 2Y3 (a division of Pearson Penguin Canada Inc.)
Penguin Books Ltd, 80 Strand, London WC2R 0RL, England
Penguin Ireland, 25 St Stephen's Green, Dublin 2, Ireland (a division of Penguin Books Ltd)
Penguin Group (Australia), 250 Camberwell Road, Camberwell, Victoria 3124, Australia (a division of Pearson Australia Group Pty Ltd)
Penguin Books India Pvt Ltd, 11 Community Centre, Panchsheel Park, New Delhi – 110 017, India
Penguin Group (NZ), 67 Apollo Drive, Rosedale, North Shore 0632, New Zealand
(a division of Pearson New Zealand Ltd.)

Penguin Books (South Africa) (Pty) Ltd, 24 Sturdee Avenue, Rosebank, Johannesburg 2196, South Africa

Penguin Books Ltd, Registered Offices: 80 Strand, London WC2R 0RL, England

10 9 8 7 6 5 4 3 2 1

Library of Congress Cataloging-in-Publication Data

St. Crow, Lili.
  Betrayals : a Strange angels novel / Lili St. Crow.
      p. cm. – (Strange angels)
  Summary: For her own protection, sixteen-year-old Dru is taken to a secret training facility that feels more like a prison, but she faces great danger there and learns that a traitor who was involved in her mother's death now wants Dru dead.
  ISBN 978-1-59514-252-8
  [1. Supernatural–Fiction. 2. Schools–Fiction. 3. Psychic ability–Fiction. 4. Werewolves–Fiction. 5. Vampires–Fiction. 6. Orphans–Fiction.]  I. Title.
  PZ7.S77432Bet 2009
  [Fic]–dc22
                                    2009021856

Printed in the United States of America

*For Gates. Keep holding the line.*

## Acknowledgments

*Without Miriam, this book would not be. Without Jessica, this book would not be any good. Without you, dear Reader, this book would be lost. Thank you all.*

*Love is whatever you can still betray.*

—John le Carré

Windshield wipers struggled *back and forth, clumped with snow. The mingled breath of three teenagers fought with the defroster. Thank God the truck was still running, even after they'd driven it through a wall.*

*"So you're sending us somewhere you know there's a traitor." Graves's chin dipped even further, resting harder on the top of my head.*

*I thought about all this, felt nothing but a faint, weary surprise.*

*Christophe sighed, "I've got friends at the Schola—they'll watch over her just as I would. She'll be perfectly safe. And while she's there, she can help me find whoever's feeding information to Sergej. She's been drafted."*

*Graves tensed. "What if she doesn't want to?"*

*"Then you won't last a week out there on your own. If Ash doesn't find you, someone else will. The secret's out. If Sergej knows, other suckers know there's another* svetocha. *They'll hunt her down and rip her heart out." The windshield wipers flicked on. "Dru? Do you hear*

*me? I'm sending you somewhere safe, and I'll be in touch."*

"I think she hears you." Graves sighed. "What about her truck? And all her stuff?"

"I'll make sure they get to the Schola too. The important thing is to get her out of here before the sun goes down and Sergej can rise renewed. He's not dead, just driven into a dark hole and very angry."

"How are we going to—"

"Shut up." He didn't say it harshly or unkindly, but Graves did shut up. "Dru? You're listening."

Oh God, leave me alone. But I raised my head, looked at the dash. There really was no option. Hair fell in my face, the curls slicked down with damp, behaving for once. "Yeah." It sounded like I had something caught in my throat. The word was just a husk of itself. "I heard."

"You were lucky. You ever put yourself in danger like that again and I'll make you regret it. Clear?"

He sounded just like Dad. The familiarity was like a spike in my chest. "Clear," I managed around it. My entire body ached, even my hair. I was wet and cold, and the memory of the sucker's dead eyes and oddly wrong, melodious voice burrowed into my brain. It wouldn't let go.

That thing killed my father. Turned him into a zombie. And Mom . . . "My mother." The same husky, flat tone. Shock. Maybe I was in shock. I heard a lot about shock from Dad.

Silence crackled, but then Christophe took pity on me. Maybe. Or maybe he figured I had a right to know, and that I'd listen to him now.

When he spoke, his voice was harsh, whether with pain or with the cold I couldn't guess. "She was svetocha. Decided to give it all up, stop hunting, married a nice jarhead from the sticks and had a kid. But the nosferatu don't forget, and they don't stop playing the game because we pick up our marbles and go home. She got rusty and she got caught *away from sanctuary, drawing a* nosferat *away from her home and her baby." Christophe put the truck in gear. The windshield was clearing rapidly. "I'm . . . sorry."*

*"What else do you know?" I pulled away from Graves, his arm falling back down to his side. He slumped, looking acutely uncomfortable, a raccoon mask of bruising beginning to puff up around his eyes. His nose was definitely broken.*

*"Go to the Schola and find out. They'll train you, show you how to do things you've only dreamed of. God knows you're so close to blooming. . . ." Christophe stared out the windshield, his profile as clean and severe as ever. His eyes were bright enough to glow even through the gray daylight. Drying blood coated his face, a trickle of fresh red sliding from a cut along his hairline. He was absolutely soaked in the stuff, but it didn't seem to matter to him. "And when you hear from me, I'll set you a challenge worthy of your talents. Like finding out who almost got you killed here."*

*The truck was still running like a dream. Good old American steel. Dad's billfold sat in my jacket pocket, a heavy, accusing lump.*

*Christophe measured off a space on the wheel between two fingertips, looked intently at it. "So what about it, Dru? Be a good girl and go back to school?"*

*Why was he even asking? Like I had anywhere else to go. But there was another question. "What about Graves?"*

*The kid in question glanced at me. I couldn't tell if he was grateful or not. But I meant it. I wasn't going anywhere without him.*

*He really was all I had. That and a locket, and Dad's billfold, and a truck full of stuff.*

*A shadow crossed Christophe's face. The pause was just long enough for me to figure out what he thought of me even asking that question, and that he was weighing my likelihood to be difficult. Or just letting me know I didn't have anywhere else to go.* "He can go with you. There are wulfen there, one or two other loup-garou. He'll be an aristocrat. They'll teach him too."

That's all right then. *I nodded. My neck ached with the movement.* "Then I'll go."

"Good." *Christophe took his foot off the brake.* "And for the record, next time I ask for the keys, hand them over."

*I didn't think that merited a response. Graves scooched a little closer to me, and I didn't even think about it. I put my arms around him and hugged. I didn't care if it hurt my arm and my ribs and my neck and pretty much every other part of me, my heart most of all.*

*When you're wrecked, that's the only thing to do, right? Hold on to whatever you can.*

*Hold on hard.*

\*\*\*

Ten hours later the black van pulled around in a neat half-circle. "End of the line," the dark-haired boy said. "Let's go."

Darkness crouched around the huge building. I had a confused impression of cold, high-piled gray stone. Towers and two wings going off to the sides, the whole thing raked back like a Gothic spaceship. Two big smooth concrete lions on pedestals faced out from the long circular driveway, glaring down the thin ribbon of blacktop that had peeled off the county highway and brought us here. Weird ropy ivy crawled over the walls, like long bony fingers. Morning fog was a thick gray blanket, and the trees dripped silently on all sides, pushing against the building's frigid personal space.

Graves held my hand, still, so hard my fingers had long ago gone numb. The driver and the dark-haired boy in the passenger seat hopped

4

out neat as you please, taking the shotgun and the AK-47 with them.

"You okay?" Graves asked for the hundredth time.

I coughed a little, cleared my throat. The motion of the van had almost lulled me to sleep, especially since it was warm and I was exhausted. My back ran with pain and I'd stiffened up, moving like a creaky old lady when I moved at all. Plus I had to pee something fierce.

Horror movies never tell you that—about how most of the time when you're faced with the unspeakable, the biggest thing you take away from the experience is the need to find some indoor plumbing. My hair was greasy, frizzing out because it had air-dried after being drenched with snow. The wild mass of curls unraveled on my shoulders and I really, really wanted to wash it. Not to mention the rest of me. If I scrubbed hard enough, maybe I could rinse all the fear off. The thick, cloying fear that coated me like chocolate—only not so sweet or warm.

I clutched my bag with my free hand—everything I had in the world, since Christophe had the truck keys and my truck to go with it.

I was now completely at their mercy, and I wouldn't have minded so much if they would just give me a bed and let me *sleep* for a little while. Then they could do whatever they wanted. Up to and including killing me.

*Not really, Dru. Don't even joke about that.*

"One of them's going up to the door," Graves muttered. He'd done that all along, giving me a play-by-play as if I didn't have eyes. It was academic—I kept said eyes shut most of the time. I just didn't care. "The guy with the big gun is near the front of the van."

*Of course.* "Standing guard." My throat was scraped raw. I wanted a drink of water almost as much as I wanted to pee. It was ironic. "Just in case."

"How you doing?" Graves turned away from the tinted window

5

to peer anxiously at me, green eyes firing in the gloom, just like the silver skull and crossbones dangling from his left ear. His hair was a tangled mass of dyed black. It was predawn, gray and hushed, and now that the van had stopped you could tell it was cold outside.

A warm car never stays warm for long. Heat is like love. It drains away.

I searched for something witty to say, settled for bare honesty. "I want to pee."

Amazingly, he laughed. It was his usual bitter little bark, but heavier and deeper now. He sounded tired, and his proud, beaklike nose lifted a little. Under his half-Asian coloring, he looked so exhausted he was almost gray. There was very little left of the baby-faced Goth Boy he'd been.

Getting your life yanked out from under you will do that, I suppose.

Graves's laughter petered away. He sobered. "Yeah, me too. We haven't been left alone since they picked us up in that chopper, either. Do you think—"

Whatever he was going to ask me was lost as the kid with the AK-47 opened the van door. "It's clear." He gave me a smile that looked like it was trying to be reassuring. He was even sharply handsome, with a button nose and dark flyaway hair, an engaging smile, and light brown, almost yellowish eyes. But the gun and the way he glanced back over his shoulder, checking the space between the van and the front door of the big pile of stone, was something I'd seen a few times following Dad around while he hunted the things from the Real Word, the world of stuff that goes bump and crunch and yowl in the night.

Professionalism. It sat uncomfortably on his young face.

Every single person from the Order looked like a teenager—except my dad's friend August, who looked about twenty-five. I wasn't sure what to think of that, and just sat there staring at the rapidly strengthening foggy daylight outside the van for a moment.

"Miss Anderson?" He leaned forward a little, the mouth of the gun pointed carefully down and away. "It's okay. We're at a Schola; it's safe."

*Nowhere's safe. Not anymore.* But I moved a little, and Graves took that as a signal to slide across the seat, letting go of my hand, and hop down. He turned, awkwardly, as if he wanted to help me.

But the dark-haired kid shouldered Graves aside and offered *his* free hand. "Here. Really, everything's all right." Another one of those smiles, and his eyes glittered at me.

I made it down out of the van, ignoring his hand. As soon as my feet touched down, he slammed the door behind me. "Let's get you inside." He made little waving movements with his hands, like he was trying to herd chickens or something.

It was the crowning absurdity. Cold air pressed against my cheeks; I smelled ice and damp leaves and the particular rot of a forest in a cold winter. The fog pressed close, deadened every sound. I scrubbed at my face, surprised to find my cheeks were still wet. Had I been crying?

The steps were huge and granite, and the massive iron-bound oak door atop them opened slowly. Mr. AK-47 herded us up toward it, and my fingers fished around blindly until they hooked on Graves's and squeezed. Both of Goth Boy's eyes were puffed up with bruising, and the bridge of his nose was a little flattened, but the swelling had gone down remarkably quickly. He made the stairs easily. I had to stop on each one because my back felt like it was going to shred itself. My knees creaked. I glanced up at the sky—featureless iron. It didn't look like snow, and I was happy about that. I've had enough snow to last me a long time.

But it was *cold*, and it smelled like early morning. Like metal against the tongue, and like sodden, frozen plants. And the flat white heaviness of fog. My chin dropped toward my chest. The soft muffled wingbeats of an owl echoed inside my head.

Gran's owl, the warning of danger. I should have told Dad I'd seen it that week and a half ago. Maybe he would have stayed home, and he'd still be alive.

Jeez. Just over a week was all it took for my life to implode. It was some kind of record.

"Jesus," a boy said softly, up ahead of us. "It's really true."

I didn't even look up. We reached the top of the stairs, and Graves squeezed my hand before we were separated and I was whisked off by three boys who didn't seem as young as their unlined faces would have me believe. They were murmuring over my head, various cryptic things, and I paid no attention. They took me through halls, and I heard whispers as kids clustered in doorways. It was like running a gauntlet or something, and I pulled into myself, concentrating on one foot in front of the other.

There was a long flight of stairs at last, and then a room with blue carpet. "You look pretty tired," someone said. "Are you hungry? Thirsty? Anything we can—"

I saw an empty bed-shaped object and let out a sigh. "No thanks. No. I just want to sleep." *I just want to lay down and die.*

"All right." He was a faceless blur, I was so tired. I couldn't even ask where Graves was. "You just try to rest, then. The bathroom's through there, and—"

I didn't hear whatever he said after that. I made it to the bed and sank down in a cloud of softness. The coverlet was blue too, I figured out that much. I didn't even think about warding the walls. Gran and Dad would have been on me about that.

The thought was a pinch in a numb place. Gran and Dad. Both gone.

*I should get up and pee*, I thought, and then darkness swallowed me.

I dreamed of Gran's owl, moonlight edging its feathers as it winged through blackness. A fuzzy sense of danger enfolded me, but I was too tired to care.

And that was how I arrived at the Schola.

# CHAPTER 1

**A** **week later I** was already in trouble.

The thing with a school full of boys being taught to kill suckers is that sparring gets to be a group event. It's like a fight in a regular school, only here the teachers don't intervene—or at least, they hadn't in any of the other four fights I'd seen since I arrived. You get a mob of onlookers, all shouting, and it can turn into a melee easily enough. Things don't stop until someone's bleeding. Or worse. Being able to heal just makes the boys more likely to hurt themselves.

I couldn't heal like they could yet, because I hadn't "bloomed." So much for being special. Here I was just as fragile as a civilian. But when you've spent most of your spare time learning how to make the best of what you have against things that go bump in the night, you don't give up easy.

I came up from the floor with a punch, getting my feet under me, and Irving grabbed my wrist. He used my momentum to whip me past him, but I'd expected that, hooked my other fingers, and got a handful of his face. That's what Dad would have called "dirty fightin'," something he approved of in a girl.

Hey, there are no rules in a *fight*. Thinking there are "rules" can get you killed. Dad drilled it into my head over and over again— you fight to win, to survive. Not to look good or give the other guy a chance.

*Stop thinking about Dad, Dru.* I had other problems.

Irving had bet he could best me in under two minutes. We were at ninety seconds and counting, and I was winning.

A bet like that doesn't go unchallenged. Not when your former Marine dad's been teaching you how to kick ass for years. Not when there's a hot boiling bubble of acid right behind your breastbone all the time. Not when you're practically alone in a school full of teenage boys.

Not just any teenage boys, either. Boys who can turn into fur rugs with bad attitudes at the drop of a hat. *Djamphir* boys who are born with the eerie stuttering speed of suckers, blurring through the slow stupid daytime world like a cheesy special effect at the drop of a hat. Boy *djamphir* don't have to wait to "bloom," oh no. They're stronger and faster from the start, and they only get better once their voices break and they "hit the drift" in puberty. Some of them hit it later, in their mid-twenties. But even before they hit the drift they're more than a match for any human.

I twisted, my sneakers digging into the frayed mats, and kicked back. That caught him in the knee, and I heard bones popping and loud growling. I hit the dirt, the mats scraping against my elbow because I was only in a tank top and jeans.

I'm not stupid. When you hear the distinctive noise of werwulfen changing into the furry shape that makes them almost impossible to kill, that's the reasonable thing to do.

Except Irving wasn't wulf. He was *djamphir*, and he was already committed to his leap. So where was the sound coming from?

I rolled over just in time to see Irving hanging in the air over me, pale face alight, golden highlights slipping through his chestnut curls as the aspect took him. The world slowed down, moving through syrup just long enough for me to scramble, the clear heavy weight of physicality straining against every muscle in my body. The *snap!* like a rubber band popped off expert fingers rang through my head as time sped back up again and he rammed down into the mats a good three feet away from where I was now but exactly where I'd been. His knee hit too hard—without my face to cushion it—and he let out a short, sharp cry. The lines across his cheek from my fingernails flushed an angry red, and his hair stood up, writhing.

Now he wasn't just a teenage boy needing to save face in front of the crowd. Now he was *serious*. And we were at twenty seconds left.

*Good.*

I gained my feet in a rush and skipped back twice. The mass of onlookers exploded away, giving us enough room to move. Irving bounced up like he was full of helium, his curls moving just like in a shampoo commercial, and he threw himself across the intervening space with the weird blurring speed I wasn't even close to getting accustomed to.

The speed I couldn't use—yet.

So instinct took over. It wasn't precisely a bad instinct—brace yourself and punch the guy straight in the face. But Dad would have yelled at me for being stupid, since Irving was so ungodly fast, and straight-on force, like in karate, doesn't work so much for me. I'm built too thin and rangy. I don't even have moderately big breasticles. They just look like—well, never mind what they look like. At least they stay strapped down when I worm into a sports bra.

It doesn't quite suck being a girl, but sometimes it's close.

I *should* have grabbed Irving's arm, twisted, and slid him past me, using his own momentum to help him right into the stone wall across the room. Instead, I hit him. There was a crunch as my fist met his nose, and he collided with me like a freight train. We were heading for the wall, and the thought *this is going to hurt* flashed through me like electricity popping through a lightbulb filament.

And it would have, too, if something hadn't hit us both from the side, roaring. I got an elbow in the face and went tumbling, slapping the frayed, stained mats and wrenching my back a good one. I just lay there for a second, bells ringing inside my skull and the entire world seeming very far away.

It took a long time for me to blink, looking up at the arched, ribbed vault of the ceiling. This part of the complex had been a chapel, but now it was the armory and a sparring space unfolding with mats that had seen better days and the smell of healthy young boysweat. Underneath was the ghost of incense, and if it were daytime, shafts of weak sunlight might slip between the bars and pierce dusty dimness.

During the day, though, the Schola sleeps. Right now it was just past midnight, and I was in deep shit.

"Dru?" Someone was bending over, shaking me. I tried to push them off, but my hands wouldn't quite work right. A dreamy sort of panic slid through me then, and I heaved back into my body with another elastic *snap!*

I was doing a lot of that lately. The air was full of rumbling and muttering, and there was a lot of shouting going on.

*Oh God. This might've been a bad idea.* I grabbed at a waiting pair of hands and hauled myself up. My head was ringing and my back hurt something awful.

"What the bloody blue *hell* is going on here?" The words sliced through the hubbub, except for that deep thrumming growl. I shook my head, a sliver of warm wetness threading down from my nose, and pushed between two *djamphir* boys—Clarence, his straight black bowl-cut damp with sweat and excitement, and Tor, his aspect on and thick streaks of buttery yellow sliding through his hair. Both of them were taller than me, but I shouldered them aside and found myself in the front row.

Graves had Irving down, his long, tanned-looking fingers closed on the *djamphir*'s throat. His eyes were chips of green flame, and the growl was so thick it blurred the air around him, the sound of a very pissed-off skinchanger. He probably couldn't talk, either—his jaw was subtly modified, accommodating fiercer, longer teeth. The crackle of bone had been *him*. He wouldn't get furry—he was *loup-garou*, not wulfen, only half-imprinted with the thing that made them able to shift—but he was pretty motivated to do some serious harm, and angry enough not to care about hurting someone.

It had happened three or four times by now. Twice back in the Dakotas, each time when we were in danger—or when he *thought* we were in danger, since Christophe had turned out to be on our side after all. And on the first evening I'd woken up at the Schola, I'd almost walked right into a shoving match between him and a *djamphir* in the cafeteria. From what I heard, the *djamphir* had asked him something about me, and Graves had turned on him. The result was shove, shove, growl, shove some more, yell, and me wading in to make them cut it out.

I didn't think I'd gotten the whole story, but Graves wouldn't talk about it. And now there was this.

"What the—" Dylan said again, elbowing his way through the throng.

I tuned him out and stepped forward. My right leg felt funny, and something dripped onto my upper lip. Three steps, four, my boots dragging a little against the mats. When I laid my hand on Graves's shoulder, the buzzing going through him felt like I was resting my hand on a juiced-up power transformer.

He actually snarled, his dyed-black hair curling, all but standing up and snapping with vitality. The sharp, strong bone structure of his face was subtly off-kilter now, nose less proud and cheekbones taking on the higher wolflike arc instead of the broadness of "human." Rich color flooded through his skin, making his perpetual tan deeper.

"Calm *down*," I managed. Only I sounded like Elmer Fudd, because I had a stuffed-up nose. My eyes were smarting and watering, too. "Jesus." It came out like *Jebus*, and I could have laughed. Except it wasn't funny.

"Everyone *shut up*." Dylan folded his arms, his leather jacket creaking. The noise went down. Here at the Schola, when a teacher talks, you *listen*. "And back up. Back up!"

Graves growled again, and Irving choked. He was turning an awfully deep shade of crimson. His fingers plucked weakly at Graves's hand, but with his arm twisted underneath him and an angry skinchanger on top of him, he couldn't get any leverage.

I hauled back on Graves's shoulder. A bolt of pain went down either side of my spine. "Come *on*, asshole. Calm down. This is getting ridiculous."

"Why didn't you wait for me?" Dylan addressed the air over my head. "I'm getting a little tired of—good God, girl, you're *bleeding*."

Graves let go of Irving and flowed to his feet, shaking me off. His lips were pulled back, teeth gleaming, his eyes awash with feral phosphorescence. I realized the wulfen had settled into a bloc behind him, and the tension running through them was palpable.

A few of them had gotten a little hairier, too. The tension made the wulf boys bulk up as well, shoulders straining at shirt seams. They don't take on werwulf form unless they really have to, but you can tell them from the *djamphir*. It's in the way they move—like they're shouldering fluidly through sunlit grass, instead of with the sharp hurtful grace of the half-*nosferat*.

The *djamphir* don't change, but the aspect ran through all of them—their hair moving and rippling with color changes, eyes glowing, and one or two of them showing little dimples of fangs touching their lower lips.

Boys. Jeez.

Dad had always taught me that wulfen and suckers didn't get along. I was beginning to think it was genetic. As far as I could figure, *djamphir* and wulfen were on the same side against the suckers. That was what the Order was about. But they sure as hell didn't seem to like each other much.

I pulled Graves back, and we only had a bit of a problem when I stepped in front of him and he tried to shove past me. I grabbed him by his used-to-be-bony shoulders and shook him. My fingers sank into muscle, and I didn't worry about hurting him. His head bobbled, but his gaze snapped down to mine and the snarl petered out.

I held his eyes for what seemed like a very long time. He blinked, and his shoulders relaxed a little. That's when I turned and found Dylan, arms crossed, standing over Irving with one winged black eyebrow raised and the rest of the *djamphir* utterly still behind them both. The *djamphir*'s eyes gleamed and their fangs were out.

Oh, the testosterone. You could have cut it with a cafeteria spoon.

"We were sparring. I got stupid." I took another two steps, my heels landing harder than they should have and pain jarring up through my entire spine. "You all right?" This was directed at Irving, who was coughing, a deep rasping sound. But he didn't look almost purple now.

He glared at me, and I felt sorry. It had just been a little friendly workout, nothing big. I should have just rolled my eyes and let his posturing pass.

But instead, I'd gone off on him. And I was supposed to be so much more mature than boys at this age.

"Sorry, Irving." My back seized up again, and I breathed out through my mouth. The muttering growl behind me receded a little, and I put my hand down to help him up. "I should have grabbed you and helped you into that wall instead of trying to punch you in the nose. Go figure." It was really hard to sound conciliatory with something dripping and dribbling off my top lip. I was hoping it wasn't snot. That would be gross.

I sniffed, and the rest of the nosebleed let loose in a pattering gush.

Irving froze, staring up at me. His pupils shrank. A spatter of bright-red blood hung in the air, then splashed —

— right on his clothes, starring the mat next to him too.

"Shit," Dylan said, and leapt on him. "*Get her out of here!*"

Hands grabbed me, hot against the bare skin of my upper arms. I was dragged backward, and the world threatened to turn over without me attached to it. The ringing inside my head got worse, the sound of owl wings brushing the inside of my skull in frantic bursts. The wulfen hauled me out, and I heard Irving screaming as Dylan held him down, the bloodhunger turning his voice into a harpy's shriek.

*Yeah. Just another night at the Schola. The fight doesn't stop until there's blood on the floor.*

But when the blood is mine, it can send the boy *djamphir* a little crazy. It's something about me being *svetocha*. Super-happy stuff in my blood even before I "bloom," something that reaches down and wakes up the crazy in anyone with a touch of *nosferat*.

After the blooming hit, I'd have my own superhuman strength and speed. And that super-happy stuff in my blood would make me toxic to suckers just like Raid is toxic to insects.

But now it just made me vulnerable. I smelled like a really nice snack.

Dylan had been drilling it into my head for the whole week now, on and on, that I couldn't spar with the *djamphir* students. They couldn't control the bloodhunger very well, I could get seriously hurt, yadda yadda.

Christophe had never told me about that.

There were a lot of things he hadn't told me.

The wulfen dragged me out into the hall, and the rushing noise inside my head got bigger. I think I probably passed out. At least, the world got really faraway and dim, and the only thing that mattered was hearing Graves. He could talk now that the rage had passed, and he was saying the same thing over and over again, a catch in his voice right before my name.

"It's okay, Dru. I promise it's okay."

He didn't sound like he believed it either.

# CHAPTER 2

**T**he ice pack stung, but holding it against the bridge of
my nose meant less swelling and bruising. I sighed, shifted
uncomfortably, and blinked away the hot welling of reflex
tears. Graves had thought to grab my jacket, too, so the goose bumps
on my arms were covered.

"It was my fault," I repeated stubbornly. "I should have pulled
Irving past me instead of trying to paste him on the nose."

"That's not the point." Dylan sighed. Some days he sighed more
than others, and some days it seems like he did nothing *but*. He had
a face that could have been on a Roman coin, and I'd heard his real
name was something unpronounceable and Goth. Not like black-
lipstick-and-angst, but actual barbarian.

Around here, you never knew. Even the teachers looked like
teenagers. The really old ones look about twenty sometimes. But
they're late drifters, and they never get to looking thirty. My dad's
friend August—the one I'd called to confirm Christophe's story—

must've been one of them. I wondered about it, but it didn't seem polite to ask.

Dylan pushed a hand back through his dark hair and settled more firmly in his chair. His desk was stacked with papers, and a large silver blob I stared at the first time I was in here until I realized it was a skull dipped in shiny metal. The skull had long canines and long pointed incisors, and I decided not to ask if it was a real sucker skull for the thousandth time.

Behind Dylan, shelves of dusty leather-bound books stood frowning down on me, cobwebs ghosting up near their tops. The place smelled like leather, dust, and the musky smell of teenage hormones, but it still felt like the principal's office.

I've been in principals' offices all over America. Before I figured out the best way to get by was to just keep my head down.

I've kind of been sucking at that lately.

Graves stood just behind me. Dylan didn't offer him a chair. I didn't like that, especially since Dylan had refused to talk *or* sit until I sat down. His office had windows, with the obligatory iron bars. I'd made some sort of joke when I first got here about whether the bars were to keep us in or the suckers out, and the dead silence and pained look on everyone's face had told me to shut up.

Outside the barred windows, the lawns were painted with moonlight. Trees stood guard, silvered with threads of fog, a white wall sending spectral fingers up to touch naked black branches.

The ice pack crackled as I held it to the bridge of my nose, then peeked out at Dylan.

"Look." He had that I'm-being-patient tone again. "Combat training for you is going to take a while, and it won't really get started until after you bloom. If you *must*, you should be practicing with the teachers, not the students. And Graves . . . he can't be interfering every time he thinks someone's insulted you, or whatever it is. It's not safe. For either of you."

Dylan was magnanimously leaving out the part where I drove Irving into the hunger by bleeding all over him. Nice.

I waited for Graves to say something, but he remained stubbornly silent even when I looked up at him. His eyes glowed from under a thatch of dyed-black hair, his coloring back to normal. A bruise ran up his cheekbone, turning a mottled purple as it swelled.

It would be gone by tomorrow. *Loup-garou* heal even quicker than wulfen. They get all the benefits of the change, like speed and strength, without the allergy to silver or the risk of losing control.

Go figure. I'd learned more about wulfen in one week here than from all the painstaking work Dad and I did with moldering leatherbound books and years of hunting weird stuff.

Graves's mouth was set, pulled down at the corners, and he looked mulishly defiant. Only his earring sparkled a bit, peeking out from all that hair. He stood behind my chair and glared at Dylan.

No help from that quarter. It was all on me.

"It was *my* fault," I finally repeated. "None of the teachers have time to spar with me. They treat me like I'm glass, and the classes you have me in are remedial shit I could get in any normal high school. I'm not going to get any better if they keep putting me through kindergarten work."

"You're *svetocha*, Dru. You're precious. You have no idea what you're worth—dead for the *nosferat*, or alive to us." Dylan rested his elbows on his desk. Paper crackled. "Should I say it again? You haven't bloomed yet. Once you do, you'll be able to handle harder sparring, but until then—"

"Until then I'm just supposed to sit around and look pretty? No thanks." I could feel my chin jutting forward, a sure sign that I was Being

Difficult. "I want to *help*. I was out hunting with my dad when most of these kids were probably taking basic how-to-ID-a-sucker classes. Keeping me in kindergarten isn't going to *work*." Why couldn't he get that through his head? I wasn't some nine-to-fiver, some Kmart shopper.

I was a hunter too. I'd been Dad's helper, hadn't I?

"Oh Lord. Not this argument again." Dylan sighed. His eyes were bloodshot and dark-circled with fatigue. He always looked tired and stressed out. It didn't make him ugly, though. "You have bad habits from your time as an amateur, Dru. It's time for you to unlearn them from the bottom up, and that means low-level classes just like everyone else. That's what the control directive said. My hands are tied." He gave me an odd look, his dark eyes unreadable, then continued. "Irving will heal completely in less than twelve hours, your *loup-garou* friend there in under eighteen. You're stuck with longer healing time and less speed, strength, and stamina. You're not even ready for a practice run, let alone some of the junior cleaning expeditions. Not to mention the fact that any *nosferat* who gets wind of your existence will try to drain you to fuel their own hunger, or take you to—" He stopped dead, swallowed hard.

"Sergej." I said the name. It burned my tongue, made the air tighten. Here they didn't talk about it. Naming a sucker is bad luck, and who knows if they can hear? Even hunters like Dad wouldn't say a sucker's name out loud. They'll use initials, or code words.

But I'd said it before.

Dylan didn't flinch. He did, however, sigh. Again. "Dru. You have not bloomed. You can't hold a candle to even the prefects or the senior students, and there's nobody with enough control if something—God forbid—happens and you start *really* bleeding. If—" He caught himself just in time.

"If Christophe was here, things would be different." I made the words a singsong. "Come on, Dylan. I'm not stupid. Christophe isn't here, and nobody else is going to be allowed to train me, even though he's disappeared and nobody will talk about him. Even though he saved my life. What's the deal?"

"It's very complex." He looked at the silver-dipped skull on his desk, and his jaw set. Every boy at the Schola had good skin, bright eyes, sparkling teeth. It was like being trapped in a goddamn sitcom. You could only tell the teachers from the students by seeing them actually teaching. Or by the way certain older ones had of stopping and tilting their heads, becoming absolutely motionless.

They didn't even seem to breathe when they did that, and it was usually a sign of Restriction. Which meant being sent to my room while everyone else manned battle stations. Twice in the past week, and I heard there were regular Restriction drills, too. Just like fire drills out in the stupid daylight world.

Yeah. My favorite thing ever, being stuffed in a room while someone else goes out and fights. The ice crackled again as I shifted my weight. Somehow I'd bruised one of my ass cheeks, it felt like. "Well, I'm a smart girl. Try me."

"It's not a question of your brains, Dru. It's a question of what is safe for you, since Christophe feels there's a mole in the Order. You're the only *svetocha* we've been able to save for a good thirty years—you're rare, and any other *svetocha* we manage to locate are killed before we can bring them in. We want to make sure you don't come to any harm, and part of that is making sure you're properly trained from the beginning. Though why they've sent you out here and given us such a confusing directive . . ." Maddeningly, he stopped again.

A conversation with Dylan is like that. He stops in the middle of sentences, refuses to go any further, just stares down at his desk with a mournful look. You could almost feel sorry for him.

I dropped the ice pack into my lap. A thin trickle of wetness kissed the knee of my jeans, soaked in. "Why don't the teachers have any time to train me if I'm so goddamn important? Why are we waiting for Christophe when this Council of yours has such a problem with him? And why—"

"The Council doesn't have a problem with him. A *significant minority* of the Council does. It's not the same thing, and it's not anything you should be worrying about. You have enough to deal with." He eyed me. "That's going to swell more. You should go take some ibuprofen and a turn in the bath."

In other words, *la di da*, I was dismissed. "You're not answering my questions." I hauled myself upright, clapped the ice pack to my face again. "Thanks for nothing."

"You're welcome. At least I'm not putting your friend there in detention for interfering and making things worse." He probably regretted it as soon as he said it, because I wheeled around and caught him closing his mouth with a snap. But Graves finally did something—he grabbed my shoulder and hauled me out of Dylan's office suite, past the twin suits of rusting, cobwebbed armor glowering at the door, and into the quiet hall.

"Let it go, Dru." Graves finally spoke up when we got to the end of the hall, and the stairway loomed in a cochlear spiral. "He's just threatening."

*Oh, so you finally open your mouth?* "Thanks a *million*. I know that."

"You're welcome. Come on, let's get you down to the bath." He let go of me and dug in the pockets of his long dark coat until he came up with a battered pack of Winstons.

*He* got to go off-campus to get smokes almost every day. He got to hang around with the wulfen without a tide of whispers following him everywhere. He got to spar and go to classes with them, and he

24

was starting to catch their jokes and make a few friends.

Me? I was the only girl in a boys' school, and I was kept inside like a goddamn hamster while everyone went out and had fun. Not that I wanted to go anywhere for a while, after being plucked out of snow and insanity and deposited here. The food was okay, they'd ordered jeans and T-shirts for me, and there was no shortage of drawing paper or anything else I might want. All I had to do was let Dylan or another "advisor" know and then, wham-bam, it would show up at my door the next morning. Or evening.

It was creepy. Especially since every time I wanted to take a walk, even outside on the quad of cracked pavement and dead winter garden squares, an "advisor" would show up as well. Usually Dylan, who didn't even pretend to be looking something over or just walking around.

No, he stared right at me with a mixture of worry and weirdness on his face. And that was thought-provoking too.

I just didn't know what thought it was supposed to provoke.

"How long have we been here?" I peered at him around the ice pack. "About a week, right?"

He got that prissy precision look on his face again, just like every time he corrected me. "Nine days, give or take. Yeah." He hunched his thin shoulders. Between that and the beak nose he looked birdlike. But there was something else in the set of his face now. Graves was looking more worried and adult than ever. "Seriously, you should get into the baths. That's puffing up and looking pretty bad."

The ice pack was leaking. Cold water slid a questing tendril down my wrist, soaking into my jacket sleeve — or Dad's jacket sleeve, since it was his spare army-surplus green one.

His billfold was under my bed. It wasn't the safest place in the world, but . . .

That thought hurt my chest too. The unsteady ball of fury and something else behind my ribs got a little bigger. I grabbed my temper with both hands, shoved it down. Let out a gusty sigh. "Fine, I'll go to the bath. Jesus. By the way, why did you jump on him?"

As if I didn't know. But maybe this time he'd say it.

But he didn't. He just looked away down the hall, hunched down even further, his long, clever fingers fiddling with the cigarette pack. "You were bleeding."

I opened my mouth to tell him that I hadn't been. But then I sniffed again, my skin crusted with copper-smelling dried blood, and thought that if a wulfen's nose was sensitive enough to tell right before a bloody nose started, a *loup-garou's* would be too. "Well, thanks." I tried to sound gracious, and the ice crackled again. More cold water from the leaking bag slid down my sleeve.

*Great.*

"No problem, Dru. We're going out for burgers tonight. Want me to bring you some?" He sounded hopeful.

My chest squeezed down on itself. "No." I hated to rain on his parade. "They'll be cold by the time you get back. I'll just grab something in the caf."

And all the way down the stairs, listening to his silence behind me as I stamped away, I kicked myself for not saying yes.

\* \* \*

On the boys' side of the sparring chapel there was a long room with a ton of individual stone-lipped tubs sunk in the floor. They had lot of partitions and community tubs too, and I'd heard there was always someone in there.

On the girls' side, the long room was just as big. There were four tubs large enough to drown a couple girls apiece in. Six bathroom stalls. Granite flooring, all kept pretty spic and span. Except for the grotty corners that meant it had been damp in here for a long time. Even chlorine won't work that funk out.

Still, it was warm and steamy, and the tubs were always bubbling. But there was never anyone in here but me.

I lowered myself into the tub on the farthest side from the door. My clothes lay tangled a few steps from the rim. I'd hurled the ice pack halfheartedly at the shiny new garbage bin set by the sinks, and it hung over the edge, melting water dribbling onto the floor.

I couldn't even care.

The cloudy not-really-water bubbled. It smells like minerals, a flat palate-coating tang, and it doesn't feel like regular water. It's too jelly-thick. For a few seconds it's so hot it stings. Then it coats the skin, and the bubbles turn sheer instead of translucent. Time spent in the tubs speeds the healing process up like crazy. Which is a good thing, because the combat training here is full-contact.

If you're a boy.

I'd felt kind of weird about walking around in the locker room by myself. It was like having a whole suite to myself while the boys slept in dorms. And none of them had empty bookshelves, or a CD player of their own, or a personal advisor watching over their every sneeze. Or a computer all to themselves, with Internet shopping sites already bookmarked and a credit card registered to "Sunrise LLC" lying in a neat paper sleeve next to it on a rosewood desk, plus an info sheet telling me where to get stuff delivered to—PO box and mail stop.

Creepy. Dad never used credit cards. Not his own, anyway. Liquid resources for hunting were best. But these guys were the Order. They were big—it took money to run a place like this.

Still, it didn't seem as big as Christophe had made it sound. Which was something else to think about. And I never went to any useful website, like a GPS ping to find out exactly where I was or county records to find out who owned this chunk of land—not to mention going hunting to find out if there were any news reports about my disappearance or Graves's. That kind of information would have been useful, but there was no point in leaving tracks on a machine I knew wasn't private.

So, no shopping and nothing useful about the computer. It might as well have been a mute hunk of plastic.

A class schedule—Aspect Mastery, History, Algebra, Civics— had been tacked to my door two days after I'd gotten here, but after the first day of stupid boring remedial crap I'd wadded it up in a ball and started bugging Dylan to give me something challenging. Even the Aspect Mastery class was nothing special, just a social hour for a group of five boy *djamphir* who spent the time telling nasty jokes and watching me in their peripheral vision. History was run by some blond teacher who stared at me very hard between sentences, as if he was willing me to disappear.

I hadn't stayed in any classroom for very long. Hanging out near the armory seemed like a better deal.

Graves was always on me about it. *You shouldn't skip, Dru. It's important.*

Yeah. Like I needed a civics class, for God's sake. Like anyone cared what I did as long as I stayed inside. Like *I* cared, now that my whole world was upside down.

Now that Dad was gone.

*Don't think about that.*

The stone was slick and gritty at the same time. I found a bench and coughed, cupped some of the heavy not-really-water in my palms and smoothed it over my face. It crackled, soothing heat working its way past the ache of a pair of developing black eyes, and I let out a sound that was half-sigh, half -sob. Echoes fell flat against every clean, hard surface. The mirrors were fogged, as usual, but sound bounced off them nevertheless.

I wondered, like I did every time I sat here, if my mother had ever chosen this tub. If she'd ever sat here and heard her own voice bouncing off the stone and glass and metal. If she'd ever felt lonely.

She'd been a part of the Order, or so Christophe and Dylan had told me. But nobody would really talk about her, as if she were an embarrassment. And I didn't know if she'd ever even been here; this complex was big enough but still tiny in the scheme of things.

Small school, about four hundred students. It wasn't the kind of place that could scramble helicopters on short notice. But I could have been confused, since Christophe hadn't exactly been giving out information left and right.

I was just avoiding thinking about it for as long as I could. It wasn't working.

My eyes flew open, not-water cracking and falling away in little shards of white. Wet hair hung in strings, the curls struggling to spring up. I touched the smooth curve of metal at my throat and winced as if I'd poked at a bruise.

The locket lay just below the notch between my collarbones. Heavy silver, as long as my thumb, the heart and cross etched on the front and spidery, foreign-looking symbols on the back, their edges resting against my skin. I'd gotten so used to seeing the silver gleam on Dad. He never went anywhere without it.

Now whenever I caught sight of it in the mirror or brushed it with my hand, a shock would go through me. Like I'd stuck my finger in a light socket. It was just *wrong* to be wearing it.

The next hurtful thought arrived right on schedule. I couldn't put it off any longer.

Dad.

*He walked down the hall, and the buzzing got so bad it shook everything out of me, the dream running like colored ink on wet paper, and as it receded I struggled to say something, anything, to warn him.*

*He didn't even look up. He just kept walking toward that door, and the dream closed down like a camera lens, darkness eating through its edges.*

*I was still trying to scream when Dad reached out his free hand, like a man in a dream, and turned the knob. And the darkness behind it laughed and laughed and laughed. . . .*

I shut my eyes again. Loosened my legs and slid under the unwater's surface. It closed over me like a dream, like a balm, and the heat worked in toward my bones. Only there was a coldness inside me, too deep for it to reach. A freeze that wasn't physical.

*He's dead, Dru. You know who did it. You know why.*

Or did I? I knew Dad had been expecting to come back. He *had* to have been—there was no way he would leave me in a house all alone for good. He'd always come back for me, sooner or later.

Well, he *had* come back. Just not alive. I'd shot a zombie in my living room, and it had been my father.

Christ. Of all the things that will fuck a kid up, that has got to have a category all its own.

I knew who had killed him and turned him into a zombie. The same person Christophe and Dylan and everyone else said killed my mother.

*Sergej.* The *nosferat* who looked like yet another teenager, with oily black curls and eyes that could swallow you whole. The same sucker who had tried to kill me. The reason why I was stuck inside the complex that was the Schola, barely even going outside to walk in the barren leafless winter gardens. I *could* go outside, but not without someone showing up to stare at me.

Standing guard. Because Sergej—or another *nosferat* like him—might come back. He was a big wheel among the suckers, the closest thing to a king that they had, and he knew I was alive.

I shuddered all over. My lungs burned. The not-water fizzed around me, heat burrowing in through my muscles, soothing and healing. My face gave one last heave of red pain and subsided. The shuddering got worse as I floated, and for a moment I thought of opening my mouth and letting the stuff in the tubs rush in, coating everything down to the back of my tongue and—

I surfaced in a rushing splash. The stuff dribbled away from my hair, slicked my face, crackled as it hit open air, and instantly formed a weird, wax-white coating over every inch of my exposed skin. Rinsing it out of my hair would take ten minutes in the shower.

I blinked away the clinging on my eyelashes and inhaled, mouth gaping open to take in a deep wallop of steamy air.

White light hit my eyes, scoured through the mishmash inside my head. My breathing deepened, evened out, with a hitching at the end of each exhale.

Underneath the weird white paraffinlike coating of whatever was in the baths, the tears were hot and oily. They slicked my cheeks, but there was nobody around to see. Or to hear.

I settled back onto the stone seat, drew my knees up so I could hug them, and sobbed. Then I went up to my stupid room and cried some more, until dawn came up through a pall of cloud and I finally fell into a thin, troubled sleep.

# CHAPTER 3

The cafeteria was a long, narrow space, every railing and molding made of dark wood. The walls were stone and half-paneled with heavy, age-varnished oak, but the floor was garish blue linoleum. Both were chipped and worn from hard use. The tables and the squeaking plastic chairs could have been in any high school in America.

I sat alone near the exit to the halls leading to the west class wing instead of the other branch going to the infirmary and library. The trays were red plastic, bunged-up and warped. The plates were white industrial china, the silverware stamped steel.

I missed my kitchen. I missed my dishes, even the mismatched ones, and Mom's black-and-white cow-shaped cookie jar. I missed my mattress, my clothes, and my CDs, and all Dad's weapons. I'd spent all morning—evening, whatever—hanging out in front of the armory, making excuses to stand in front of the counter and breathe in the smell of metal and gun oil. I missed the boxes and my truck and everything.

I even missed cooking, and god*damn*, I never thought that would happen. The food here wasn't bad, but it was job-lot industrial, and I could never see anyone in the kitchen. Just indistinct shapes through a cloud bank, like the fog that rose out of the forest every night. It said something about my life lately, that a screen of shifting steam that dispensed food was only moderately weird to me.

The food was set out on steam tables right in front of the weird wall of vapor. Pasta and salads and desserts. Burgers and pizza and fries for the younger ones, or the ones who liked to eat like real teenagers. Raw and rare meat for the wulfen, including livers and other stuff I didn't look too closely at. There were also boxes and mini bottles of wine, but I stayed away from those.

Today it was bow-tie pasta in a cream sauce, with prosciutto and peas. Salad with fresh tomatoes and your choice of dressing. Garlic bread that wasn't half-bad. Only it just sat there on the plate, congealing. There was a carton of chocolate milk, and an energy drink in a blue can. The blue of the can against the red of the tray, the white of the plate, the green specks of peas—if I had my colored pencils, I'd draw the whole shebang and call it *Still Life with MSG*.

I ached to draw something, anything, but as soon as I settled down with a pad of paper the urge left me. It was the first time in my life I hadn't been sketching furiously. My dreams were Technicolor weird, but they didn't push me to scribble. I just felt itchy, like I was waiting for something to happen.

It was loud. The walls reflected a hundred conversations going on, and the occasional hijinks. A bunch of teenage boys in a lunchroom is a recipe for trouble most of the time. The wulfen had their tables, the *djamphir* theirs—usually in prime spots, like right off the end of the line or near the exit to the infirmary. Even here there were cliques.

Nobody sat at my table. A few of them tried, but I wasn't really interested in talking and they drifted away. It was like being the new girl all over again every damn day. Irving had tried to say something to me earlier, but I'd just put my head down and walked off. I still felt bad over making him lose his shit in front of everyone. It was embarrassing. What on earth could I say?

I wasn't used to being such a failure at everything. And Jesus, I wasn't looking to make new bosom buddies. Why bother? I mean, something was bound to come up. It always did.

I'd never been at any school longer than three months. Not since Gran died.

Dylan kept saying I was important, but none of the teachers would make any time for anything useful, like combat training. The only time I did my katas in the sparring chapel there was a whispering audience, and that was horrible. I was used to Dad just watching quietly, maybe offering a suggestion when I finished. Now a tide of whispers followed me everywhere.

So I did my tai chi in my room once or twice, but even that didn't help. The calm and grace that always used to wait for me if I just did the movements long enough was gone. Everything that used to make it okay enough to cope with was just not working.

I just sat there, feeling the eyes on me. I hate that feeling.

Irving was sitting two tables away. He kept glancing over, and he finally put his palms on the table and made as if to stand up. But then he dropped back down and looked at his tray.

Graves pulled out the chair next to me. "Hey, kid."

"Hey." I dropped Mom's locket against my chest as if it had stung me, looked up and grinned. It felt strange on my face, but then the happiness caught up with me and it turned more natural. Relief burst behind my breastbone like a mortar shell. "How was your morning? Evening? Whatever."

He set his tray down, dropped into the chair. "Full of new information. You know some brain-damaged vampires can't cross running water or major interstates? And the most common type of poltergeist feeds almost exclusively on the bioelectricity of teenage girls." He wagged his unibrow at me—nobody had held him down and plucked at the caterpillar crossing his forehead yet. I thought about saying something about it, decided not to for the hundredth time. His green eyes burned, and it wasn't just my imagination. His face *was* different. Less baby, more sharpness.

He was looking more like a wulfen now.

"Yeah, I knew about that. The poltergeist, I mean. There was this one time, in backwoods Louisiana . . ." The sentence died. I didn't want to think about that. Dad had held the girl down while I did the taking-apart-the-poltergeist thing, with salt water and Gran's rowan wand. The thing had hurled all sorts of small household items at both of us, clipping Dad a good one on the head with a teacup before I'd remembered to circle the bed the girl was tied to, cutting off the poltergeist's access to her. Weakening it enough for me to tear it apart.

Dad hadn't said a single thing about that—he didn't need to. I kicked myself all over for *that* one. And here they were wanting to put me in boring, normal, *remedial* classes. Jesus.

Graves snapped his fingers. He had two lattes in paper cups, and handed me one of them. "Earth to Dru. You wanna tell me about it?"

"Not really." I hunched my shoulders. "I didn't know that about *nosferatu*. Brain damage?"

"We did this experiment with holy water today and slides of tissue—big fun. If I get a good grade in the basics, I can start doing computer modeling for vampire migrations. Put my math mojo to good use." His eyes lit up, and he sucked at his latte before casting a shrewd glance over my tray. "Want a burger?"

He got to do real classwork while I was stuck in civics. I shrugged. "Not that hungry. I wish I could see who's doing all the cooking."

He nodded, in that way that told me he understood completely. "Yeah, I can't even smell anything through that cloud stuff. It's why I try to stick to fried instead of baked or boiled. Can't quite handle the raw meat yet. But I found out something interesting." The corner of his mouth curled up into one of his bitter little smiles. "Come on. Ask me."

The unwilling grin on my face just wouldn't go away. "Okay, I'm asking. What did you find out?"

"The kids here are troublemakers from wulfen families. Mommy and Daddy Wulfen pack the boys off to Scholas. The girls stay home and are taught to fight by their parents. Isn't that interesting?"

*Wulfen girls get to stay home. So there is more than one Schola.* That answered those questions, at least. "Why are the troublemakers sent here? Is this, like, a reform school?"

He brightened again, like I'd handed him exactly the right question. "Yeah, sort of. Tight discipline, tough love, all that. But there's something else. It's not just the troublemakers, but all boys get sent to Scholas. It's the treaty. An agreement between the ruling wulfen packs and the *djamphir* running the Order. The Order's not the only ones out there fighting, but they are the *official* ones, and they've a big infrastructure in place to keep the kids safe while they're being trained, *and* they promise to support the ruling wulfen families as long as they send a quota of their boys every year. They call it the Tithe."

*Well, that answers that.* "Are there *djamphir* families?"

"Some *djamphir* marry or shack up with normal girls. Most of them live incognito because of the vampire-hunting teams, and a lot of them only stick around long enough to find out if the girl breeds more *djamphir*. Sometimes they don't. You really *should* come to class, Dru."

*Eww. There's a word for guys like that.* "Uh-huh. When they put me into classes that are as cool as yours, I will." I took a cautious sip of the latte. It was a little too hot, but okay. It wasn't like Dad's coffee.

I almost flinched. There it was again.

"So how are you doing?" Graves picked up a burger and took a massive bite. Settled into chewing. It was the same thing he asked me every mealtime.

Every mealtime he was here instead of off running with his new friends, that is.

Across the room, a shoving match erupted between a dark-haired *djamphir* and a tall, skinny wulf. The noise changed for a minute, growls and yips running under the surface of the crowd roar, and a wulf teacher—leather pants, a Kiss T-shirt, and muttonchop whiskers that looked odd on his unlined face—stepped in, sending the wulfen one direction and the *djamphir* boy another. The *djamphir* boy waited until the wulf teacher's back was turned, then made a nasty gesture to all and sundry.

I'd kind of expected that kids who knew about the Real World wouldn't act like jock dipwads. Guess I was wrong.

I let out a sharp breath I hadn't been aware of holding. "Fine." I set the paper cup down. "Wanna go for a walk?"

Graves swallowed hastily. "I've got sparring after this. It's hell. I never knew I could get so sore."

"Sparring practice, huh?" They would teach *him* to fight. No problem. But nobody had time for me. "What are they teaching you?"

He shrugged. "Shanks is teaching me some basic stuff. He says I've got to get over that afraid-of-getting-hit thing. He also says I'd better train hard, because when I go all loco it's going to be training that saves me."

"Shanks?"

His hair flopped over his face as he nodded. "Bobby. That's his nickname—he's tall, especially when he changes. Grasshopper legs."

"Oh." *Aren't you just making friends all over.* "You going out again after classes?"

"Yeah, we're going running. There's going to be a full moon in a couple weeks; some of the kids are going to do their first Change. If I do my parkour practice right—"

"Parkour. That's a funny word." I said it for the hundredth time, and watched him grin for the hundredth time.

His eyes really lit up. He actually looked happy. "You'd really like it. Freerunning is *awesome*. And once they teach you how to fall and leap and stuff, it's super easy."

"But just for wulfen?"

Another shrug. "You could come along. Some of the *djamphir* do it too. The practice, not the actual runs."

"Graves! Hey, Graves!" someone shouted, and he looked up. A curly-headed wulf yelled something across the lunchroom, and Graves whipped him the bird almost faster than the eye could follow. A tide of growling swirled through the room, but it subsided as Graves looked steadily at the wulf in question, his green eyes narrowing.

Back in the Dakotas, Goth Boy would never have done that. He'd been on the bottom of the food chain, same as me. But now, he was actually, sort of, kind of . . . well, popular. Or at least getting there. It helped that he was *loup-garou*—all of the benefits of being wulfen without the crazy part. He didn't get seven feet tall and hairy like an overgrown toupee. Christophe had said it would make him a "prince" here.

And Graves was all over it in a big way.

I stared back down at my tray. Nothing on it looked even remotely edible anymore, so I took another gulp of my latte. It splashed in my stomach, gurgled a bit, and subsided. "What was that?"

He shrugged. "Nothing. They like to tease."

"About . . .?" *About you sitting next to the Typhoid Female?*

"Nothing, Dru. Here." He scooted my tray away and slid a small plate off his, setting it in front of me. A burger, a mound of fries. "It's hot. Eat."

I picked up a fry. He had packets of ketchup, too, and squeezed one out on his plate. We lapsed into silence, a bubble of companionable quiet almost deep enough to swallow the empty chairs ranked along the sides of our table.

Maybe I had some sort of social plague. Besides, I didn't want to talk. Except to Graves, and there was really nothing to say.

I found out I was hungry after all. He'd even dumped pickles on the burger and left off the onions. He must've been sure I'd eat. "Thanks."

"Hey, no problem. First one's free."

I dredged up another unwilling smile. "This isn't the first burger you've gotten me."

"Won't be the last, either. It's the first one I've gotten you today, so just eat, all right? I've got a half hour before I have to be down to get my ass beat up. So talk to me. You get anything ordered to your room finally?"

"Nope." The clothes I was wearing now had shown up in packages with a post office box number on them, a number different than the mail stop on the info sheet in my room. I'd written it down and stashed it in my bag—information like that might be useful later. Someone had guessed at my sizes and done a handy job of it. And the wulfen had taken Graves "into town"—there was something close by, even though this place sat on a few acres of Sticksville—to get kitted out.

But not me. They couldn't have anyone knowing about a *girl* up here at this school.

I wondered where all the money came from, then decided maybe I didn't want to know. I had a roll of cash in my battered black canvas bag, and it's usually no big trick to get more.

But still. I'd never had to get more on my own before. I knew *how*, sure. But Dad had always been there, and—

"Hello? Earth to Dru?" Graves waved a broad, long-fingered hand in front of my face. "Whatcha thinking? It must be deep."

I shrugged. Took another french fry. "I was just wondering where all the money comes from. This isn't a cheap operation they've got going. I wonder if the other schools are bigger. Which still leaves the question of how they pay for this."

Graves studied me sideways for a moment. That adult look was back, as if he was listening to a song I couldn't quite hear. "That's true. I thought about that too. Want me to see if I can find out?"

"Sure." Another fry, and another bite of burger and sip of latte. "Can I come with you? To sparring?"

His pause was long enough that I knew what he'd say. *Probably not a good idea, Dru.*

I wanted to hear him say it, anyway. The bubbling ball of acid inside my chest swelled another few notches. "Why?"

He hunched his shoulders. It was no good—he wasn't as bird-like-thin as he'd been a couple of weeks ago, before he'd gotten bit. He couldn't look small anymore. "No offense, but you like to pick fights too much. And I hate having a chick see me get my ass handed to me. It's a guy thing."

My face felt funny, so I let my hair fall down between us, curtaining my expression. Long hair is good for some things. And since we weren't in Midwest Podunk anymore, my hair had actually been behaving. Go figure. *"This* chick could hand your ass to you, you know."

"One of the teachers would jump me or throw me out of here if we got into it, Dru. Let's not."

"They wouldn't throw you out. I'd leave too." *I'd go just about anywhere to get out of here.* But I couldn't, could I. Not with the vampire king looking for me, right?

"We'd both end up dead." He sounded uncharacteristically serious, and his free hand came up, touched his opposite shoulder. Right where he'd been bitten. He rubbed at it a little, as if it still hurt. "Please, Dru. Let's not do this, okay?"

I dropped the burger. It splatted down on the plate and I pushed my chair back. My lips were greasy. Chewed food sat in my stomach like a bowling ball. "Fine. Let's not. Have fun at sparring."

"Dru—"

But I got up, shoved my chair back under the table, and fled. When he came by my room later, I kept the door closed and locked. He knocked for a while, but then he went away. And I sat there on the bed, fingering my mother's locket and wondering how much longer I was going to be trapped here.

# Chapter 4

**ap. Taptap. Tap.**

T I turned over restlessly. Sleep retreated like a cat, on soft little feet. I didn't want it to go, clutched at it with dreaming fingers. I had been dreaming of something important, a warning, owl wings brushing the air around me.

The bed was wide and deep and soft, a maple four-poster with filmy, dusty blue curtains drawn back. The whole room was blue, from the indigo velvet quilt cover to the pale-sky wallpaper figured with gold crosses, to the tinted varnish on the seven bookcases and the heavy cobalt velvet drapes. The rug was sapphire, and thick enough to lose dimes in even though it was older than me. The window behind it didn't have iron bars, because it opened onto a little private garden completely enclosed by high, blank walls—three stories down, with a barred door I could reach only by going out my door, making three turns, and going down two flights of stairs.

A lot of effort to spend if I wanted to walk outside into a raw, blustery little plot of ground with gravel paths and leafless, pinched-looking things that might have been rosebushes—in spring, that is. If I really, truly wanted to wander around thorny stabbing vines under a gray sky.

Instead of bars, there were heavy iron shutters, with little hearts and crosses punched out in even rows marching down their lengths.

I left those open. When they were closed, the entire room got still and, well, dead.

My eyes opened slowly. The warning retreated. Had it been Gran? Whoever it was was trying to tell me something very important.

*Taptaptap. Tap. Taptap.*

A cool bath of dread started at my scalp and slid down the rest of me. The sound was familiar—fingers drumming impatiently on glass. Memory mixed with dreaming, conspired to pull me under as the pillow turned hard and hot against my cheek.

*There was a zombie at my back door. Its eyes swung up, and they were blue, the whites already clouding with the egg-rot of death. Its jaw was a mess of meat and frozen blood; something had eaten half its face. Its fingertips, already worn down to bony nubs, scraped against the window. Flesh hung in strips from its hand, and my stomach turned over hard. Black mist rose at the corners of my vision, and the funny rushing sound in my head sounded like a jet plane taking off.*

*I'd know that zombie anywhere. Even if he was dead and mangled, his eyes were the same. Blue as winter ice, fringed with pale lashes.*

*The zombie's gaze locked with mine. It cocked its head like it had just heard a faraway noise.*

*I let out a dry barking sound and my back hit the wall next to the hallway, smacking my hip against a stack of boxes.*

*Dad bunched up his rotting fist, the meat chewed away from finger bones by something I didn't want to imagine or even think about, and punched his way through the window.*

I sat straight up, gasping for air, fighting free of the heavy blankets. Threadbare sateen sheets slid sweat-slick against my skin, turned into wet fingers clutching me at hip and ankle. My fists balled up and I hit nothing but air, the scream dying in my throat. The soft brush of feather-muffled wings filled the room for a moment, but Gran's owl — the bird that had sat on her windowsill while she died, the bird that had warned me of danger and led me to Dad's truck a week and a half ago — didn't show up.

*Something is very wrong here, Dru. You should beware.* But the voice receded as soon as I lunged into wakefulness, and I found I was clutching my mother's locket in one damp hand.

I blinked again, trying to separate dream from reality.

*Tap. Taptap.* The sound was real. And it was coming from my bedroom window.

I rolled out of the bed, hit the floor hard. Teeth clicking together — lucky I didn't have my tongue between them. My hands were too clumsy and slow, patting the top of the nightstand for a weapon. At home I'd have a gun. But here, there was nothing but the silver-loaded stiletto — all the weapons were signed into the sparring chapel or the armory, including the gun I'd had when they rescued me. Except for the switchblade that had been forgotten in my pocket, the one I didn't tell anyone about.

It just seemed like a good idea not to, that's all.

I pressed the button for the suicide spring. The blade snicked free and the tapping stopped.

I blinked, fisted sleep-crusties away with my free hand. Thin swords of pale winter daylight shifted position as whatever was outside my window moved.

Daytime. Of course it was — that's when the Schola sleeps, because that's when it's safe. Or at least, safe from *nosferatu*. Some of the older werwulfen students haunt the grounds during the day, running patrols in human and not-so-human form. I thought maybe a few of the *djamphir* teachers did too, but I hadn't bothered to ask. It had seemed enough just to sleep during the day and be up all night, even when my body clock had a little trouble adjusting.

My breath turned stale in my throat. I crouched beside my bed, weighing my options.

*Click.* The window catch snicked up. The stiletto turned itself in my hand, blade flat against my wrist and forearm. Silver loaded along the blade would hurt just about anything evil, and I would at least give a good lick or two in any fight. I took in a deep lungful of still, dusty air, my heart crawling up into my throat but a strange sense of calm descending on me.

Everything else in this place left me at sea. But something weird threatening to crawl into my bedroom window?

I knew how to deal with this. It was *familiar*. Once in Louisiana we'd tangled with a voodoo king, and we'd had a hex climb in through the window carrying roach spirits. But I'd seen Gran's owl before and told Dad, so when the window had broken with a silvery tinkling sound and the first huge roaches spilled through, we were ready.

When whatever-it-was came through the window, *I* was going to be ready.

This was what I'd been waiting for, without even realizing it. Everything else was just treading water. This, with my heart in my throat and my entire body suddenly awake and tingling with fear, was real.

And I didn't have to think about being alone or lonely when I was afraid.

I was still crouching there, my tank top twisted and the boxers I'd been sleeping in crawling up my crack, when I realized the thin blue lines of energy running through the walls weren't sparking and crackling. It had been a job to do the warding without Gran's rowan wand, but I'd managed. The wand was, after all, only a symbol—as Gran had endlessly reminded me. *Ain't nearly as good as the will behind it, Dru. You just remember that.*

She was always saying something like that. *You just remember, Dru. Just remember.*

That was the trouble. I was starting to get stuff I'd rather forget stuck in my head on repeat. Stuff like a zombie at my kitchen door, or a small dark space full of stuffed animals and the smell of drowsy little-girl fear.

What would wards not react to? There was a short list of things. I began running through them frantically.

The window opened. A breath of chill, rain-laden air puffed past the curtains, and they separated just enough for him to shimmy through. His boots landed on the carpet, the window closed with a slight squeak, and he turned around. Weak gray daylight touched his sleek dark hair, the blond highlights slipping through and retreating like fingers combing the silk-heavy strands.

His eyes swept the room once, then settled on me. Burning winter-blue eyes, glowing in the half-dark. He was in a hip-length, rock-star leather jacket, and he passed one hand back through his hair, shaking it down as water flung itself free. That cold blue gaze came to rest on me, and I suddenly smelled apple pies baking.

"Hello, Dru." His mouth curled up in a grin. I had forgotten how the planes and angles of his face all worked together, making him not handsome but just . . . *right*. How his eyebrows slanted up a little, and how his shaggy haircut looked expensive and relaxed all at once. "Have you been a good girl? Your guardian angel wants to know."

I stared at Christophe, my mouth open slightly, and realized how ridiculous I probably looked just as he slid the curtains closed and the room turned dark.

"Jesus," I whispered. "Where have you *been*?" It was about the most useless question in the world, and it came straight out of my mouth.

"Out and around, around and about." He paced across the room with long, springing strides, stopped at the door, and touched the chain lock, the deadbolt, and the bolt I'd shot home before lying down to sleep. "Very good, barring your door and warding your walls. You're not such a careless little bird now."

*I wasn't ever careless!* But there were more important things to open my mouth about. Every single question I hadn't been able to get answered in the past week and a half fought for place in the line, but they lost out to two inconsequentials. "Where's my truck? And all my clothes?"

Well, maybe not *inconsequential*, but I could've asked something else. Like, *Why didn't you tell me about the bloodhunger? Or, Was this my mother's room? Or even, Why does it seem like they were waiting for me here? What did you tell them? Why won't they teach me anything real?*

Christophe turned on one heel, surveyed the rest of the room, and finally looked back down at me again. I still crouched right by my bed, the knife ready in my fist. "I have taken good care of everything of yours, little bird. The truck is in a storage facility downstate under another name, safe and sound." He raised one elegant eyebrow, slightly. "They didn't give you any clothes? Or an expense account?"

My cheeks turned so hot I'm surprised they didn't glow. I straightened, suppressing the urge to pick at my boxers. Fixing a wedgie is *so* not the way to look competent. "Of course they did. But I was *sleeping.*"

"All safe in a little blue nest. I wonder why they put you here?" He shook himself again, water spattering. He was soaked. "Did you miss me?"

*Oh, for chrissake.* I set the knife down on the elegant little nightstand and pulled the hem of my tank top down. "I'm going to get you a towel, and I'm going to get some clothes on. Then we can—"

One very blue glance, before he pushed his hair back with stiff fingers and gave the rest of the room a once-over. "A towel would be nice, but you don't need to bother getting dressed. You're not going anywhere."

Silence filled the room. He looked steadily at me, I looked back, and the flush died on my cheeks. The smell of apple pies filled up the space between us, and I suddenly was pretty glad I wasn't bleeding anywhere, or even scabbed up. I knew how strong and fast Christophe was. If he decided to go all bloodhungry on me, what chance did I have?

Which all of a sudden made me think of something else. What if Irving had been taking it easy on me? Or if he hadn't, and Christophe was stronger, why the hell *was* he that way?

How old was this *djamphir* who'd rescued me? He was pretty obviously an "advisor," and they tend to be older.

Like, *way* older.

"There's a lot of things you didn't tell me." I tried not to sound accusing. I was suddenly very aware of the tank top clinging to me and cool air touching exposed skin. My legs felt very long, very skinny, and pretty unshaved.

Hey, I wear jeans all the time. You couldn't pay me to wax, and who has time to drag a razor over everything every day? When we'd lived below the Mason-Dixon I'd kept up with it, but moving up with the polar bears and finding out I was a lot deeper in the Real

World than I'd ever guessed didn't leave me with a lot of time for hair removal.

I thought I might make some time from now on, though. My cheeks were so hot I was amazed steam wasn't rising off the skin.

"Dru." He took two steps toward me, his boots crushing the carpet. "I didn't have time for a lot of niceties. You realize that, right?"

I crossed my arms over my chest. Jeez, it was cold in here all of a sudden. And had he always smelled this good? Was it a cologne? *Eau de Christmas Pie?* "I guess," I said finally. There hadn't exactly been time for a lot of note taking, but he still could have told me a few things.

Would I have believed him? All I had to do now was look around this pretty little room and think of the bars on the other windows. Or of the first Restriction, when the bell jangled and everyone leapt for their stations, and Dylan dragged me up to this room and told me to lock the door.

*But why?* I'd wanted to know, and Dylan had showed his teeth, fangs curving down as his aspect slid over him.

*Because this isn't a drill,* he'd said. *And you are what we're going to die for if they break through the outer defenses. Now lock your door.*

Christophe shook his head again. Water flew like jewels. "A towel *would* be nice, Dru."

"Yeah, sure. Fine." I stamped barefoot toward the door between two bookshelves. I had my own bathroom, while the boys in the dorms had to make do with communal ones. And I still couldn't figure out who cleaned it, though it wasn't as old-grungy as the caves downstairs. And I don't make much of a mess, either.

Living with Dad taught me that much, at least.

The towels were blue too, and a little threadbare. Bright blue like a summer sky. The color of our truck, the color of Dad's eyes—

warmer than Christophe's, even when bloodshot after a night of sipping Beam, or when he was in what he called a "damn bad mood."

I had to stop and take a deep breath. Right next to the squirrelly panic-feeling of being left behind again was a hot wash of relief, as vivid as oil paint. It was a familiar feeling—the relief I felt each time Dad showed back up to collect me.

What did I have to be relieved about? Nothing except the fact that *someone* had come back for me. When you've spent your life waiting to be collected like a library book or a piece of luggage, the intensity of that relief gets a little ridiculous.

But at least Christophe hadn't forgotten about me.

I grabbed a bath sheet and stamped back out. Christophe hadn't moved. He was staring at the empty bookcases with a peculiar look on his face. I'd tried to make them look a little *less* empty by arranging some of the knickknacks—including a blue glass elephant with its trunk lifted—on different shelves. My books, my CDs, my mattresses—everything was in the truck. Nothing here was mine. It didn't even smell right—when a place hasn't been lived in for a while, you can tell. The air itself gets stale. Moving into a place where nobody's been breathing for a while is like trying on shoes that don't fit quite right and hoping they'll wear in.

Shoes never do. I've never spent long enough in a house that felt this unfriendly, I don't know if they ever relax.

Still, I was beginning to call a truce with some of the knickknacks. They'd stopped looking like prissy little disapproving things and started to look a little easier with the idea of me. And when I came back after going down to the caf, at least it smelled a little bit more like a hotel each time instead of a crypt.

"Here." I tossed the towel at Christophe, who caught it with a clean, economical motion. "Start talking."

"What if I just came to see you?" He scrubbed at his hair, wiped his face and hands. The jacket squeaked a little. His hands were wet, and I saw deep red, dripping lines crisscrossing his palms and scoring his knuckles before he shook his fingers out. They were pale and perfect again when he held one up and examined it critically, exhaling.

My heart made a funny flipping movement. "Oh, please. You wouldn't have waited if you really wanted to see me that bad." *And you wouldn't be sneaking in through my window if everything was all right.* I found a big plaid flannel shirt Graves had gotten on one of his shopping runs and shrugged into it, my fingers fumbling with the buttons. It smelled vaguely of cigarette smoke, boy, and harsh deodorant soap. Another odd flush of relief spilled through me. "Where have you really been? Driving here? Are you okay?"

"I'm fine. Touched that you care." He rubbed behind his ear and grinned like a cat. The blond highlights sliding through his hair were darkened by the wet, but still visible. He shucked out of the jacket, too, and looked for a place to put it. I pointed at the creaking office chair in front of the computer and he hung it up, muscle moving under his thin black V-neck sweater.

I looked away at the drapes pulled closed over the window. It was pretty dark in here, and I was kind of happy about that.

But there was plenty not to be happy about in the dark, too. I flicked the bedside lamp on—an antique brass number with a blue stained-glass shade—and turned to find Christophe watching me. His eyes were even bluer than the room, but oddly bleached.

Winter eyes.

"How old are you, anyway?" I didn't cross my arms, but I did pick up the stiletto again. I did not try to push the blade back in, just held it loosely.

It made me feel better. My hair was all messed up and my boxers were on weird, but at least I felt equipped to handle this if I kept a grip on the knife.

*Why? He's not going to hurt me.* The relief burst inside my chest again, but under it was the bald edge of fear. Now I'd seen what a *djamphir* could do.

It was stupid not to be frightened of them.

Christophe kept very still. He was staring at my breastbone, where my mother's locket glistened. When I moved a little bit, pulling the top of the flannel shirt closed, he finally examined my face instead. My cheeks were hot as stove burners.

"Just a little older than you, Dru." He flicked a quick glance at the rest of the room again, like he expected there to be someone hiding in the shadows. "This reminds me of your mother's room. She was the last *svetocha* we managed to save." *There,* his tone said. *Does that answer the question you were really asking?* He shook the towel and glanced around the room again. A breath of pie scent touched my cheek. "She had books, lots of them. They're probably in a holding room. Waiting for you."

My hand made a tiny movement, wanting to touch Mom's locket. I forced it down. "They won't train me." It burst out in a cascade I tried not to make into a whine. "You said they would. No combat training or *anything*, they treat me like I'm—"

"Glass?" He tilted his head. His rain-wet skin was perfect, like damp silk. "Like you're fragile? Precious? There are worse things, *moj ptaszku.*"

*Not from where I'm sitting.* "Look, I'm not going to get any better if they keep treating me like—"

I didn't even see him move. One moment he was all the way across the room, with the towel in his hands and his head cocked.

The next, he was nose to nose with me, a warm draft smelling of apples and spice pushing at my hair, kissing my cheeks.

I half-fell back, slashing up with the knife. Warm steel bands closed around my wrist and *twisted*. My arm shrieked with pain, the knife plucked from my suddenly nerveless fingers, and my knees buckled. His other hand clamped at the back of my neck, under my hair. My shoulder wrenched, screaming as it twisted in a way it wasn't built for.

*Move it, Dru!* Dad's voice, filling my head. There was only one way out, and I took it—bending forward, kicking up to roll, my shoulder giving a high, hard pop of pain as Christophe's fingers loosened. My bare foot hit his knee, heel grinding in. It was a good kick, and he let out a short, sharp sound like a laugh.

I hit the floor and rolled, came up in a crouch. The knife was nowhere to be seen, and Christophe bent his leg a little, shaking it out. He should have looked ridiculous on one leg, but instead he looked like a cat flicking one paw, the rest of him perfectly poised.

*Stay down. If he comes at you, you've got a better chance of shaking him off.* I flicked a glance at the door. No help there—it would cost me too many precious seconds to unlock, unbar, unchain it.

"Good," he said. "Looking for escape, since I'm too fast. Very good. But I'm already here and you have no weapons, *moj mały ptaszku*. What do you do?"

*No weapons my ass. There's always a weapon.* I cast around, found nothing but knickknacks for throwing, and heard the muffled beat of feathered wings again. They brushed the air of the room. My hair lifted on a faint breeze that seemed to come from nowhere, and I went very still.

I half-expected to see Gran's owl. But nothing happened. I watched Christophe carefully.

"There it is." He nodded. His hair had gone slick and dark as his aspect rose to the surface. You could either have a weak aspect or a strong one, and the ones that came out "externalized" in another form—usually an animal nobody normal could see—were the strongest of all.

It was also the part the bloodhunger came from. A deep, dark place that drove you crazy when you smelled the red stuff.

Christophe sank down, slowly, until he was crouching. One hand was tented on the carpet for balance, and his gaze never left mine. "You're very close to blooming, Dru. You have a certain natural facility, especially when you're in a high emotional state. But you can't count on that. It could be that you haven't been allowed into sparring sessions because they're designing a program for you, or importing teachers. Or there could be other reasons."

Something told me he was more in the "other reasons" camp. Still not telling me what he knew, or what he guessed. "Dylan said it was because you weren't back yet." I didn't relax. Neither did he. The tension was a rope between us, a nameless heat through my bones.

"Ah, Dylan. How is he?" The smile that spread over Christophe's face wasn't nice at all. It was the grin of a cat in front of a mouse hole. "Did he tell you he was in love with her?"

*Huh?* "What?"

"We all were. She was a moment of light, your mother. Sergej stole her away, though not before she left us of her own will. We were all . . ." He straightened slowly. The stiletto spun around his fingers, silver-loaded blade blurring in a complex series of half-arcs as his hand flicked. "That's enough for today, Dru. You can stand up."

I stayed where I was. This was more than I'd gotten out of anyone, and besides, I didn't trust that he wouldn't jump me again just to prove a point.

I should have been more scared. But I wasn't, despite the fact that my heart was pounding hard enough to force its way out through my throat-pulse. My breath came in short, sharp little puffs, and all of me tingled with adrenaline.

It was the first time since I'd gotten here that I felt actually awake and reasonably alive, instead of numb and terrified.

"Stubborn as usual." He sighed, tossed the knife back on the nightstand. It clattered against the lamp's base. "I have about a half hour until I can leave. I won't waste it tossing you around the room."

"Gee, thanks." I couldn't sound more sarcastic, but I was willing to give it a try. My breathing evened out. "What are you here for, then? Tea and cookies?" My mouth wanted to water. He smelled like cookies. Cinnamon ones, with dabs of apple-pie filling.

But my stomach had shrunk to the size of a dime. Climbing in through the window plus "a half hour until I can leave" didn't equal anything good. I had that much figured out, at least.

Every speck of amusement was gone. He looked a lot older, suddenly, even though his face hadn't changed. "To find you and make sure you're safe."

*Well, isn't that nice of you.* My heart gave another pounding leap. I made my knees work, pushing the rest of me slowly up. My shoulder ached fiercely. "They won't even let me go outside alone."

"It's not outside that worries me. Much." Christophe let out a sigh. The sweater clung to him, and his jeans were soaked through, especially the knees. Which brought up another question.

"How the hell did you get in the window, anyway? And what are you worried about in here?"

"A traitor." He looked at the bed, visibly decided he'd better not sit on it, and stretched his hands in a curiously helpless motion. "Someone who gave away the location of an Order-approved safe house, one even I wasn't supposed to know about, to Sergej. Which, incidentally, made it possible for him to lie in wait for both of us."

I tried not to shiver at the thought. Christophe flying through the wreckage of the wall on the truck's hood, just like Superman. Graves behind the wheel, terrified and hanging on. And me, almost drowning in Sergej's dark, oily eyes. "But we kicked his ass, right? Even though someone gave that away. And—"

Christophe shook his head, and for a moment he looked sad. He moved and I flinched, but it was just to walk over to the computer chair and drop down as it squawked slightly. "It was a draw, Dru. Barely that. If it hadn't been daytime, if Juan and the others hadn't believed me rather than a control directive, if your friend hadn't trusted me, if you hadn't already fought Sergej with more skill and power than anyone expected, if, if, *if*. You would have died." The snarl that crossed his face was there and gone in an instant, so fast I might have imagined it. "I would have lost you."

He said it like it had just occurred to him.

Another uncomfortable silence filled the room up, pushed against the curtains and made the rain-filtered light seem dimmer. I stared at him.

"And you're not supposed to be here." He took a deep breath. "I assumed you'd be sent to the main Schola. I don't know how you ended up in this satellite, among . . . well, this type."

Well, we'd already answered that question—this wasn't the only Schola. But what was he going on about? "What type? Wulfen? There are *djamphir* here, too, you know."

"Never mind. Maybe . . . they . . . decided you'd be safer at a smaller school. And it does make things easier for me."

"What kind of things?" I sounded suspicious even to myself. My cheeks were on fire again, and my knees didn't feel too steady.

"Things like watching over my careless little bird until she blooms. This Schola is fairly well known to me. No, your mother was never here."

*Thanks, Christophe. I didn't ask.* But it felt sneakingly good to *know*. Another one of those uncomfortable quiet spaces between us. I tried not to hunch my shoulders. "What else haven't you told me?"

"Nothing important. Nothing critical. But you want me to talk?" His chin tipped down and he stared at me. "So, *skowroneczko moja*, come sit at my feet and listen. We don't have much time. And I have something to give you."

# CHAPTER 5

**sat on my** bed, my arms wrapped around my knees. Sometimes I moved so my legs didn't fall asleep. Most of the time, though, I just sat and stared at the thin gray daylight coating the window, sleet beating in waves now. He'd gone out through the window and just . . . vanished, even though I ran across the room and stuck my head out like an idiot, peering after him.

Christophe left behind the fading smell of baking apple pies, wet footprints on the carpet, a soaking towel with spots of rust, a sodden computer chair . . . and the two wooden things.

*Practice swords?* I touched one handle. It was warm, the wood worn down and oiled, dark with use. Fine-grained, and very hard.

*No.* Christophe had touched one of them, just the way I was touching it now, running his fingers gently over the curves. *These are* malaika, *made of hawthorn. They are not made for practice. These are for killing things that walk the night, and they were made for a* svetocha's *hands. Very few* djamphir *are skilled in the use of the Kouroi's traditional blade anymore.*

*But what good are wooden swords?* Long, slightly curving, oddly leaf-shaped blades. They looked like they belonged in a high-budget chop-saki movie, the kind I'd seen a hundred times on late-late-night cable while waiting for Dad to come back.

I winced at the thought. It was much easier and nicer to think of Christophe's measured, even voice.

*Hawthorn is deadly to* nosferatu, *and even deadlier when wielded by a Kouroi. How much more deadly, then, when wielded by you? Be good, and you'll learn to use them. When it's safer, and I come back.*

And he'd left them here. Weapons. They might have been wood, but their edges were bastard sharp. To prove it, Christophe had sliced off a little bit of his hair. The small lock of blond-streaked brown lay on the nightstand next to the stiletto. A *keepsake,* he'd said. *So you know I'll return.*

And I'd blushed, again, like an idiot. It was absurdly comforting to know that *someone* would be coming back for me. Now that I'd lost everything—*everyone*—else.

I stared down at the swords, the hot flush dying in my cheeks, sliding back down my throat to settle in my chest next to the acid bubble. The locket was a warm spot on my breastbone.

Pale gray light ran over every curve. They looked like they belonged here on the bed, against the rucked-up velvet of the quilt cover. More than I did, at least. There was a fresh scab on my unshaved knee, a rash of red rug burn on my other leg.

As the afternoon wended toward evening, I got up. My legs were a little unsteady from sitting curled up on the bed for so long. I carried one of the wooden swords into the bathroom. There was a mirror over the sink, a nice big one. The light in here was good too, warm gold from the dusty bulbs. It ran over my tangled hair and the hollows under my eyes.

Just one average teenage girl, rangy and awkward. Cheekbones too big for her face, blue eyes a different shade than Christophe's. My eyes were all Dad's, right down to the faint lavender lines in the irises. My hair was Mom's, but without the sleek glossiness of her ringlets. The curls tangled every which way, but they weren't the halo of frizz they used to be.

I wasn't breaking out anymore. The bath, I guess. I couldn't even feel good about that. I was too dead-pale. Between the rings under my eyes and the two fever spots on my cheeks, I looked like a ghost.

And I should know. I've seen a few.

I lifted the sword, tipped its curve down, back up. "*Malaika*," I whispered. It *did* look like it belonged here. With the velvet and the satin and the chipped stone.

But not me. The circles under my eyes were the remains of bruises. My upper lip was too thin, lower lip too fat, my nose too long, and my hair was hopeless. The plaid shirt was a glaring mixture of red and yellow and green, and my sleeping boxers had penguins on them. They were still crawling up my ass crack.

Yeah. I'd never win any prizes.

I was tough, though. Wasn't I? I could spot Dad, no matter what he was benching. I'd gotten Graves away from a crazed wulfen and out of a deserted mall, through a snowstorm, and faced down Sergej on my own. So what if I'd had to be rescued? I'd still gone a couple rounds with him, shot him in the head, and managed to come out still breathing.

*Dad. And Gran. And Mom. All gone.*

Something too hot and sharp to be tears rose up in my throat. I was the only one left.

*If you are a good girl, go to classes no matter how boring, and keep your ears open; I'll teach you how to use these. Your mother was a master of the* malaika. *I don't know why she left hers behind.* He had touched a hilt again, his fingers oddly gentle and his mouth drawn down bitterly. *I have the pair she used in a safe place. When you're ready, they're yours.*

My breath hitched in my throat. I let myself remember my mother. It was the most painful of all, because . . . well, just because.

Her hair always smelled of warmth and fresh perfume. Her heart-shaped face and the prettiness of even her smallest gestures. Her dark eyes and Dad's picture of her kept in his wallet, with a shiny place rubbed in the plastic over her face.

That shiny place was still there, though the picture was gone. If I dug out Dad's billfold, I would find the photo missing and the place where I always ran my thumb while getting out a twenty or a fifty would glare at me. If I stared long enough, I could probably even see the curves and lines of her face from a long time ago.

*Oh God.* I pushed away the memory that wanted to rise to the surface, but not nearly quick enough. You can't ever stop thinking something quick enough. Something that hurts always gets the knife in too fast for you to slam a lid on it and shove it away.

*We're going to play the game, Dru.* She'd hidden me in a closet and gone out to fight Sergej. Dad had left me at the house and gone to face Sergej alone. Gran had tried to stay with me, but old age had taken her. Her body had failed right out from under her, and I could tell she'd hated leaving me. She'd held on all through summer, but the first cold wind coming up the valley had been too much for her, and the hospital . . .

There it was again, a hurtful thought. I let out a long, slow breath, as if I was working through a cramp. It didn't help. This cramp was on the inside, someplace no deep breathing could touch.

I wasn't as pretty as Mom, or as smart as Dad. I wasn't good at everything I touched, like either of them. I was just one scrawny punk-ass girl.

I met my own gaze in the mirror. I didn't look like I should be holding the wooden sword. I clasped it awkwardly in one hand, away from my body like a baseball bat I was afraid might bite me.

*Just me. Just Dru.*

The girl in the mirror was smiling a little, which I suppose meant I was, even though my face felt frozen. I cautiously put my hand down, let the sword dangle.

I stamped back to the bed and slid the swords underneath the dust ruffle with Dad's billfold. I wasn't supposed to let anyone know I had them. I wasn't supposed to tell anyone I'd seen Christophe—but there was one person I *had* to tell. If Graves wasn't too busy running around with his new friends, if I could get him alone, he could . . . what could he do?

Was it even fair to dump this on him too and ask him to help me figure it out and deal with it?

Most of all, I wasn't supposed to let anyone know I had a job now, one Christophe had given me. And that was trying to find out who at the Schola had wanted me dead bad enough to betray Christophe as well.

*So I'm not pretty or smart or any other hundred things. But I'm stubborn. And tough.*

It was time to start using what I had.

# CHAPTER 6

**afeteria noise washed** over me in waves. Catcalls, conversations, laughter—everyone was at breakfast. I stabbed at my scrambled eggs with a fork. The pancakes had been steaming hot and fresh; now they just sat there.

Like me, just sitting here. It was just after dusk, class started in forty-five minutes, and I was really feeling the urge to go back to bed. I mean, I've never loved school, and I was determined to start *doing* something, even if it was putting up with the stupid remedial classes.

But getting up and getting dressed, braiding my hair back, and dealing with the cafeteria was really testing that determination. My shoulder still ached from the little tango with Christophe, but not as bad as it could have. Those baths worked wonders.

A shadow fell over me. I was hard-put not to twitch. But it was just a young blond wulfen with dark eyes and a gentle face. He was pale and gripped his tray so hard his knuckles were white. He looked about ready to break something from sheer nervousness.

I seconded that emotion.

His mouth moved, but I couldn't hear whatever he was saying under the noise. The screen of steam that the food came through hissed underneath all the crowd sounds.

"What?" My fork clattered on my tray. He flinched, shoulders hunching under a blue cable-knit sweater. He was built slight and narrow-hipped for a wulfen, but long corded muscle stood out on his forearms beneath the pushed-up sweater cuffs.

"Dibs," he croaked. "Name's Dibs."

I closed my mouth with a snap. I've seen shy all over the United States, and this kid had a bad case of it. My conscience poked at me, hard.

I pushed out the chair next to me. "Hi. I'm Dru."

The way his face lit up, you'd have thought I'd just given him a winning lottery ticket. He dropped down, and his tray held a huge pile of raw meat slopping over the edge of a plate. I saw two T-bone steaks and a mess of hamburger, and my stomach turned over. I swallowed and reached for my coffee.

"Hi." He scratched at his leg through his jeans and grinned. White teeth gleamed, and his hair was a buttergloss sheen. Girls would probably love him—he had the big-eyed look of a nervous deer. "I, um. Hi."

"Hey." I took a mouthful of scrambled eggs. Tried not to look at his plate. "So what is it?"

"What?" He looked genuinely confused.

"Nobody wants to talk to me. Why are you here?" I was glad of the company, especially since Graves was nowhere in sight. But I've been the new girl in schools all over the country. You don't ever trust the first boy who wanders up to you. Or at least, you learn to look for what they might be thinking they can get out of the new kid in town.

Of course, Graves had been the first one to approach me back in the Dakotas. I wasn't sure what to think about that. It had been lucky, I guess. Maybe.

Not so lucky for him, since he'd got bitten and ended up here.

"You looked lonely." He hunched over his plate, his long fingers almost but not quite touching the meat. "And they bet I wouldn't do it, since I'm sub. Sometimes you have to show them they're wrong, even the doms."

"Sub?" *Doms? Oh boy.*

"I, um, was born that way. Born, not bitten, and born sub, too." He blinked. "You don't know about that, huh? Graves said you knew a lot, but not some stuff."

"He did, huh?" I shoved in another bite of egg. Dibs relaxed a little. "What else did Graves say?"

"That if anyone messed with you, he'd call 'em out. He got into it the first day he got here, proved he was dom. He sleeps in a top bunk." Even though he was showing his teeth, Dibs's expression was gentle. He scooped up one of the steaks and bit into it, teeth scissoring effortlessly through.

*Isn't that interesting.* "And you don't?" I played with a line of syrup on my plate, dragging fork lines through it and swirling.

"There're lots of beds, but not every wulf sleeps in one. It's complicated." He took another massive bite. The meat splorched a little, and I felt distinctly queasy.

*Deal with it, Dru.*

But I remembered a werwulf's teeth tearing through flesh and grinding down on Graves's shoulder, and the thought made me feel green all over. Not a nice springtime green, either.

"Hey, dogboy!" A yell from a passing *djamphir*—one of Irving's friends, a slim dark-haired kid in a red shirt and jeans, slouching past with that eerie gracefulness. "Put your dish on the floor!" He sneered a little as he passed, elegantly.

Dibs hunched up even further, and the ball of acid inside my chest boiled up as if something had been dropped in it. I slid my chair back, my legs tensing, but Dibs's hand came down on my wrist with surprising strength.

"Just let it go," he whispered under the crowd noise. "It doesn't mean anything."

"It *does*." I tried to pull my hand away. "It means something."

A ripple ran through the caf. I turned my head, keeping the *djamphir* in sight. He dropped down at Irving's table, one of the prime spots of cafeteria real estate, and laughed. His friends were laughing too. My braid bumped my back as I tried to pull away from Dibs again.

*Mark.* Memory served up the *djamphir*'s name just as my free hand curled into a fist. *I'm pretty sure his name is Mark. He even looks like a Mark. Go figure.*

"Wow. You really do care." He laughed, a shaky little sound. "Just let it roll off. I'm not upset, see? You'll just make trouble if you say anything. Keep your head down."

The tension simmered down a notch, but it didn't leave me. My shoulders were a rigid bar under my T-shirt and hoodie, and I'd lost every ounce of appetite I'd had.

"You don't argue with them." He let go of me, finger by finger. "Not over a wulf. They won't make it hard for you, get it? They'll make it hard for me. But don't worry, the doms will take care of it. Sooner or later. They always do."

"Jesus." I let out a long, shaky breath. It had bothered me before, the dismissive way Christophe treated Graves; as if he was somehow tainted. Somehow *less*. It bothered me here, too—the *djamphir* were the top of the food chain.

I'd thought things would be different somehow. I'd thought the Real World didn't play petty bullshit high school games. But here, it was just the same old thing. It was depressing. Could you ever get away from it?

But picking a fight the day I'd decided to turn over a new leaf wasn't a good idea. I should start this out right.

Dibs was watching me anxiously, a vertical line between his golden eyebrows as they wrinkled together. He looked like a retriever I'd seen once, a sweet dog that lived in a trailer park outside Pensacola. The way he tilted his head and chewed at the same time reinforced the impression.

*Scratch behind his ears, who's a good boy?* I swallowed hard, disgusted at the thought. I wasn't like them, the dismissive, pretty *djamphir* boys. I'd always been an outsider.

I stabbed at my pancakes like I was stabbing at the face of stupidity. "Do they all act that way? The *djamphir?*"

"Yeah. I mean, except you. Graves said you were different. He said you—"

"Hey, Dru." Graves yanked out the chair on my other side and dropped into it. He smelled like cold air and cigarette smoke, his long black coat still carrying a chill from outside. A bloom of red up high on his cheekbones did good things for him, and his earring glittered. His eyes were sparkling, too. "Dibs. Nice to see you, man."

Dibs shut up so fast I was surprised he didn't lose a chunk of his tongue. He busied himself with tearing at the steak and chewing, with a guilty hangdog look.

"So you're a dom, huh? Nice." I stabbed my pancakes again. "Kinky."

"You're the one who ties people up, babe." Graves's gaze flicked past me, touched Dibs, and returned. "What happened?"

Dibs shrugged, took another mouthful.

My tone was hard and dismissive. "Some *djamphir* asshole just catcalling, that's all." Stab, stab, the fork hit the plate hard. "I'm about due for class."

"I'll walk you—we've got first period together. Glad you decided to show up." He looked smug. Insufferably smug. His smile was a wide V, so big a dimple came out on his left cheek. He wasn't so baby-faced anymore, and was that dark stubble spreading up from his chin? His hair was starred with little beads of moisture—it must have been raining outside.

Yeah. He got to go outside and smoke, and then come back in and—

*Jesus.* I grabbed the edge of the table with both hands. The fork mashed itself against fake wood. My teeth gritted together so hard my jaw ached. I'd been mad before, plenty of times. Kid-mad. This was a new feeling, and it swallowed me whole. I actually saw little sparkles of red around the corners of my field of vision, and my arm ached with the need to punch that fucking smile right off his face. Arm? No, my whole *body* vibrated with the urge.

"Uh-oh." Dibs's chair scraped as he pushed back. "Graves? She smells red."

I shook. The wave of trembling passed through me. What the hell was I thinking? It was Graves. He was pretty much my only friend here. Was I really going to go ballistic on him? Over *what*?

"She's fine." Graves just looked at me. His face didn't seem nearly as smug now. Just thoughtful, and familiar. "She gets a little antsy sometimes, but she's okay. Right, Dru?"

And just like that, the rage evaporated, leaving only the sour little red-hot bubble in my chest. I found my voice. "Right. Antsy." *Where did that come from? What was that?* "Jesus." It came out sounding breathy and exhausted.

The cafeteria was curiously hushed. Tension ran under the surface of that quiet before my ears popped and I relaxed a little bit more.

"You're wound pretty tight," was all Graves said. "Hey, you should eat something other than that. Want some bacon?"

*Christophe visited me. I have to talk to you.* The words died on my lips. Dibs crunched down on something next to me. It sounded like bone, and my stomach did a funny sideways jigging movement. "I, um, I'll just stick with toast." To prove it, I picked up a half-slice of sourdough covered in butter. It was cold, but I put it in my mouth and bit down. My teeth were tingling. It was a weird feeling, like they were waking up from novocaine. I mean, I've never had a cavity, but I can imagine.

Graves nodded. A shadow of relief slid through his green eyes. "'Kay. Hey, we're going out for burgers again after classes. Want me to bring you some?"

*No. It'll be cold when you get here. I don't want any grease, thanks.* "Maybe a milkshake one of these days. I haven't had a milkshake in a while."

Not since he'd handed me one in a mall food court and asked me what was wrong. The memory pushed through my head, tinted with panic, and I let out another shaky sigh.

"You got it. If you're still awake when I get in." His hair fell over his face as he nodded, the dead-black strings looking normal on him. His skin had cleared up, the caramel coloring nice and even. "Sure you don't want any bacon?"

*Yeah, if I'm still awake when you condescend to come back? No thanks.* I took another hurried bite of toast as Dibs cracked down on another bone and made a happy, humming little sound. I suppose I should have been ready for that. It was one thing to feel lonely because nobody would sit with you. It was another thing entirely to have a wulf chowing down right next door. "Nah, I'm good. Really." I made the words come out through a mouthful of cold soggy toast and congealed butter, and told myself I'd better start eating my food while it was hot.

Maybe I shouldn't tell him about Christophe at all. I mulled over this until the bell for first period rang, and was still mulling over it hours later when I fell asleep in the gray light of predawn. Graves didn't show up with that shake. But it wasn't like I was expecting him to, either.

Yeah, right.

# CHAPTER 7

**M**y **second week** at the Schola ended in a hard freeze. Temperatures plunged, especially at night when the stars became hard clear points in a naked inky sky. Ice dribbled over the windows, and I couldn't even feel relieved that the constant fog had drawn back. All the wulfen were complaining because this kind of weather kept them indoors. And believe me, if you've never been stuck inside a room with twenty restless young wulfen while a teenage-looking *djamphir* drones on about the anatomy of suckers, well, you've missed a real party.

A Schola classroom generally isn't like a regular classroom. They're concave, most of the time. The teacher stands in the bottom of the bowl, and the students sit on benches or couches in concentric circles. It was couches in first-period history class, which meant Graves was sitting right next to me, leaning forward with his elbows on his knees. He looked like he was paying attention, too, under the mess of dyed-black hair falling in his face. His nose jutted out, and his chin was set. The usual black coat strained at his shoulders.

The intensity in his green eyes was new, though. I'd never seen him concentrate this fiercely.

I still felt sorry for dragging him into this.

On my other side, the only other *djamphir* student in the room leaned away from me, taking notes on a yellow legal pad. It was Irving, his curly hair slicked down a little. He'd apparently forgiven me for the sparring thing. He didn't seem the type to hold a grudge.

His friend in the red shirt wasn't here, thank God.

Everyone was freshly showered and bright-eyed for the first class of the evening, and it was so cold I was in layers—T-shirt, Graves's flannel, and a blue wool sweater. I'd have preferred to be hanging out in front of the armory, but at least the lecture was something I hadn't heard before. The teacher had thrown out the textbook and was teaching something new.

"For the wulfen attacking, the primary target is usually the unprotected belly." The instructor, a pale blond *djamphir*, had stopped staring at me. He still halted every once in a while, glancing at me and going completely motionless for a few seconds. It was eerie. "This bleeds a *wampyr* out, and has the added bonus of leaving a blood trail should the thing escape."

Irving raised his hand. "Why not the throat?" He looked like a bright student giving the teacher an opening. His eyes had lit up, and he leaned forward. "Wulfen claws are more durable than plenty of weapons."

"Good question." The teacher nodded. I still hadn't figured out his name yet. "Anyone?"

A shaggy dark-haired wulf perched in one of the very back rows spoke up. "Throat's too small a target." His upper lip lifted for a moment, a gleam of teeth. "Plus, gets you too close to the thing. Arm's length is safer."

"And?" The teacher's eyebrows rose. Nobody said anything.

I tentatively raised a hand.

Immediately, every pair of eyes in the room fastened on me. "Yes?" The blond wasn't sneering now. Instead, he was looking attentively at me, eyebrows raised.

*Oh Lord. I'm going to feel stupid.* My heart was going a mile a minute. "Wulfen fight in packs?" I hazarded. "I mean, I haven't seen much, but they seemed to be pretty good at fighting as a unit. I guess *djam-djamphir*—" I stumbled nervously over the word and immediately felt like a dumb-ass. "Well, I don't see them working together a lot, not in a case like that."

"*Very* good!" The teacher beamed like I'd just handed him Christmas. "Striking for the belly is a strategy with greater returns if the creature is distracted by other team members. What are other strategies for distracting a *wampyr?*"

I felt like I'd just won a prize. And this was *real.* It wasn't like a stupid history class where they aren't telling you the truth anyway, just the regular collage of corporate-approved lies to suck all the interest out of everything.

No, this was about the Real World. How many times had I told Dad high school wouldn't prepare me for anything? We'd gone round and round over it.

The thought of Dad hurt, so I tried thinking about something else. Now I felt kind of bad about skipping all the time and fighting with him. Maybe if I hadn't—

I didn't want to think that all the way through either. I sat up a little straighter.

Graves gave me an unreadable glance. He didn't bother to raise his hand. "Blood," he said. The single word dropped into the room like a rock into a pond. "Spill enough and the animals go crazy."

A ripple ran through everyone. Irving made a single restless movement next to me. The couch creaked.

The teacher's mouth made a weird little twitch. He didn't quite dart Graves a venomous look, but it was close. "The hunger."

"More like a thirst, actually." Irving shifted again. I got the idea he was trying to get the teacher's attention. "Why do we call it hunger, anyway?"

"Putting a pretty face on it?" Graves suggested sweetly. I cottoned onto what he was doing a little too late, and the teacher actually stiffened.

*Oh Lord. Here we go.* I sighed internally and threw a question in I wouldn't have asked if I hadn't been trying to distract everyone. "What I want to know is, why don't I have it? And does it really make suckers go nuts?" I moved, and my elbow whapped into Graves's side. *Hard.*

I hoped it looked unintentional.

The room went still again. I was almost getting used to the way everyone shut up whenever I asked a stupid question. At least I'd been learning for a few days now, even if Civics and Aspect Mastery were still total wastes of time.

Maybe this wasn't so bad.

Blondie looked relieved, but he darted a little glance at Graves. Then at me, and I swear I saw a flash of anger. "Some *svetocha* have the bloodhunger, but not until blooming. And yes, even a small amount of vital fluid can drive a new *nosferat*—or an older one— into a state of severely diminished rationality. It depends on how long ago their last feeding was, and—"

*Feeding. Like, on people.* I shivered, but didn't have a chance to finish the thought. The low clear tones of a bell sliced through whatever Blondie had been meaning to say, and everyone in the room leapt to their feet.

*Shit. Restriction.* Maybe it was a drill. I grabbed Graves's arm, the decision made almost before I was aware I'd touched him. "Come with me."

"I've got to—" He tried to step away, stopped, and looked down at me.

The wulfen were jamming up at the door, some of them half-changing already, fur running up over their bodies. Irving paused just at the door to look back, his aspect sliding through his curls with golden highlights as his eyes lit up. His lower lip was dimpled, the tips of his fangs just slightly touching the flesh. The teacher was already gone, vanishing on a wind that smelled of some fancy-dancy cologne.

But *he* didn't smell like a Christmas candle. Only Christophe. Who could I ask about that?

I kept hold of Graves. "Please. I'll go nuts if I'm locked up in my room again without anyone to talk to." *And I haven't been able to get you alone, you're always hanging out with the hairy boys. I do want to tell you about Christophe. Go figure.* "Graves. Please."

He shrugged, shoulders lifting and dropping. "I'm supposed to go to the armory. It's detention if I don't show up."

*What, you won't get involved unless I'm getting beat up? And since when are you worried about detention, for chrissake?* A sour taste filled my mouth. "Fine." But I didn't let go of his coat. Dylan would probably be along any second. "Go on, then."

"You don't understand—" Maddeningly, he shut his mouth and glared at me, like I was the problem. The bell rang again, urgently, and he tore himself free and headed out the door, the coat flapping around his calves.

Leaving me all alone in the empty classroom. My fingers stung, like from rug burn. My mother's locket was a cold, heavy weight under my layered shirts.

The bell finished ringing, and the weird staticky silence of the Schola under siege crawled into my head.

The boys all had jobs when that bell rang. Battle stations, some of them in the armory passing out weapons, others meeting at pre-determined points and waiting. The oldest students and the teachers went out to sweep the grounds.

Last time, some of them had come back beat up pretty bad. Bleeding, even. From the suckers.

I stood there for a few seconds, my hand scraped raw from the rough cotton of Graves's coat, yanked free of my grasp. This made the fourth Restriction. Someone always showed up to take me back to my room.

Not this time. Seconds ticked by, one after another. The fluorescents buzzed, and cobwebs in the upper corners drifted like seaweed. Some of the ceiling tiles were crumbling too.

*This place is falling apart. Jeez.*

It occurred to me that this was the first time I'd been really alone outside my room since I got here. I hunched my shoulders, pulled my sweater sleeves down, and realized I was waiting for someone to show up and tell me what to do. The switchblade was a heavy weight in my ass pocket, covered up by the sweater and the edge of Graves's flannel shirt.

*Way to go, Dru.* There was probably something else I could be doing. Anything. I'd been Dad's helper since Gran died, moving from town to town, getting rid of the nasty things that go bump in the night. Just standing here wasn't going to help anything. And waiting for someone to come back and shove me into my room wasn't going to help either.

The silence took on a new quality, static draining away, replaced with breathlessness. I blinked hard, twice, and turned around sharply. My hair fanned out in an arc, I moved so fast.

Perched on the back of the couch I'd sat on, Gran's owl ruffled its white feathers, each tipped with a shadow of gray. Its black beak looked unholy sharp. Yellow eyes held mine, and I let out a sharp sigh of mingled relief and pain.

*Oh, thank God. Where have you been?*

It was the first time I'd seen Gran's owl since I got here, outside of dreaming. The usual ringing started in my ears, a high clear thin tone like a bell stroked over and over. It filled my skull like cotton wool.

The owl cocked its head, a *what's up, boss?* look. I blinked. Dust motes hung suspended in the air, and the round clock fastened up over the door had gone silent. It wasn't even ticking.

This was the space between precognition and something weird happening. Something weird or Seriously Bad. It was too soon to tell which.

*Whoosh.* The owl took wing in a flurry of feathers. It was a big bird, almost too big for the room, turning in tight circles and heading for the door. Its wings *thopped* down just as it was about to hit them on the jamb on either side; it turned, smart as a spaceship in a movie, and was gone out into the hall.

Sudden certainty filled me. I was supposed to follow it.

Gran had always told me to trust this feeling, and Dad always told me not to let the backwoods foolishness take the place of clear logic. But he also never stopped me when I got that look on my face—the look that said I was seeing something he couldn't.

Gran was famous for "the touch" for miles around, and I'd always assumed I'd gotten it from her. After all, she'd trained me, right?

But now I was wondering just what I'd gotten from where.

The owl had shown up on my windowsill the last morning I'd seen Dad alive. Last time, the owl had led me to Dad's truck—and Christophe. The streak-headed werwulf that had bitten Graves had also been there, but that was incidental.

Wasn't it?

I didn't have time to sit around. I bolted after Gran's owl, my legs full of heavy unwillingness. The world slowed down to something covered in hard goopy plastic, a clear fluid I had to force my way through to move anywhere. This was also part of the space-between, that heaviness. I didn't have time to wonder if I was moving too quickly for the world to catch up, or if I just had to reach through a little more space to reach the body I moved around in on a daily basis.

My bruised shoulder clipped the door on the way out, and a zigzag of red pain shot all the way down my ribs. My sneakers slapped the stone floor, and I got up a good head of speed even through the clinging flood of whatever slows the world down when you're following your dead grandmother's owl.

The hall receded like a mirrored passage in a fun house, the kind where everything is multiplied into infinity. The yellow-pale glare of fluorescent lighting crawled into each crack and chip in the walls. Stone floor with occasional bursts of worn industrial carpet or old linoleum blurred under my squeaking sneaker soles. The Schola receded around me, its halls warping. One sleeve of the too-big blue sweater unrolled and flapped around my left hand, but I didn't have time to pull it up. It was hard work keeping the owl in sight as I slipped and skidded, bouncing off walls and on the verge of tripping countless times. Until it banked again, zooming down another short hall, and a pair of double doors was in front of me.

*I hope they're not locked.* But the right one threw itself open as soon as I hit it, the little pump-thing on top that made it close without slamming giving a high hard pop and a clatter as bits of it rained down. The door smacked the stone wall, and its hinges gave a scream. Chill night air poured in, blowing my hair back.

I leapt the threshold at warp speed, and the cold was a hammer blow against every inch of exposed skin. It cut right through me, and my tongue stuck to the roof of my mouth. The thick clotted taste of wax and citrus poured over my palate. The owl banked in a tight circle again, then headed away at a good clip.

The taste of oranges is bad trouble; Gran would call it an *arrah*. She meant "aura," like when people with migraines get weird tastes or smells right before their heads decide to cave in. Me, I just get a mouthful of fake rotting fruit, kind of, when something *really-bad-weird* is about to happen.

Like, say, when a sucker is about to come out of nowhere and paste you a good one. I mean, I also get it—but with a different tang—when I'm about to see an old friend, or things are going to get weird but not dangerous.

I wasn't going to slow down to find out which flavor of weird this was going to be. Not with that sudden sureness in the middle of my chest pulling me forward. Urging me on.

The woods pressed close into the building's personal space, and ribbons of greasy white threaded between black naked branches. It smelled wrong—too powdery for fog, with an undertone of the ugly dry smell of a snakeskin. And the cold was more than weather—it was a weight pressing against skin and heart and bone.

I took the three stairs down with a leap and landed hard, gravel crunching underfoot. Almost slipped, but pulled up high and tight like a ballerina, and flung myself after the owl. Here there were gardens—it might be pretty once spring came. Now, however, ice rimmed the wooden boards holding long rectangular plots of winter-dead garden back and dripped in icicles from the fog-ribboned trees. It was the east side of the complex of buildings that was the Schola, and I wondered in a dreamy sort of way how the hell I'd gotten over *here*.

Right behind the panic beating like a second heart inside me. And the fear soaking through my entire body. Something bad *was* about to happen, I was sure of it now. I could only hope I'd received the warning in time, and that I would be able to get away from it fast enough.

Past the gardens the land ran downhill in a gentle slope, toward the river. A ribbon of paved path curved down toward a shack of a boathouse, crouching against the moon-silvered water. The moon was half-full, shedding her light over a gray and white landscape that looked exactly like an ice sculpture with streaks of oil-soaked cotton wool hanging from every sharp edge.

The fog was closing around the Schola in grasping, veiny fingers.

Halfway down the hill, saplings and bushes started springing up, the forest's outliers. Then the trees rose, dense and black even though they were naked and festooned with shards of ice. The owl soared, came back, circled me as I ran, and shot forward down the hill, leaving the graveled path behind and crossing the paving, heading for the inky smear of trees.

My breath came in harsh caws of effort. I ran, and the owl returned, like it was pressing me to go faster. It wheeled over my head again, and I thought I heard Gran's voice. *That's a wise animal what muffles its wings so the mouse can't hear it, Dru. And it's a wise animal what hides even when it's quiet. You never know when somethin's up over the top of you lookin' down.*

The first time I'd seen the owl was on the sill of Gran's hospital window, the night she died. I'd kept quiet about it ever since. Only Dad knew about it, and he was—

*Stop thinking and run.* This time it was Dad's voice, full of quiet urgency. The only place their voices were left was in my head. It was better than being alone but it was so, so lonely.

I tried to speed up, but the thick clear goop over the world was hardening. My heart rammed against the walls of my chest, pulsing in my throat and wrists and eyes so hard, like it wanted to escape.

The world popped back up to speed like a rubber band, and I was flung forward as if a huge warm hand had reached down and tapped me like a pool ball. Almost fell, caught myself, and leapt over the last garden box, clearing it with feet to spare.

Sound rushed back in. Ice crackling, gravel flying, my own footsteps a hard tattoo against frozen ground, the harsh rhythm of my breathing—

—and behind me, padded footsteps and a high, chilling howl, queerly diluted through the odd, gleaming fog. The taste of oranges ran over my tongue again; I couldn't spit to clear my mouth and wouldn't have anyway, since it wasn't just waxen oranges. I knew for sure now it meant something totally and completely bad was going down.

I ran for the trees like my life depended on it. Because I knew, deep down, that it did.

# CHAPTER 8

**B**ranches slapped at my face and hands. I leapt over a
fallen log, crunched down in a pile of leaves, and fell. Scudgy
leafmuck splorched up through my fingers. The darkness
scored itself with little diamond holes of moonlight, sharp frozen
reflections. I scrambled to my feet and took off again, dodging a
creeping streamer of fog. The locket was a lump of ice on my chest.

Behind me, another howl lifted to the cold sky. This one was
edged with broken glass and razors. It burrowed into my head, scraping against the inside of my skull.

*They've found my trail.* I didn't know who *they* were, or even why
I was so sure they'd run across my scent. I just . . . knew, the way you
know how to breathe or to pull your hand back from a hot stove. The
way I knew to avoid the creeping little fingers of vapor rising from
the ground.

The same way I knew to keep running. No matter how many
times I fell.

I scrambled and floundered on. The owl's soft passionless *who? who?* slid through the woods, bouncing off the steel-hard bole of each frozen tree. There was a kind of halfass trail running along the leaf-strewn floor; I broke through the hard shell of a deep puddle and gasped as icy water grabbed at my ankles. Leapt and landed badly, my ankle almost rolling, stumbled on. The owl called again—*hurry up, Dru.*

Another inhuman scream lit the night, digging into the meat behind my eyes with razor claws. I let out a miserable, thin, gasping cry and stumbled forward, my hands coming up to clasp my head until the pain was cut off in mid-howl, just like a flipped switch.

*What the hell was that?* But I had no time to figure it out. I pulled myself into a fist inside my skull, just like Gran taught me. When another scream lifted out of the night, somewhere off to my left and a good ways away, it didn't scrape along the inside of my head. It just ran hard over my skin like a wire brush dripping with acid, and if I hadn't been throwing myself forward so hard, I probably would have yelled, too, in miserable surprise and pain.

That's the trouble with getting involved in the Real World. Once you're in, you can't shut it out and go back to daylight nine-to-five. You're stuck running through the woods at night, risking a broken leg and even worse, while something horrible chases you.

The thin track petered out, the way false trails in the woods do. One minute you think you're following the road back to somewhere you know; the next you leap sideways to avoid fog that shouldn't be moving like that, tip into a bunch of friendly thorn bushes, and wonder what the hell happened.

Except when you're running for your life, those bushes aren't friends. They spear through your clothes and rip at your skin, and by the time you thrash almost free, the footsteps behind you have drawn much nearer. So near you can hear every shift of weight and crackle of twigs breaking, each splutch of muck on the forest floor as they leap, higher and faster than a human ever could.

Gran's owl was now nowhere in sight. I froze, tangled in a bunch of thorny vines, and tried to control my gasping. My lungs were on fire; my heart was just about ready to bust out through my ribs and go sailing.

But I tried to be still and quiet. The bushes crackled, thorns scraping. One of them touched my cheek, a cold pinprick. I wanted to shut my eyes, lying tangled on my side, but the idea of being in the dark woods with my eyes closed just didn't work.

Even the fog was making a sound now. A small rasping, like scales against glass.

My hip, pressed against the cold ground, turned almost numb. Wetness seeped into my sweater and jeans. A cloud hung in front of my face—my own breath, gauzy and translucent.

The footsteps slid around me. There seemed to be two sets, circling each other. I squeezed my eyes shut, lost the battle with myself again, opened them. A line of thorns pressed into my sweater's back. My sneakers were soaked and my feet were so cold they had vanished into numbness.

Crashing. Snapping branches. Moonlight trickled in, spots of false color whirling in front of my light-starved eyes. The greasy white vapor pulled close, questing through tree branches and reaching down to puddle against frozen leaves with that tiny, horrible sound.

Soft, stealthy movement under the crashing. I couldn't tell where it was coming from, and locked my teeth over a helpless noise. Swallowed hard. The fog was creeping closer, closer, little drablets of it touching under leaves. It looked like claw-tipped fingers plucking at the fabric of the forest floor.

Something moved in my field of vision. Once I saw it, everything resolved into sharp focus. Anything moving is easier to see at night. The trouble comes when whatever it is stops and goes motionless, but this figure had a patch of shaggy white up near the top. It moved like a wulfen, with thoughtless grace, the fur blurring its outlines as it sidestepped a long white rope of seeking fog.

There was only one streak-headed werwulf I knew of, and I'd already tangled with him before. I'd shot him in the jaw, but not before he bit Graves. Christophe had shot him, too, right in front of Dad's truck. Sergej's pet, a wulfen broken to his will.

I didn't think he was here to offer me cookies.

*Ohshit. It's Ash.* I pulled in a soft breath. My lungs were starving, crying out for air. I lay still, and a cough tickled at the back of my throat. It always happens when you're hiding—a cough, a sneeze, something. It's stupid. The body decides to screw around with you, even though it knows being quiet is the only way it's going to go on living.

Ash stopped, head upflung, and sniffed. The tickle got worse. His head ducked a little, lean muzzle dipping, testing the air. He stepped sideways, utterly silent, and stopped again. The fog cringed away from him.

*Keep moving. Oh God, let him keep moving.*

Another soft call from Gran's owl marred the sudden silence, but I couldn't see it. The crashing and snapping had stopped. Everything was still, even the spots and shafts of moonlight holding their breath, trapped in reflective veils of white vapor.

Too late I remembered the stiletto in my ass pocket. If I'd thought to get it out, I could be armed now, instead of lying helpless in a tangle of thorns.

The streak-headed werwulf took another three steps, quick and eerily graceful, to the side. His head turned, and the mad gleam of his eyes seemed to pierce the darkness and burn into my skin.

*Did he see me? God, oh God. Did he?* My hand twitched, wanting to get at the knife. But if I did, I'd have to roll over and make noise. And good luck getting it out of my jeans in time to do anything about the werwulf.

God, how I wished for a gun. *Any* gun, even a .22. A nine-millimeter would be better. A .45 or an assault rifle would be the best. And someone to work it who had a bead on this thing would be awful nice too.

*And while I'm dreaming, I'd really like a pony.* My heart hammered, thudded, and basically tried to make me gasp again. I couldn't even start moving my hand toward my pocket—if I could see movement at night, a wulfen damn sure could. If he couldn't already *smell* me.

Why was he hesitating?

The tension stretched, unbearable second after unbearable second, and the taste of wax and dead oranges burst on my tongue, so hard I almost gagged.

I *hate* that. My eyes rolled as I tried not to swallow it, my mouth was full of spit—Jesus Christ, I was going to start *drooling* now. I know that taste isn't real, I know there's nothing in my mouth, but fuck if I'm ever going to swallow it.

The streak-headed werwulf folded down like a toy, a slow fluid movement. His shape rippled, becoming more slump-shouldered animal than vaguely human. The white streak got more vivid, or maybe it was a spot of moonlight pulsing on his pelt. A slight wheezing, chuffing noise came out of him. He was facing away from me, and I wondered if some of the teachers from the Schola were in the woods now.

*Ohplease. Please, God. Help me out a little here, come on. Please.*

Another shape resolved out of the moon-and-tree chiaroscuro, fog melding around it in a cloak of greasy cotton. Vaguely human-oid, tall and broad-shouldered. The moonlight picked out a white blur of face and two white blurs of hands, the rest just a shadow.

"Isn't this *nice*," the newcomer hissed, an affront to the silence filling the woods. The rasp underneath the words ran over my skin like a wire brush, again. I tried not to flinch. "Where is the little bitch? I can smell her."

Ash growled. The growl held not even the approximation of words, but it was chock-full of warning. Fur rippled, and the white streak on his head glowed.

"Shut up and *find* her!" The words held a slight lisp, and I knew why.

Because the tongue didn't work right around fangs. This was a sucker, a *nosferat*. I could tell by the way his voice sucked at the world around it, oily and cold.

And it sounded like he was after me.

*Well, duh, Dru. Big deal. Stay still.* The maddening tickle got worse. It was like a sharp stick digging into the back of my throat. Re-flex tears built up in my eyes, hot and aching. A thin finger of fog was creeping closer and closer to my feet, and I *knew* that it would touch me, and when it did the sucker would know I was here, and—

The werwulf's growl changed pitch and tone.

"Don't presume to bark at me, beast. The Master wants—"

I didn't get to find out what the Master wanted, because the werwulf sprang—*away* from me.

He collided with the sucker like a runaway freight train, a crunch that echoed between the fog-hung trees. The sucker let out an amazing, blood-chilling howl. They rolled over and over, hitting and splintering trees, bones and teeth snapping.

*Move move move!* Dad's bark in my head, as if I was on the heavy bag again, popping punches and sweating, wanting to make him proud. Or as if we were dealing with those roach spirits again, me passing ammo through the window with shaking hands and—

I scrambled to my feet, thorns raking every exposed edge and pulling at my sweater like they were trying to tell me to stay down, and bolted. Leapt over the fingers of vapor crawling over the ground like I was doing football tryouts or something, skipping too fast to really keep my balance. It didn't matter where I was heading, as long as it was *away*.

The woods got deeper and denser, and I tore through them. Trees whipped past, some of them clutching at me like they were on the sucker's side, trying to slow me down. More thorny vines snaked across my path, but the fog had retreated. I floundered through, making a hell of a lot of noise, and heard a high, chilling howl behind me.

I thought wulfen howls were bad when I heard them in my own garage. Hearing the high, glassy cry in the middle of the woods at night is infinitely worse, because the howl sounds like it could be words if you just listen hard enough. The horrible thing is that it pulls on that deep hidden part in every person—the blind animal part.

The part that knows you're the prey.

But the worst thing about it?

Is when it sounds *right behind you*, and something hits from behind, tumbling you into another thorn-spiked mess of vines and branches, leaf mold and dirt filling your nose, and a huge, hot, hairy hand winds in your hair.

# CHAPTER 9

**tried to scream,** but the other paw-hand had clamped over my mouth just before I could get enough air in. Hot breath touched the top of my head as we both lay for a second, me with the sense knocked out of me, stunned and scraped all over.

*Goddammit, girl, that ain't gonna cut it!* Dad's voice yelled in my head. *Let's see some action here!*

It's what he used to yell when I was working the heavy bag, so tired my arms were about to fall off. It meant I was going to have to do more, be more, in order to help him. He needed his helper, and that was me, and death doesn't wait for when you're rested and ready. It sneaks up on you when you're exhausted and hungry and cold and so scared you can't even see straight.

I thrashed, flung my head back and clipped a wet, cold nose with my skull. It hurt and the wulf made a little pained yowl, like a puppy running into something. My elbow sank into his midriff, and he huffed out another sound with a whine at the end. His hand loosened from my hair, but that was only so he could grab me by the waist as I struggled and he braced himself.

His arms clamped down like steel bands, and he growled. Terror short-circuited everything inside my head, and I still don't know how I got free, rolling away along a slippery, gucky strip of rotting leaves.

He growled again and scrambled fluidly to his feet. I scooted backward, my filthy palms skidding in muck and dirt, and hitched in a breath to scream, as the wulf gathered himself, the white streak glowing at his temple like a neon sign, and leapt—

—straight *over* me, colliding with a shape in midair and both of them falling less than three feet from me with a jarring thud, squirts and puffs of fog evaporating. Hissing, tearing, bone-ripping sounds filled my head as I lunged away from this new madness. They rolled, the white streak bobbing, and an unutterably final crunching sound was followed by a hot black gush that splattered the trees in every direction. Sucker blood smoked where it landed, and some of it whizzed past my face, speckling my sweater and sending a stripe of thick warmth up the left leg of my jeans. I cried out, a small sound of disgust lost in the larger noise as the streak-headed wulfen threw back his head and growled, a shattering thunderous noise.

I was still trying to get away, scooting backward in wet jeans, the smoking vampire blood puffing into that same greasy mist once it had finished eating through denim. I was going so fast, in fact, that I ran smack into a tree for the first time that night. Which was pretty miraculous, you know, it being only the first time instead of the fourth or fifth.

A keg of dynamite went off inside my head, and my ribs screamed in pain. I was pretty much full of agony all over, and pretty goddamn sure I'd pulled something in my back again, too. God, if I lived to be an old lady I would probably have so many back problems—but it looked like I wouldn't be around that long.

The streak-headed werwulf hitched himself up and jerked across the space between us. Furrows of dead wet leaves exploded up, and he dug his claws in and stopped, his snout in my face and his breath touching my wet skin. The fog retreated behind him, pulling back like singed fingers.

I let out another small sound, this one cut in half as my breath hitched, every aching muscle tensing in preparation. His breath chuffed in, chuffed out, and it smelled oddly like peppermint and copper.

His eyes were inches from mine, his longer, sleek nose almost touching the tip of my just-human one. A long, long inhale, and I leaned back into the trunk as far as I could. The gleam in his dark eyes was horribly human, and just as terribly hurt and insane. The white streak glowed at me, so bright I thought another random beam of moonlight had gotten caught in his fur.

He sniffed me again and made a low, painful sound. His mouth couldn't shape a human word, so I had no idea what he was saying, whether he was threatening me or . . .

Or what? Why was he just *crouching* there, staring into my eyes? The tree behind me was an icy wall of rough steel, and my legs were still twitching, trying to push me right through it. The werwulf leaned forward again, making that queer, horrible noise, and I smelled hot copper.

Blood. Someone was bleeding. Was it me? Had I just not felt it when he clawed me open?

A rushing noise filled my head, and I heard the beat of mufflefeathered wings just before the werwulf dipped forward, his cold nose-tip pressing my cheek for a moment. Then he melted away. He ran across the small clearing, hitching and favoring his front left paw-hand, and vanished into the trees just as I heard someone yelling my name.

"*Dru! Dru! Goddamn you Dru where are you?*" It was Graves,

screaming-hoarse, and I was faintly surprised. I was even more surprised not to be dead. There was no fog now. The trees were silvered only by moonlight and festooning ice.

I sagged against the tree, vampire blood smoking all over my ruined, filthy clothes, and I did the single most inappropriate thing I could.

I began to laugh. High-pitched, whistling laughter as insane as the broken thing peering out through Ash's eyes.

# CHAPTER 10

"Let me get this straight." Dylan's hair was wildly mussed, his aspect shining through as he struggled to retain his composure. The way his fangs kept popping out and retreating was not happy or helpful. "Three dead *nosferatu* on your trail, you're beat up and covered in their blood, and you can't remember what happened?"

I couldn't stop shivering. I just nodded. My hair dripped muddy water, and I smelled like I'd been dipped in death.

Graves had his arm around the blanket he'd wrapped me in, and he made a restless movement. "Come on. Let's get you somewhere warm." He gave Dylan a green-eyed glare and started up the hill, half holding me up.

"Wait a goddamn second." Dylan didn't think much of this. "The Schola was broken into. They went right for her classroom. She somehow escaped a trio of hunters—none of whom we can identify yet, all three of them eviscerated out here in the damn woods. She needs to tell us what happened so we can—"

"Have her die of hypothermia? Good plan. Jesus Christ, you guys are jackasses." The hem of Graves's coat flapped as he sped up. "Look at her, dammit. Her lips are blue and she's covered in crap. Is she bleeding? Do you even care? No wonder there's no girls around."

I wondered what that had to do with anything, couldn't figure it out, and hiccupped out another long string of half-hysterical, muffled laughter. I kept glancing around and flinching whenever I saw white moonlight.

Dylan's eyes glittered in the dimness. "Shut *up*, dogboy. Just because you're a prince among your kind doesn't mean you can—"

That hot pocket of rage bubbled up inside me. This was getting ridiculous—but I welcomed the heat, because it was anything other than the dazed, panicked numbness. "Dylan," I heard myself say, between two choked giggles and a coughing snort, since there was mud in my nose. "You call him a nasty name again and I'm going to knock your teeth out." I found that my wet feet could still grip the ground, and— even better—my weak shivering legs could still carry me. "Graves . . ." The word died in a spate of deep bronchial almost-retches.

"Just relax, kiddo," Graves muttered. His arm was tense over my shoulder, pulling me closer to his warmth. The food around here was bulking him up big-time. Or maybe I just felt so small, the way I hardly ever do. "Christ."

Yeah, I felt small. And vulnerable. And very, very terrified.

Dylan shook his head like I hadn't even said anything. "Why did you leave the Schola, Dru?"

*Because something was coming to kill me, duh. When Gran's owl shows up, I follow. It's that simple.* I was too tired to even begin explaining.

A running mass of shapes clustered at the top of the hill. Some had thought to bring flashlights, and golden beams scoured the darkness. It was useless—*djamphir* and wulfen could both see way better than the average human after sunset. But those swords of light were a welcome sight, because they weren't greasefog or moonlight on a crazy wulfen's pelt, and I let out a half-sob. Graves's arm tightened again over my shoulders. "It's okay," he called. "We found her!"

Dylan cursed. They started down, a mass of boyshapes. The wulfen leapt ahead, some of them blurring between fur and skin in that clay-under-water way they do, and I swallowed another harsh sound. It's always weird to see them change and to hear the crackle of bone shifting, flesh running, and fur sprouting. . . .

Yeah. It about makes your lunch want to escape, even if you haven't had any. And even if you were used to Bigtime Weird.

"Goddammit." Dylan made a short, sharp movement, and his voice dropped into a hurt-angry whisper. "I can't help you if you don't talk to me, Dru."

*Yeah, I don't think you could help me even if I did talk to you. There's just not enough words in the world.* My brain hurt, and the rest of me was clumsy and cold.

I couldn't stop coughing. Or laughing, little hitching noises that spilled out of my throat between the harsh rasping. Graves just pulled me along, and the wulfen reached us in a tide of fur and bright eyes. They flowed around me, some of them clapping Graves on the shoulder, most of them sliding between human form and furry, loping kind-of-quadruped. The sudden babble, after the silence and terror of the woods, broke over us both.

"Is she okay?"

"She all right?"

"Dru?" Dibs stepped close, was pushed aside, but not before his fingers brushed my wrist—a fleeting, warm touch. I let out another choking sound.

"Is she all right?"

Behind them, the *djamphir* came crowding. Irving was pale, his curls springing as his aspect slid over him and retreated. They started asking if I was okay, too, but Graves just dragged me through, the wulfen moving with him and somehow everyone getting out of his way, until we got to the doors on the east side of the Schola.

The doors were blown outward, shards of wood lying over the steps, and I blinked. *I didn't do that.*

But maybe something behind me *had.* Once more, Gran's owl had led me out of danger. Or into it, depending.

And oh God but another memory was rising up, the owl on my window ledge the last morning I ever saw Dad alive. I started coughing in earnest.

I didn't want to think about that. I'd rather cough my lungs out.

The hall I'd run down was a mess, splattered with smoking black sucker blood, the carpet torn up and the waist-high paneling gouged. Paler wood in the deep furrows glared at me. "J-j-j-j—" I was trying to express my dismay, but Graves just kept going at a good clip, his arm a steel bar over my shoulders. My feet dragged uselessly most of the time. He actually shouldered a few kids out of the way, a snarl running just under the surface of the babble of voices.

I gathered there had been two teams of suckers, one that had burst in near the sparring chapel and made a lot of ruckus, and a trio of "hunters" who had quietly infiltrated the west wing of the Schola—the one I'd had my first class of the evening in. I must have just escaped them.

*That* was an uncomfortable thought. My feet dragged along the floor. I left dirty clumps wherever I tried to step, but Graves was doing all the work of moving us along. As long as he was doing such a handy job of it, I didn't care.

The sparring chapel was a long way away, and it seemed awful cold. My teeth were still chattering, and everything seemed very far away, even the noise as some kind of scuffle and yelling started.

We reached the deserted chapel, every footfall echoing. Graves palmed open the door on the girls' side, and a gasp went up behind us. He just kept going, dragging me through, and the door whooshed shut. Thick, silky steam billowed, and I coughed again.

"Goddammit," he said quietly, and hauled me across the tiled floor. The word bounced back at us through the vapor in the air. "What the fuck is going on?"

"I d-d-d—" I was about to say I didn't know, gave up. He looked down at me, his face sallow in the steam-filled light, and his jaw set. When he looked like that, serious and determined, you could see where he would be handsome. The girls would go for him big-time, especially in any urban place where they don't value cookie-cutter looks as much. A bolt of shameful, nameless heat went through me at the thought.

"You want me to help with your clothes?" The blanket fell with a sodden plop, and he shucked his coat, almost tearing the sleeve because he couldn't get out of it and hold me upright at the same time very well. "Or, um, I can just stay at the door. In case."

"H-h-h-help. M-me." The shivers were making it hard to think or breathe. I grabbed at the hem of my sweater with clumsy-cold swollen fingers. Graves pulled it up as he braced me; I got lost in it for a second and finally struggled out of the heavy, wet wool. It landed with a splutching sound, and I wondered how much water I'd been lying in out in the woods, and why it wasn't more frozen when ice was everywhere.

Ribbons of steam in the air were white and heavy. I didn't want to think about it.

The entire world went glaring white for a minute, and the next thing I knew Graves was holding me up and awkwardly peeling the sleeves of the flannel shirt off my goose bump–covered arms. I struggled out of my T-shirt, swaying as he held me up. My teeth clicked like castanets, and he went for my jeans while looking grimly up over my shoulder. My bra was wet too, but thankfully not dirty.

My fingers were like wet sausages, too clumsy to do much. The jeans were loose, and he let out a low whistle when he saw the bruises ringing my shoulder, my ribs, and the fresh ones beginning on my arms and the side of my right leg. My socks were filthy, and I'd lost a sneaker somewhere. I honestly didn't remember *where*. I hadn't even noticed it was gone.

His hands were scorching hot; he dragged me to the lip of the closest tub and paused for only half a second, looking up at the ceiling like he was gathering himself. His beat-up black nylon wallet landed on the floor three feet away, and he pitched down the steps and into the huge tub with me, fully clothed, his shoes giving one forlorn underwater squeak before I lost my footing and cried out miserably. It felt like being dipped in hot lava, but he held onto me, guiding me down.

I'd never been in the baths in my underwear. The feeling was weird, like sitting in a hot tub full of Jell-O while wearing a swimsuit that definitely wasn't made for this sort of thing.

"Dru?" For the first time that evening, he sounded scared. "Come on. Say something."

The chattering had stopped, but I was still shivering. Somehow my arm had ended up around his waist, and he settled onto the seat right next to me. The surface of the bath crackled against his sweater. I gasped again, my skin pain-peeled like after a sunburn, and tipped my head back. Bubbling not-water turned gray, dirt swirling through it before it was whisked away by the current. A leaf fell out of my hair, hit the turbulent surface, and was pulled under. The not-water was neck-deep on me, and only chest-deep on him.

"Dru?" Now he sounded close to panic, and I realized I was making another low, keening sound. My throat was full of something too hot and nasty to be tears. "Say something, dammit."

I swallowed the weird moaning sound I was making. My mouth opened. "S-s-s-something." I paused. "D-d-dam-mmit."

He snorted. The laugh caught him sideways, his usual bitter, sarcastic little bark, and I was too grateful to still be alive to really think about the fact of being half-naked in a tub with a boy.

Besides, it was *Graves*. And his arm was still around me. I put my head down on his shoulder and forgot about everything other than the stinging heat pushing its pins and needles into my flesh.

I hadn't been this close to him since we'd both squeezed onto a helicopter lifting out of a Midwest snowstorm. I'd been crying then, too.

Now I wondered about all sorts of things. Especially about him having to fight the first night he got here. Getting Dibs alone and having him explain a few things seemed like a good idea. I wondered why I hadn't thought of it before. My head was so heavy, and Graves's shoulder was bony but comfortable.

"Talk to me," he pressed. "Don't pass out on me, Dru. Hey, I got a question."

"Huh." An affirmative noise was about all I could come up with. *So do I. Why didn't Ash kill me? And how in God's name do I start telling you about all this when it doesn't make any sense even to me?*

"What's Dru short for?"

*Jesus.* It was my turn to half-snort a laugh. "D-don't ask."

"Too late. I been wondering all this time."

The shivers started easing up. My jaw was sore when it finally unclenched. "Tell you l-later."

"Mh. So you wanna tell me what happened?" Gently, carefully, like he was lifting up a Band-Aid and checking underneath it.

"I—" The water bubbled. The door banged a little, like someone was leaning on it. The sound echoed through the locker room. I blinked, waking up inside my own head. "Oh jeez. You're in *here*."

"Uh, yeah." He didn't sound surprised. "Was thinking you might fall and hurt yourself or something. Drown. If you're okay, or—"

I kept my head on his shoulder. Pressed it down a little and made my arm tense up. "Don't. Don't leave." My teeth ached. Even my *hair* ached. "There was . . . I saw . . . okay, it was my grandmother's owl." A brief flare of panic worked up inside me—I'd never really *wanted* to tell anyone about it, and the habit of the secret was hard to break.

But this was Graves. And he didn't disappoint me. He just accepted it. "Owl." Nodded, his sharp chin dipping. "Okay."

"And it led me outside, and I ran. I think it was trying to get me away from the suckers. I ended up in some bushes and I saw . . ." The rest of it spilled out in an incoherent jumble, but he nodded every once in a while. I liked that about him. He was so smart you didn't have to hold his hand and walk him through everything. He could fill in the blanks on his own.

"You're sure it was the same one?" His eyes had half-lidded. The not-water began to calm down, bubbling and fizzing. It stung my scratched hands and spread up my shoulder in little waxy dollops, heat sinking in.

I suddenly wanted to wash my hair. My scalp crawled. My heart had finished its pounding and finally settled down. "I guess. How many werwulfen with white streaks on their heads have we seen?"

"Point." His head dipped in another nod. His hair, getting damp from the steam, fell in his eyes. He tossed it out with a shaking, sudden motion.

I let out a sigh. I couldn't keep it in any longer. It came out in a whisper. "I saw Christophe. During the day." It was more like three or four days ago, but I didn't want to tell him *that*.

Graves stiffened. A full thirty seconds ticked by, him staring at the mirrored wall through veils of steam. "Jesus, Dru."

Like it was *my* fault. "I couldn't get you alone to tell you."

"So you tried *this*?" But he was joking. He shifted uneasily, moving as if his arm was cramping, but he left it where it was, his fingers no longer burning my other shoulder. "Where did you see him?"

"He came in through my window. You can't tell anyone."

He rolled his eyes. I couldn't see it, but I could *feel* the movement. And the rolling of teenage eyes has a noiseless noise all its own. "Duh. But what was he doing coming through your *window*?"

*Hell if I know, kid.* "Giving me some things. Stuff like my mother owned. And telling me some things."

"How the hell did he have things that belonged to your mother?"

Trust Graves to boil everything down to its essentials. "They aren't; they're just *like* hers. And, well, I guess he knew her." I hadn't thought about it just that way before. He'd certainly *sounded* like he knew her. And now that I thought about it, he'd said specifically that the wooden swords weren't hers. I opened my mouth to go on with explanations.

But he asked the other sixty-four-thousand-dollar question before I could. "Just how old is he, anyway? And *who* is he?"

"I dunno." I slid down a little further into the not-water's embrace, and another cloud of dirt from my wet hair went through the bubbling jelly. *Jeez. How much guck did I get rolled in?* "I'm more worried about Ash not killing me. He had the chance. He got rid of those other suckers, and—"

"You saw that?"

"I saw one. Stands to reason he did the other two." A tremor went through the center of my bones. "Jesus." *I could have died. There's no way out of that classroom, and three suckers . . .*" He was right nose to nose with me, Graves. Nose to nose." My brain kept making a funny hitching stop when it got to the memory, replaying it, throwing up its hands in horror, and stalling like an engine. "And the fog . . ."

But I didn't want to think about the fog ever again. Thank God it hadn't touched me. If it had . . . I didn't know quite what would have happened, but it would have been bad. I *knew* that much, all the way down to my quivering, aching bones.

It's hard to argue with certainty like that.

Graves was more worried about essentials. "A wulf working alone did that? And he just . . . what, ran away?"

"Guess he heard the rest of you coming." The shaking intensified. It wasn't shivering. It was my body rebelling against everything. I wanted a cheeseburger, and I wanted to curl up and sleep, and I wanted things I couldn't even name. Most of all, I wanted to just shut my eyes and make all this madness go away.

My head was still on his shoulder. He was still holding me. He was still fully clothed and hadn't said a word about it. A long silence passed between us, full of steam and the funny burpchuckle bubbling of the not-water. It hissed a little bit as I slid down some more, more of the dirt in my hair getting whisked free.

"I don't know what to do," I whispered finally. It scared me more than I wanted to admit. I was used to knowing what the procedure was in every situation; I was used to Dad knowing what I didn't and giving me orders when I was out of my depth.

I mean, Dad never let me flounder. Not like some parents, who will just sit there and watch you flail around. I've seen that a lot, and it always looks to me like the adults *want* the kid to fail.

Maybe it makes them feel better when we do, or something.

Graves sighed. "Okay." His shoulders came up, the one I'd propped my head on, digging into my cheekbone. "We should get you cleaned up. And Dylan's going to have a cow."

"Why wasn't he there?" As soon as I said it out loud, I regretted it. "Someone always came to get me when the bell rang before. This time, nobody."

"Yeah." Not-water splashed as he moved. "I was thinking that too. Let's get you cleaned up." He untangled himself from me, and I had to lift my head. The burning had settled into a more soothing heat, soaking in. My back hurt, but not as much as it could have.

"Graves?"

"Huh?" He swung back, and for the second time that night I was face-to-face with a shapechanger. But this one had bright green eyes, and his dyed-black hair hung in damp strings, and he was the same half-ugly kid who had been the only person I could depend on since a zombie smashed its way through my kitchen door.

Less than a month, and my entire life was in the kind of mess only the Real World could make. I had no idea how to start fixing it, but he was here, and he hadn't let me down yet.

We stared at each other for a long moment. My throat was dry. I was pretty sure dirt was smeared all over my face and my hair was sticking up like Medusa's. But I leaned forward just a little, and if he hadn't turned his head a little bit, my lips wouldn't have landed on his cheek.

His skin was softer than I'd have thought under the stubble showing up, and I had to sniff because my nose was full. But I pressed my lips against his cheek and felt like an idiot. What had I been about to do?

*Okay, Dru. Time to play this cool.* "Thanks. I mean, for getting me in here, and all." I retreated, suddenly very aware I was just in panties and a bra that were probably now ruined, and that he had dumped himself into the tub without even taking his shirt off. And I probably had dirt all over my stupid face. "You're always, you know, around. When I need you. Thanks."

Of all the things to say.

*OhmyfuckingGOD, Dru, how stupid can you be?* I made it over to the other side of the tub and hoped the heat would hide the red marching up my neck to plant itself in my cheeks.

Graves actually coughed. It was kind of decent of him. "No problem." He headed for the stairs out of the tub, awkwardly swilling a lot of crackling wax around. He floundered up and out, almost slipped, grabbed the edge of the tub. "First one's. Yeah. Free."

He was probably just as embarrassed as I was. I sank back into the tub, reached out, and held onto the edge myself. I was feeling kind of like my arms and legs might fail me at any moment.

I hunched in the bath for a long while, shivering and shaking, and the only thing that got me out of there was the thought that one of the teachers might think I was drowning and come in to "rescue" me.

Or, you know, kill me. Because it seemed pretty obvious that the Schola, where Christophe had promised me I'd be safe, was a pretty damn dangerous place.

# CHAPTER 11

**W**hen you're up all night all the time, midnight is the middle of the day. It's not late enough to be lunch yet, but it's too late for breakfast, and when you've been chased and have rolled around in muck, are you hungry anyway?

I was. I was *starving*. But instead of being in the caf, I was sitting in Dylan's office again. Looking at the shelves of leather-bound books and waiting. It *was* just like the principal's office, and Graves had vanished after handing me a fistful of dry clothes brought from my own room through the door of the girls' locker room.

I didn't like that. It was just numbers one and two on a list of things I didn't like. Someone—maybe even Graves himself—would have had to go through the rosewood dresser in my room, and whoever it was even brought panties, for God's sake. It was creepy. Thank God I hadn't hidden anything in there. I mean, the panty drawer has *got* to be the first place anyone's going to look, right?

And where was Graves? I had a funny squirrelly feeling in my chest when I thought about him not being here. I wanted to see him.

I wanted to see any friendly face. Nobody else here qualified except maybe Christophe, and he was nowhere around. I didn't have any clue *where* he was.

Dylan was off doing whatever it was he did when he wasn't sighing at me, or preparing to come in and sigh at me. Which left me all alone, my hair washed clean and dripping and my teeth clenched together. Not to mention with my head full of questions, and arms and legs that didn't feel too steady. I slumped in the usual high-backed, carved chair, staring at the books. They were a treasure trove of titles about the Real World, from demographic surveys on werwulfen to a whole section on witchcraft and black hexes, their spines lettered with crimson foil.

I bit on my right index fingernail, chewing along until it was nonexistent. Moved to the next nail. *What I wouldn't have given to have a crack at some of those while Dad was alive. He might've liked it too.* I wouldn't have minded a peek at the hex books. Dad preferred human intel—asking questions in occult shops and bars where the Real World congregated. I'd been in and out of those places ever since Gran died and Dad came to pick me up, and I was beginning to think it had been a lot more dangerous than even he had thought. Every time he took me into another place to get the lay of the land, he got really tense.

Now I wondered if it was because I was with him, or because a misstep could have meant both of us ending up dead. And I wondered why he never told me about Mom being *svetocha*. Why hadn't he said something? Anything? Was he planning on telling me when I was old enough? How old was "old enough"? What the hell had he been waiting for?

Or had he not known? Had it been my mother's secret?

How *could* it have been?

I started chewing on my right ring fingernail. Then again, Dad never was a touchy-feely say-everything kind of guy. We could spend whole days not talking, just getting things done. I was always proud of knowing exactly what to do without him having to tell me every time. Gran hadn't been a big one for talking either, preferring to teach by example, but next to Dad she was positively chatty.

And how would Dad have told me, anyway? *Dru, honey, your mother was part vampire, which means you are too. Sorry about that.*

My heart hurt. I squeezed my eyes shut, tried not to think about it.

The door opened. I stayed slumped in the chair, even though my heart leapt nastily and I had to swallow a gasp. I grabbed at the chair's arms, and my feet slid in a little bit in case I had to stand up in a hurry.

Almost dying will make you a little jumpy.

"Here she is." Dylan sounded tired. "*Entrez-vous*, my space is yours."

I heard a light step and a swish of something. A spicy, pretty smell filled the air, and I craned my neck, opening my mouth to ask Dylan where the hell Graves was.

The words died in my throat as the advisor stepped to one side, closing the door and standing at attention right in front of it. A shadow slid past him and glided toward me.

She was tall for a girl, and her hair was a glory of reddish curls. Narrow shoulders, wide blue eyes, a pointed chin, and a long, old-timey dress of red silk. That hair was perfect, held back from her heart-shaped face with two black-velvet bows. She half-turned, leaned back, and hopped up to perch on Dylan's desk, shoving paper back with her skirt.

I stared. Her boots were pointed and heeled, and rows of tiny buttons marched up her shins. She crossed her ankles and looked at me. Her eyes turned a little lighter as dark streaks slid through her hair, the curls becoming looser and longer as her aspect flooded her. The twin points of delicate little fangs touched her pink-glossed lower lip.

*Holy shit.* I stared some more.

"Dru," Dylan said, calmly enough. "This is Lady Anna. Milady, this is Dru Anderson."

"Hello, Dru." She had a sweet, chiming voice. I stayed where I was, nailed in place, my mouth half-open. "Is that a nickname? What is it short for?"

I was *so* not going to answer that. But my mouth opened anyway. "You're *svetocha*." The words just fell out. "Jesus Christ. I thought I was—" I sounded accusing, and Dylan straightened self-consciously, his jacket creaking. "Holy *shit*."

Her smile faltered for a moment. "I'm a well-kept secret. If the *nosferatu* suspected, they would attack every place we own, even this small satellite of the Order, with far more frequency. Already, with you here for such a short period of time, we've had several students injured and a marked increase in the number of . . . incidents."

*So that's my fault? Jesus.* A hot ugly feeling welled up inside me. I closed my mouth with a snap. We looked at each other for a few minutes, her fangs retreating and the curls in her hair tightening up, until she looked just like a storybook impression of a princess.

"We are hoping that the attack on this Schola was merely routine, a matter of them probing our defenses. Though it seems unlikely, doesn't it?" She tilted her perfect head. "Hopefully none of them escaped to carry tales."

I finally dug up something to say that wasn't a cussword. "Where's Graves?" This was all very well, but he was the one person I wanted to talk to. I needed him here for this.

Dylan shifted uneasily. "He's in the dorms." His fangs were out, and he looked unhappy. It was just a subtle downward tilt to the corners of his mouth, but it was such a change from his generally irritated expression, it was pretty shocking. "Milady wanted to meet you, Dru. It's a high honor for a first-year student."

*Color me all impressed and shit.* "Why? I mean, why did she want to come here? If I'm such a problem."

"You're not a problem—" Dylan began, but the girl glanced at him mildly, and he shut up so fast I was surprised he didn't lose a chunk of his tongue.

"May I?" She cocked her head, and Dylan spread his hands helplessly. She smiled a little bit. Those teensy little fangs were creepy as hell, especially when she tilted her head and looked cat-content. "You are unruly, Miss Anderson. You have been here barely two weeks and have already pressured a Kouroi into sparring with you, with unpleasant results. You seem to have no pride in your heritage—which isn't your fault, given your upbringing, but it is distressing. You have so much potential, but you seem content to waste it on pointless intransigence." She was solemn now, her mouth turning down like she tasted something a little unpleasant but was too polite to spit it out. "That's our fault. We have not expressed to you the reasons why we do things as we do, and I confess I have been very busy making arrangements for your continued safety, as well as other . . . arrangements for the safety of others in the Order. The work has taken up so much of my time that I have been unable to meet with you before now. And . . . well, I suppose the best way to say it is just to *say* it."

*I don't like the sound of that.* My "wrong" chimes were ringing like mad. I shifted uncomfortably. The chair had gotten really hard all of a sudden. Dylan made a soft coughing noise, clearing his throat. His dark eyes flashed, but whether it was a warning or an allergy attack, I couldn't tell.

Anna lifted one narrow hand, and her nails were lacquered pink too. *My God. All she needs is a muff and a cute little pink cell phone all covered in rhinestones. Ugh.* The smell of her—spice and goodness and warm perfume—reminded me of something, but I didn't know just what. I was too busy staring at her flawless face, the blush rising in her matte cheeks, the arc of her eyelashes.

My next thought was sudden and chilling. *I could never in a million years look like that. I'm not sure I'd want to, either.*

"We don't know why Reynard saved you from Sergej." Her tone dropped to confidential instead of just worried and hoity-toity. "Did he tell you anything at all?"

*Reynard? Oh yeah.* She meant Christophe. "He said he was part of the Order, and—"

"He said that?" Her gaze sharpened over my shoulder, and I knew she and Dylan were exchanging a Look that could have been Parental. Or at least Teacherlike. How old was this girl? She looked about eighteen, which could have meant anything here. "Would it surprise you to know Christophe Reynard hasn't been an *official* part of the Order for a good seventeen years or so? The negotiations to bring him back to us have been . . . difficult."

"Nobody trusts him." Next to her careful, polite, well-modulated tone, my voice was harsh. I'd scraped my throat raw with coughing. "Dylan said when he came back he'd train me, because—"

"Dylan is of Christophe's camp. He's been his supporter for a long time, and indeed was Reynard's sponsor. He argued and pressed and cajoled to have Reynard accorded the honor of membership in our ranks, despite his . . . unfortunate ancestry."

"His what? Slow down and speak English." I pushed myself upright in the chair. I was tired and hungry, and I wanted to see Graves. And oh yeah, I wanted to curl up in bed and shake. I wanted to lock my door and the shutters over my window and spend a little time just trembling. It sure as hell sounded good.

There was a slow, uncomfortable silence. "You might as well tell her," Dylan said. "If you're going to."

"I suppose so." She fixed me with her limpid look, and I felt every pimple I'd ever had fighting toward the surface again. "Did Christophe tell you anything about his family?"

"Just that his mom was dead too, I think." It was hard to remember when I was thinking through soup. Come to think of it, he hadn't told me much at all. "Other than that, nothing. What's this all about? He didn't tell me a goddamn thing, and nobody's told me really anything since I *got* here."

"It would surprise you, then, to know that Christophe's given name was Krystof Gogol?" A significant pause while I shook my head, mute, wondering where the hell she was going. "And the *nosferat* you escaped from two months ago, the acknowledged king of those who hunt the night, was born Sergej Gogol?"

"Huh?" I was exhausted. That's the only reason why it took ten full seconds for what she was really saying to trickle through the fog in my head. "You what?"

Anna's shoulders slumped. For the first time, she looked a little tired too. But it was just a gloss over her prettiness. "You didn't know. Christophe is Sergej's son. The eldest and, for a time, the most proud and wicked of his progeny. He saved you from his father and disappeared. But even before that, Reynard was interfering in your family."

My heart was beating very loudly. All the breath had whooshed out of me. "Say *what?*" It was a tiny little squeak from a dry throat.

Anna hopped off the desk and faced me squarely, her hands clasped in front of her. She said what I was afraid she'd say. "We have reason to believe, Miss Anderson, that it was Reynard who gave away your mother's location to Sergej. And we need your help to find out if he did."

\* \* \*

She laid the manila folder on the desk's cluttered surface. Her pink-lacquered fingernails scraped slightly. "This is what we think happened. Your mother was in a safe location." The folder flipped open, and the world skidded to a halt underneath me.

My teeth ground together behind the frozen lake of my face. They were tingling again, and the red sparkles at the corners of my vision were back. I swallowed harshly, tasting danger and rage.

It was an eight-by-ten glossy in full color, and it showed a yellow house with an oak tree growing by the front steps. I stared at the picture and my skin went cold, then hot, then cold again. Every muscle ache twinged once, then hardened into nausea.

Have you ever felt so sick your entire body feels like throwing up? Like that.

The last time I'd seen that house was in a dream.

Or was it a dream? Something I'd woken up from with Christophe and Graves both in the room, fighting off a dreamstealer—a winged serpent sucking at my breath, a thing that slunk away to lay eggs in my neighbors. Those eggs had hatched the next morning, and driving through a bunch of young wiggling dreamstealers to escape the wulfen attack on my house had been a nightmare.

I'd thought maybe it was a hallucination, the impossibly clear and detailed vision of my mother hiding me in the middle of the night.

*It wasn't a dream.* A chill hard voice spoke up in the very middle of my head. *It was memory. That was what happened when Mom died. This is the house she died in. She hid me in the closet and went out to fight. And she got killed.*

The *svetocha* next to me flipped the photo aside. Next was another glossy eight-by-ten. This time, the oak was in full summer leaf—except for the huge scorched half of it, twisted and blackened by some horrible thing still vibrating in the branches. The screen door was busted off its hinges, and the steps were shattered.

There was something terrible caught in the tree's clutching fingers. Something human-shaped, but agonizingly distorted. The image seared itself on my eyes, burrowed into my brain.

"We think she died on the steps," Anna said softly, "but Sergej hung her in the tree and . . . well. We didn't get there in time. Your father was long gone, too, with you. We didn't even know about you until years later."

*He hung her in the tree. Oh God.* "You didn't know about me?" I sounded breathless even to myself.

When she answered, there was a faint tinge of something—bitterness? Anger? I couldn't decide and didn't care. "No. Your mother . . . left the Order for her own reasons. Nobody knows what those reasons were."

*I don't either.* I blinked hard. Cleared my throat. "I thought *svetocha* were toxic to suckers. That's what—" *That's what Christophe said.*

"We are. We poison them just by breathing, just by existing in their vicinity. But some—a very few—*nosferatu* are powerful enough to endure that toxicity for a short amount of time. And a short amount of time was all Sergej needed." Her perfect eyebrows drew together. "There is a reason he is their leader."

It was weird. Nobody else would say his name. They said *he* or *you-know-who*. But Christophe, and this chick, said it quietly. Like they were talking about someone they knew.

I didn't want to think about it. My entire body, and everything inside my head, felt like throwing up, passing out, or just sinking down on the floor and trembling for a bit. "What does this have to do with Christophe?"

She flipped that photo over too. The back of it had a scribble in blue pen, a streak like someone had slashed at it. More papers. "This is a transcript of a call between an unidentified member of the Order and a *nosferat* of Sergej's line. In it, the unidentified Kouroi gives your mother's location. Christophe is the only person who might have known—he trained your mother personally, and they were close."

*He trained her?* "Close? How old *is* he?"

"Old enough to remember the last half of the First World War, Miss Anderson. We have no more proof—the recording is gone and the person who transcribed it died in battle. Rather suspiciously, I might add." She was watching me very carefully, I realized. There's a certain way people look when they're not focusing forward, when they're tracking you in their peripheral vision. "It is very likely Christophe will seek further contact with you. If and when he does, it is imperative that you notify an advisor and stand by for debriefing. Is that clear?"

The tone of command was something new. I got the idea that when this lady said *jump*, everyone around her made like a basketball player going up for a dunk.

The words hovered right on the tip of my tongue. *He's already been to see me.* A few simple words, and I could stop feeling like there was a weight pressing against my heart. I could lay the problem in someone else's lap and stop worrying about it. I could hand it over to an adult and be done.

But I heard the sound of soft wings again, and feathers brushed my face. I almost flinched, the feeling was so real.

*Look what happened last time you tried to dump the problem in someone else's lap, Dru. You called Augustine, and things seemed like they were going to get better — and now look at where you are.*

It was a warning, delivered just like all of Gran's lessons. Simple and without a lot of bullshit messing it up. "Crystal," I heard myself say. It was the first time I'd ever sounded as weary and adult as Graves sometimes did. Did he ever feel this weight pressing on him too?

He probably did. I wanted to see him so bad my hands almost shook.

"Then I shall be on my way." She scooped the file together, and I glanced up. Dylan looked worried, as usual, and he was staring straight at me. It was like he was willing me to figure something out, his lips pressed together and his dark eyes beaming a message I couldn't decode.

"The transcript. Do I get to look at it?" I didn't mean to sound stubborn, but I guess I did. Dylan actually flinched, and Anna drew herself up.

I finally figured out what bothered me about her face. She looked. Popular. She'd never been an outcast; we all just existed to throw her own reflection back at her. There was the same unfinished, greedy kind of prettiness I'd seen on cheerleaders and female boa constrictors all over America. If she wasn't *djamphir*, she'd probably have ended up as an obese, lacquered middle-aged woman with a turned-down, bitter mouth. The kind that makes a huge fuss in a grocery store over an expired coupon, or a can of corn costing fifteen cents more than she'd thought.

The kind that always gets her way, because she's shameless when it comes to wearing you down over it. Like that.

"It's classified, Miss Anderson. When Christophe contacts you, listen to what he has to say. Remember it, and be ready to repeat it."

She nodded brusquely and tucked the manila folder under her arm. Her silk swished as she headed for the door. "My bodyguard will see me out, Dylan. Thank you."

"Milady." How he managed to say the word without choking, I don't know. She swept away, her heels tapping with little sharp sounds.

The door swung shut. Cobwebs up at the top of the tall bookcases made little shushing movements. The ceiling tiles in here were rotting too.

This place was really falling apart in more ways than one.

Dylan tilted his head, one eyebrow raised. I stood there, aching and wet with sweat. I didn't realize I was shaking until I sat back down in the chair, hard. Every part of me was quivering like electrified Jell-O. Her smell left reluctantly, heaviness coating the back of my throat—especially that place on the palate normal people don't have, the place where I taste danger.

It's like the pickled ginger you get with sushi. That always tastes like perfume to me. This was heavy, oily perfume too.

*What does that remind me of? I swear to God it reminds me of something.* But the little spring that wheels memories out of their slots and throws them into the soup of your brain was busted in my head. I just couldn't come up with anything coherent.

Climbing up the stairs to my room seemed like an awfully huge task. But the thought of hiding under the bed with the dust kitties, the *malaika*, and Dad's billfold more than made up for it. I was glad, for no reason that I could name, that Mom's locket was tucked safely under my T-shirt. The idea of Anna seeing it made my heart feel cold.

Dylan's shoulders slumped. "They're gone," he said quietly. "Are you all right?"

*What a question.* "Yeah." I cleared my throat. "Peachy. Perfect. *Not.*"

"I'm sorry." He really did sound sorry. But then, he always did. "She insisted on seeing you, and . . ."

*And what? What the fuck was that?* I stared at the space on his cluttered desk where the file had rested. I knew it existed now. I'd seen where my mother died.

*He hung her in the tree.* Her sweet little voice, saying it like it was nothing when it wasn't. It wasn't nothing. It was *my mother,* and she—

"Have you seen Christophe, Dru?" His jacket creaked as he leaned away from the wall. "I don't think I have to tell you he's in deep shit. And it's getting deeper."

I was trying to think, but he was making it harder by talking to me. "I want to go to my room." I sounded about five years old. "Please."

"All right." But he just couldn't let it be. "Dru—"

"Who was supposed to be watching me?" The space where the file had been was a hole in the world, and I wasn't sure I liked the way the wind was whistling over it. I hate that empty sound, like a storm rasping against the edges of an empty house while you're waiting for your dad to come home and collect you. That low, impatient moaning. "Who was supposed to take me up to my room when the bell went off? It's the only time someone hasn't come to get me."

"I don't know, I didn't get a chance to check the schedule. And now the duty roster's disappeared." He moved again, restlessly, leather creaking. I coughed once more, a deep hacking sound. "I was called to greet Anna's transport. We never receive any warnings for her visits, so—"

"She doesn't live here?" But I didn't care. My legs felt like they would work now. Kind of. Something else he said seemed important, but I couldn't make my brain work.

"No, she doesn't." He stopped short again, and I was getting really tired of the feeling that he wasn't telling me everything. Or even anything.

I braced myself on the chair, pushed. Failed the first time. Dylan stepped forward like he wanted to help.

I leapt up as if burned, put the chair between us, and stared at him.

"Dru—" He stopped dead. We watched each other over a couple yards of traitorous air. There didn't seem to be enough of it to breathe, but there was sure enough to press down on me from all sides. Had anyone ever drowned on *air*?

I sidled toward the door. He kept very still, like he wasn't sure which way I was going to jump. The aspect folded over him, retreated, his fangs sliding under his lips.

"I'm on your side," he said, when I was almost at the door. "I wish—"

"I don't have a side," I informed him, found the doorknob with one numb hand and fled. All the halls were empty, and I managed to make it to my room without anything *else* happening.

It was a completely unexpected gift. I half-expected there to be a fire, or another attack, or some other damn thing.

I locked the door, put my back against it, and held up my hand. It was shaking like a windblown leaf. The room was dead silent, the curtains askew just a little bit, and a square of white paper against the blue of the quilt cover.

Hot and cold swept over me in alternating waves. I set out across the acres of blue carpet. My socks whispered, and could anyone else see the faint marks where Christophe's wet feet had rested?

Even though I was jolting from the fading adrenaline overload and seriously busted up, I am not stupid. It was too wrong. Two photos of the house I'd lived in Before—before Mom died and the world changed—didn't make a case against Christophe. If the information was so secret and classified, Anna shouldn't have brought the file out at all. And ordering me around is exactly the wrong way to make me do what you want.

Yeah, I mean, I understand about obeying orders when you're under fire. That's totally different. But Dad hadn't raised a blindly obedient idiot. I don't think he was capable of it.

The paper was crisp, heavy, and expensive. The writing was careful copperplate script.

*Svetocha,*
*Be careful. Nothing here is what it appears to be. Meet me at the boathouse.*
*Your Friend*

I collapsed on the bed. If it was a code, the message was lost on me. *What the fuck?*

And what was someone—maybe Christophe—doing leaving messages on my pillow when vampires were trying to kill me? While Ash, of all people (was *people* even the right word for a werwulf?) was rescuing me?

*Had* Ash been trying to rescue me?

My brain finally kicked in, far too late. *And now the duty roster's gone.* Which meant whoever was supposed to be watching me had taken it, because they knew I'd be attacked.

*Killed. Not just attacked, but killed. Call it what it is, Dru.*

I let out a long, shuddering breath. Christophe. Sergej's son. He was right—someone was trying to kill him. But he wasn't telling the whole truth either. All these lies, crowding all around me, hemming me in. Dangerous lies.

*Deadly* lies. What happened tonight could have easily ended with me murdered out in the woods.

I could end up dead tomorrow. In my sleep, even. I shivered, hugging myself for warmth. The room was cold, and it wasn't mine.

The one person I could have talked to, the one person who could have helped me make sense of this madness, was down in the dorms. I didn't feel up to going down there. Not now.

I huddled on the bed. Outside, it was night, and the Schola was awake and alive. The not-noise of people living in a space, filling it up with their breathing and heartbeats, quivered in the air. I still felt completely, utterly alone. More alone than I'd ever felt in a house waiting for Dad to come back, and that's saying something.

# CHAPTER 12

The cold front coming down from Canada finally broke two days later. Ice melted, the river became a supple silver snake instead of a flat gray ribbon. Everything turned soggy instead of hard-frozen. Thundering storms blew in, dumped a load of rain every night, and blew out. The daylight came through a filter of overcast and dry white fog. It was like being in a glass globe, because I only saw the weather through barred windows.

I couldn't stay cooped up in the room. It was like sitting in a prison cell. So I would go to class.

Classes were a special kind of hell. I'd sit there and think, *He lied to me.* Or even better, *Someone here wants to kill me.* It would knock every other thought out of my head, stamp on it a few times, and I'd lose track of everything the teacher was saying. Dibs hung out with me at breakfast and lunch, but he didn't say much. He had all he could handle just sitting still and sometimes forcing out a *hello.* The kid's shyness was just short of terminal.

Nobody else talked to me except Graves. And he hardly talked at all. At least, not about anything important. It was all, *We went running through the park* this or *Shanks took us shopping* that or *I heard about this guy in sparring, guess what he did?* the other.

I made noises, nodded, and tried to look interested. Then the gong would go off inside my head.

*He lied to me.* Or *Someone here wants to kill me. Maybe in this very room.* And I would stare off into the distance, because I was afraid to start examining everyone around for signs of murderous intent. It wasn't like I could even tell how old any of them were. They could have all been ancient and I wouldn't know, would I?

I don't know why I felt so betrayed, really. Christophe was part vampire, after all. Like everyone else here who might want me dead.

Like me.

The taint doesn't wash out. I found out that much in the increasingly useful two-hour span that was history class. No matter how far back in the family tree the sucker is, it still makes the kids *djamphir*. They get the aspect, the speed, the strength—and the hunger. And they're all boys, except for the one-in-a-thousand girl. Who rarely ever reaches adulthood, because the suckers find them before they bloom and drink them dry, getting a big old jolt of power from it.

Nice, huh? I was just special all over the place. Me and Anna. Were there more? There could be. I might not be so special.

It also occurred to me that the wulfen were probably my best bet of surviving. They couldn't want me dead, really. Right? Because I didn't matter either way to them unless they were working for Sergej too.

There was no way of knowing for sure. Which meant the wulfen weren't that great of a bet after all.

I had no way of getting out of here. Not for a while.

Graves didn't want to hang out that much, and what could I do?

Just follow the werewolves around until they took pity on me? What if some of them had a reason, God only knew what, for hating me?

And did I even dare to figure out how to sneak down to the boathouse?

I was in history class, again, sitting on one end of the couch. The doors had been replaced and the halls repaired, but you could still see the white gouges in the paneling and the carpet was a glaring mismatch, the only patches of new flooring in the whole school. The renovated bits smelled like formaldehyde, and I pulled my knees up, resting the pad of paper on them. The doodle unreeled under my pencil, long narrow arches and stone walls. I shaded in each block of rock, the grass forcing up through flagstones, and worked all around a huge blank spot in the middle of the page.

Graves perched next to me, and the kid he called Shanks—dark emo-boy hair brushed sideways across his forehead and hanging in his chocolate eyes, bony wrists sticking out from under his sleeves, engineer boots, and a sideways smile—leaned forward on his other side, elbows braced on his knees. Irving had settled himself on the floor, knees up and arms circling them. Other than that, everyone gave me a wide berth. Even Dibs acted like he didn't know me in class.

I caught Graves and the Shanks kid exchanging pointed looks, usually every time Irving opened his mouth.

Right now Blondie the teacher was droning on about basic rules for interaction between *djamphir* and wulfen. I filled in another block of shading.

"*Djamphir* are trained for tactics and wulfen are trained for logistics. This plays to the particular strength of both. Wulfen lack a *djamphir*'s sensitivity to *nosferat* infestation, and *djamphir* lack the peculiar qualities of consensus and cooperation that come naturally to wulfen. Each is half of a balanced equation, and it was only when we started cooperating that we began to be able to clear entire territories and hold them."

"What happened before?" Graves wanted to know.

Blondie's teeth peeped out from behind his lips. Very white, but his aspect was nowhere to be found. "Before? We died. We were very close to being eradicated completely, and it was war on wulfen whenever the *nosferatu* felt like it. Those who weren't taken were killed, or they lived by the leave of the Blood Princes only. As the Broken."

That perked my ears up. *Broken to his will*, Christophe whispered inside my head.

I looked up from the paper. "Broken? What does that mean?"

I immediately felt stupid. It was probably not the best thing to ask in a room full of wulfen. They might be, you know, offended.

*Oh jeez.* A slight rustle went through the room. Shanks hunched his shoulders and settled back on the couch.

"Anyone want to answer that?" Blondie turned in a full circle, taking in the faces all around him. "No? Well, I'll go ahead then. 'Breaking' a human being, even a *djamphir*, is easy. Sleep deprivation, temporary lack of protein, a constant stream of propaganda—it's called brainwashing, and it's very simple to do. Doing it to a werwulf—or a skinchanger like Mr. Graves here—is harder, because of their resistance to both physical damage and persuasion."

"They're stubborn," Irving said, *sotto voce*, and another ripple ran through the room. It might've sounded like laughter if you weren't listening too closely.

"They are *resistant*," Blondie corrected, in the snootiest possible voice. "Nevertheless, it can be done. The most popular method was chaining in a *tatra*. This is a stone cube just big enough to allow the victim to stand upright, but not enough to turn around, bend over, or sit. The chain is fastened to a spiked collar—the spikes are turned inward, like so." His manicured hands sketched the air. "So the victim must move carefully even in that confined space. Then, raw meat is thrown onto the floor or placed just outside. The food scent torments until the meat begins to rot, and every day water is flung in through an aperture above the head. It cascades down, and the danger of inhaling it and developing pneumonia is very real. Then there are the *Revelle*, the dreamstealers, creatures bred by the Maharaja."

That got my attention all over again. Graves tensed next to me.

"The dreamstealer is brought in close proximity to the wulfen, fed carrion, and allowed to sing. Does anyone here know what a dreamstealer's song can do?"

"I know what happens when they stick their tongues in someone's mouth and start drinking," Graves muttered. "It *was* singing. I remember that much."

I didn't remember that. I still hadn't decided if I'd been out of my body or just having a really vivid dream that was my unconscious putting things together and presenting me with memory. But I did remember what happened *after* Graves tore the dreamstealer off me and Christophe stopped me retching and seizing.

*Christophe. He lied. He didn't tell me. Bastard. And someone else. Maybe that Anna chick. But she's svetocha too. It doesn't make sense. The vampires are the enemy, right? Why would anyone work with them?*

*His son. Sergej's son.*

Blondie paused, visibly deciding not to respond. "A dreamstealer's song takes hope away and drives its victim to the brink of insanity. Exposure for more than a few hours breaks down the barriers between a werwulf's conscious mind and the Other—the thing inside them that encloses and permits the change. Leaving the werwulf both psychotic and unable to reclaim his or her human form."

"They did this to *girls*, too?" Someone behind me sounded horrified. I guess chivalry isn't completely dead.

But I was thinking of the maddened, insane thing in Ash's eyes. He'd once been a werwulf like the kids in the classroom with me, all of them shifting uneasily in their seats. And Sergej had done that— chained him in a stone box and turned him into something that couldn't change back into a boy.

Blondie now looked pained. I was liking him more and more over the past couple of days, until I remembered he'd disappeared out the door and left me alone to be attacked. But right now, he was the teacher I was getting the most out of. "Sometimes," he said, quietly, "a psychotic female werwulf is nearly unstoppable. However, it is more difficult to break down a female's resistance and turn her into a Broken. Other methods were employed to force female wulfen's compliance. Anyway, once the wulf can no longer shift back into even a simulacrum of humanity, it is collared by its master and becomes an automaton with no free will of its own. It becomes merely appetite and obedience."

*Wait a second.* I sat up straight, the pad of paper sliding on my jeans. "Can you stop it? I mean—can you make someone like that human again?"

"Reclaim a Broken? It's possible, if you have a strong enough chain, enough time, and a compelling reason to do so. But the master of such a creature will rarely let it go, and will call it back with such intensity the wulf will often kill itself trying to escape. Wulfen have been known to break their own necks, chew through their own arms or legs—"

"There were reclamation projects, though." Shanks folded his arms. "My dad talks about them. There were whole *teams* of them in the 1920s." His entire body shouted *I don't like this*, from hunched-up shoulders to the uneasy way his fingers flicked and his knees joggled.

Of course, it was probably uncomfortable listening for a guy who could turn furry.

"There were," Blondie agreed. "Most of the projects ended in abject failure, or the death of those who tried to reclaim the Broken. However, when the wulfen and the founders of the Order made their compact, it became much more difficult for the *nosferatu* to abduct wulfen for their purposes." An odd smile tilted the corners of his mouth. "On this continent, we have the *wampyr* on the run. Most of the time, that is."

"But there *is* a way to reverse the damage, to fix it?" I persisted. "How exactly would you do it?"

He gave me a long measuring look. "That's a question for another time. Class dismissed."

Everyone started moving and shuffling, and Blondie gave me one last long look before striding out of the room. I folded up my pad and slid it into my bag, and hauled myself up from the couch with a creak and a sigh. Graves looked up at me, his unibrow peaking once over each eye. His entire face shouted, *What the hell are you thinking?*

I felt like I'd just been dunked in a cold bath, every nerve standing upright and shrieking. My next class was Aspect Mastery. I wasn't even sure who the teacher was, so I could miss it, no problem. I bet there was something in the school library—or even Dylan's office—that covered the Broken, and I am really good at finding shit like this out. Give me some research to do, and I am *all* over it.

It was a relief to find a concrete action to take.

A cool touch of dread stroked my nape. The note on my bed. My "friend." Was it the same friend who was supposed to have been getting me to my room when the vampires attacked? Was it Christophe? But what would he be doing in my room while vampires were attacking? Wouldn't he have heard the noise and—

God, if I could just stop thinking about it, I might've been able to get some sleep, or stop jumping nervously at every little sound.

Yeah. Like that was gonna happen.

"Walk you to class?" Graves said, cutting right across the noise in my head.

"Um." I blinked. *What exactly are you thinking, Dru?* But there had to be an explanation. Something wasn't jelling, and . . . well, it was crazy.

It was *nuts*.

But I was beginning to have an idea. It might even have been a good one, but I was so tired I couldn't tell.

Graves apparently took my *um* for a *yes*, I guess, because he stood up and tucked his hands in the pockets of the long black coat. He wore the goddamn thing everywhere. "All right. Come on, you don't wanna be late."

"They roast late students over fires." Shanks bounced up to his feet, collecting his notebook and a couple of textbooks covered with brown kraft paper. He gave me an odd look, and grinned, exposing very sharp white teeth. "But not *special* ones."

"Lay off," Graves said over his shoulder. "Jesus."

"I'm interested, actually. Wanna hear about how to brainwash a wulfen, Dru?" A crackling growl ran under the surface of the words. "Gonna start a breeding stable? They used to do that too. You can get pictures on the Internet."

Kids say horrible things to each other every day, in every high school in America. But this was something else. "I asked because I want to know how to fix it." I glared at him. "What's your *problem?*"

He made a mock-astonished face. "Oooh. You're going to *fix* it, like a good little *djamphir?*"

"Bobby." Graves half-turned, his coat flaring out and brushing my knees. "Lay. Off."

"Can she actually talk when she's not sucking up to the teachers?" He leaned forward on his toes, and the growl dropped a notch. "Or playing kissy-face with you? Got her own little *loup-garou* bodyguard. Why is she even *here?*"

Jesus. I'd never talked to this kid. I was kind of beginning to see why. "Come on." I pulled at Graves's sleeve. "Let's go."

He shook me off, took two steps forward. He was tall, but Shanks topped him by a good half-head. Still, Graves didn't look impressed or afraid in the least. "Go fuck yourself. Or get spayed. Either would be an improvement."

*Oh Christ.* Did this have to happen the instant I had an idea of something to actually *do,* instead of rattling around inside here chewing on myself? "Look—"

Fur was crawling up Bobby's thin cheeks. "Hold him back, bitch," he snarled, his shoulders hunching and hulking at once. It's always disconcerting to see muscle plumping up on a wulf when the hair pops up all over them and the jaw starts mutating. He was only halfway changed, but that's enough.

"Holy *shi*—" I didn't get to finish, because Graves hauled off and cold-cocked him. They went over the back of the couch in a tangle of fur and snapping black coat-cloth, and the other wulfen gathered around, making the weird yipping noise they sometimes did to spur each other on.

*Oh, for God's sake.* I dropped my bag and hopped over the back of the couch, then started shoving. The wulfen squeezed together, shoulder to shoulder, shouting—and I actually kicked someone behind the knee, squeezed forward, and pushed another one aside with strength I didn't know I had.

They were rolling around, Shanks half-changed and making a lot of noise, Graves growling as his eyes glowed—and then Bobby got in a knee to the nuts.

And punched him right in the face.

I heard the fist hit, the crunch of bone, and almost felt it in my own face.

*Graves!* Something inside me snapped. The red-tinted rage swelled up, coated my skin, and pushed me aside.

The world slowed down again, clear syrup hardening over every surface, and I bolted forward. This time, the weight didn't close over my arms and legs, and I had a vague idea that I was going much too fast before I *kicked*. There was a crunch, weirdly distorted and amplified, as my sneakered foot smashed into the other boy's face. He went careening back, still in that slow motion, and the fresh swell of rage that flooded me was clean and clear in its intensity.

It was a tidal wave of pure incandescent anger, turning me into a glass girl full of sparkling red fluid. I hit him twice more before he landed, both good solid shots. He crashed into a tangled knot of wulfen, their mouths open as they yelled. The entire scene was strangely soundless, and the wulfen began to scatter in slow motion.

I was on Shanks again, my hand closing around his throat and pushing him down through the syrup. His arm came up, like a sleepwalker's. I avoided the claws that would have sheared through my face and deflected the blow with one wrist, slapping it lightly away. The movement continued, my arm drawing back, and I heard Dad's voice again.

*Put your thumb outside, Dru. Tuck your thumb in and you'll break it when you punch that sad, sorry bastard. That's good. Now hit 'im hard, and hit 'im good! Good girl!*

The weird elongated noises around me drew away. Time slowed

down even further, and I knew it was going to snap and speed up soon. I had enough time to hit him but good with my cocked-back fist. I could probably break his nose, or if I punched a little lower I could crush his larynx and he'd suffocate.

*Dru, what are you doing?*

The rage still burned inside me. He'd hit Graves, and *hurt* him.

But I was seriously considering a punch that could truly disable someone, even kill them. And this was just a schoolroom brawl. Like every other schoolroom brawl I'd stayed out of, both out in the regular world and here.

Well, maybe not so much here.

*What is really going on here? Why don't the teachers intervene more?* The answer occurred to me a split second later—*they're teaching them to fight. Teaching them to hate each other, too.*

The fury was still boiling inside me. My temper frayed down to the thinnest of threads spinning over an abyss. The snap to speed everything up was coming. I could feel it, hovering on the edge of my awareness the way a sneeze tingles in your nose.

A hand closed over my shoulder, and if I was going to hit the kid I had to do it now. My fist leapt forward an inch, ducked back as the wulfen squirmed slowly, his mouth half-open, blood splattering down from his nose.

I let go of him, my fingers cramping. Someone dragged me back, fingers biting into my flesh so hard I could feel the bruising begin. I was a regular old punching bag. Jeez.

Time snapped like a thick rubber band, and this time I felt jarred all the way down to my bones. I'd just been dropped into the world again, a jolt like a car hitting a brick wall. There was shouting and screaming going on, and my hair hung in my face.

I watched, hypnotized, as blonde streaks slid through my curls.

They stretched out, longer and looser, into sleek waves instead of frizz. The golden streaks retreated, darkness eating them up, and my hair was my hair again.

*Holy shit. Was that—*

"Get *back!*" Graves yelled, dragging me back further as the wulfen closed over Shanks's still figure, lying on the floor against the bottom of a couch, the blood red and startling. Several of them had turned my direction and were advancing, fur crawling over their skin, shoulders and legs hulking up. "I'm *fucking warning you!*" It was an actual roar, his entire body vibrating. It shook through me, his voice, and I'd never heard him sound that way before.

That voice had a snap to it. A *bite.* I could almost see it shoving the clustered wulfen back. *Dominant,* I realized. *That's a* loup-garou's *command voice.*

They halted, all snarling. Even pale, gentle Dibs, who rarely spoke above a scared whisper. Their faces wrinkled up, teeth growing, fur sliding and rippling over their boy-forms.

Graves pulled me back another few steps. "*Stay where you are!*" he snapped, still in that shake-the-world voice. Everything actually rattled, including the inside of my head.

Then I realized I was making a weird sound too, a high keening noise with strange stops when my windpipe closed up and I had to breathe. The smell hit me—copper, hot, and good. It smashed into a place in the very back of my throat I never knew existed before, right next to the spot normal people don't have. The one that tells me when something weird is going to happen. That red coppery smell reached all the way down and ripped the world apart. I pitched forward again, fighting against Graves's hands on me, but he'd somehow gotten his arm around my waist and was hauling me away. I lunged again, almost dragging him with me, and I realized what I wanted to do.

I wanted to knock all of them out of my way and put my face in the wounded werwulf's throat.

I wanted to *drink*.

A roaring thirst crawled out from the middle of my throat, spread through my entire body. I was dry, cracking and burning, and the only thing that could quench the fire was the sweet red fluid I could smell all over. It tapped inside my head, whispered and cajoled, and my teeth turned achingly sensitive. I could almost feel them lengthening, sharp tickling crawling over the enamel. My hair tingled, and every inch of me was awake again. The persistent exhaustion of the last few sleepless days vanished, replaced with high, crackling energy.

Graves's other arm came around my throat and he choked up as I writhed, pitching back and forth. My teeth snapped together, making little clicking sounds. The wulfen snarled back, but Graves made that weird, world-shaking sound again and they stayed away.

I wish I could say I was relieved when Shanks rose up out of the middle of a knot of werwulfen, his face a mask of blood and his eyes blazing. But I wasn't. I wanted to lick the stuff off his face and put my teeth in his throat, and I *wanted to drink*.

He snarled, Graves rumbled back. And I don't know what would have happened if a flood of *djamphir* hadn't burst through the door and surrounded me. They held me down as I started screaming, shouldering Graves aside. But he stayed, holding onto my hand even when my fingers bit down and bones in both our hands crackled.

It was the first time the bloodhunger had struck me. And now, oh God, I understood so much more.

Graves didn't leave me, even though everyone was shouting. He stayed right there, making a noise over and over again, and I finally realized he was saying my name. The hunger crested, and when it finally retreated, I started crying. Graves was the one who pulled me close and hugged me. I was sobbing and shaking like a little kid, and some of them started telling him to leave, but he just shook them off and kept holding me.

I clung to him too. They couldn't pull me away.

# CHAPTER 13

**G**raves set the stack of books down on the wooden table with a thump. My teeth still ached. So did my entire body. But all in all, it was apparently no big deal at the Schola. Shanks was in the baths, and Graves was skipping whatever he was supposed to be doing, and I'd been told to "just go somewhere else and calm down."

Yeah. Calm down. Two of the most useless words in the English language. But Dylan told me the danger was past, and I wasn't going to go and bite someone. He said it was normal, because I was so close to blooming. And that I'd get used to it.

I wasn't so sure.

He also said they hadn't had a death "from student interactions" at this Schola for about sixty-two years, which wasn't as comforting as it could have been either.

The library was full of the smell of dust and old paper. Barred windows let in sharp swords of golden evening light between heavy antique wooden bookshelves—the sun had finally come out, too late in the day to do any good. Nobody was behind the circulation desk.

It was a good thing. I could still smell the blood. My teeth were still sensitive, as if I'd just gone to the dentist's. Every nerve in me was raw, and I sat with my arms cupping my elbows, hugging myself.

"It's fucking crazy. *You're* crazy," Graves said flatly. "What are you going to do, tie him up in your room? They'll kill him."

At least he was talking about something other than me growing fangs and wanting to go all *nosferat* on someone. He just plain refused to discuss *that*, and I was grateful.

Well, as grateful as I could be with my brain refusing to work right and my hair changing color and Jesus God, what the hell was happening to me?

Who was I anymore? When I looked in the mirror, would I still see myself?

It was like vanishing into a funhouse to ask yourself that question—I mean, seriously ask yourself, in a funhouse where the horror is real and anything but fun, and see what happens. Asking yourself that sort of question makes everything inside you that's not nailed down do a funny jigging dance.

I had precious little that was nailed down anymore.

If I focused on something else, I could probably get through this. "Something just doesn't add up." At least I wasn't lisping around fangs. My teeth were normal, but I kept running my tongue over them, testing. They *felt* normal. Except for the aching in them, and the thirsty place at the back of my throat. "He was *this close* to me, Graves. And he didn't do anything but sniff me. I—"

"Shut up." He dropped down into a chair and glared at me. "What the hell is going on with you, Dru?"

*You mean, other than having my dad murdered, finding out I'm part sucker, getting chased and beaten up, and turning into a blood-craving fiend prepared to really, really hurt someone? Jeez, I'm pink. I'm perfect. I'm the picture of health.* I opened my mouth to say something smart or at least less stupid than usual, but closed it again because, well, what could I say?

It was hopeless. I looked down at the mellow glow of the wood's surface. Heat rose behind my eyes, the unsteady ball of rage caged in my ribs kicked up another notch, and I swallowed hard. Kept my temper down through sheer force of will.

Now that I knew what the bloodhunger did, would I ever be able to look at myself in the mirror? Or at any of the *djamphir* without flinching?

"Come *on.*" He was still glaring at me, I could *feel* it. "Say something, Dru. Don't just sit there and look like I've stabbed you. Christ."

The sunshine faded as dusk took hold. I slumped back in the chair, hugging myself. The whirling inside me wouldn't stop. I breathed in, breathed out, trying to make it slow down a little. If I freaked out now, what the hell *else* might happen?

Would I jump on Graves? Would my teeth get long and sharp, and would I want to put my face in his throat and *drink?*

My chest hurt. I hugged myself harder.

"Come on." His tone gentled. "What are you doing? You keep shoving everything down like this and you're going to give yourself an ulcer or something. I'm here, okay? I've taken everything this place could throw at me. I'm not going anywhere."

That just made me feel worse. He was here because of me. Great. "Do you ever want to go home?" I had to fight to keep the words steady. My chest hurt. It was the same old pain, the breathless feeling of sitting in a hospital corridor once Gran was dead, just repeating over and over, *My dad is coming, he'll take care of it. He's on his way.* And hoping it was true.

*Praying* it was true. But this time I was left behind for good. There was nobody coming to get me. Not in any good way, at least.

And the sooner I started dealing with that the better. But oh God, the thought scared me, way down deep.

He was quiet for a long few moments. "Shit no," he finally said. "Look, I don't know if you caught this, Dru, but I don't have a fireplace and picket fence to go back to. I was *homeless*, okay?"

I'd suspected, but it was a different thing altogether to hear it out loud. "You had—"

"That room at the mall? Fuck, what kind of kid lives in the mall? Here at least there's enough food. There's a bed I earned, and I'm keeping it. Nobody's trying to peddle my ass or beating me because he's drunk." He inhaled sharply, blew the air out. "At least here, there's *rules*. Werwulfen and vampires I can handle. It's the adults back in that other world I can't. They . . . At least here the evil has reasons. It's not just . . ." He searched for the word, his face twisting in on itself for a second as he struggled to articulate. "It's not just *senseless*."

*What happened to my dad was senseless.* I didn't say it. How could you say something like that to someone? "You wanted to be a physics professor." My throat had closed up; I could only whisper.

"Yeah, well, things change. Now I want to be here." Another long, seconds-ticking pause. Dust danced in one fading gleam of gold coming through a low window, following long lazy swirls down to the ground. "With you."

I stared at the motes suspended in the air, all dancing to music nobody could hear. I read somewhere once that dust could even be bits of exploded stars, falling to earth. How far does a bit of star-stuff fall and float before it gives up and just gets pulled into any planet's orbit?

Did it matter?

The sun slid below the edge of the horizon, and the Schola sighed, settling into itself.

"I don't know who I am anymore." The words were throttled halfway out, died in the library's silence. I expected the world to crack open and the sky to fall once I said it.

Nothing happened. The library still held its breath, and Graves still stood there looking at me.

"Nobody does, Dru." It was the same quiet, oddly adult tone he'd used that first evening, sitting in the mall and asking me just how bad everything was and if I needed a place to sleep. "It's called growing up."

The whirling inside me had gone down a little. I could finally unreel my arms from around my chest. I pushed my hair back. The curls felt weird—not frizzy but silky, clinging to my fingers. "I'm sorry."

"Yeah, well." Was he *blushing*? "I'm never going to live it down that a *girl* knocked Bobby on his ass defending me. Jeez."

Something tight-sprung inside me eased a little bit. The rage retreated. There was enough room to breathe, and I took in a sharp deep lungful. "Well, next time I'll let him mess with you. Happy?"

"Yeah, well. I had him handled, but still. Anyway, you wanna take half these books?"

The world was seeming manageable again. How did he *do* that? "What for?"

"Well, if you're so interested in rehabilitating Broken werwulfen, these seem like a reasonable place to start. Haven't you been in here before?"

"Once or twice." *But you're right, this is a good idea. Dad always said research is what saves you.*

Yeah, right on schedule, the most uncomfortable thought in the room was moving into my head and calling it home. I should start charging uncomfortable thoughts rent. Except what would they pay me in? Probably something even worse.

"You've been going to class more." He separated the stack into two equal piles, and it was official. He *was* blushing. High flags of color stood out on his face, so deep they were damn close to maroon. An ugly bruise was spreading up his jawbone, too.

I'd thought he was half-ugly before. Unfinished-looking. It was hard to believe. "Yeah, well, nothing else to do." I took the pile he pushed toward me. "Doesn't it bother you? That I . . . well, that I wanted to . . . suck his blood?"

His Adam's apple bobbed as he swallowed. The silver earring winked mischievously at me, catching a stray gleam of sun. "Nah. You wouldn't, you'd have stopped yourself."

I wasn't so sure, and I opened my mouth to tell him so.

"Besides," he said, flipping open the first huge leather-bound book with a thump, "it's kind of hot." A smile hovered around the corners of his mouth, fighting to stay hidden.

*What?* I stared at him for a few seconds. My jaw had officially dropped. "You're *insane.*"

"Pot calling kettle, anyone? Start reading."

I wasn't sure I'd be able to concentrate, but I did. The sensitivity in my mouth retreated, and after a little while I couldn't smell the blood anymore. After another while I could actually read the page in front of me without the tears welling up and making all the words blur. I made like I was brushing dust off my cheeks, when I was really smearing hot salt water over them.

Graves didn't say anything about me leaking. But he didn't turn a page for a long time either. When it was time to go to his last class of the night he walked me back to my room first, carrying a double armful of books that we piled on my bed. I finally fell asleep with one of them propped against the headboard, and slept all the way through until morning's faint blush against the sky.

I could have slept longer, but I had something to do.

# CHAPTER 14

took a shower, braided my hair back. The hall felt weird. I stood on my side of the door, my hand spread against its chill heaviness, and felt someone outside listening intently. It was the same feeling I used to get right before I told Dad a certain motel or house wasn't safe.

He'd never argued.

So that left just one option. I didn't like it, but it was better than sitting around moping.

Weak sun slid through the stamped holes in the iron shutters. I pushed them as wide as they would go, struggled with the window. I had to walk a fine line between wrenching it open and trying to be quiet about it. A drench of cold air heavy with the promise of rain flooded through, and I glanced down into the dead rose garden.

The paving-stone paths looked very hard from up here.

It was a long way to fall. I swallowed, hard. *Wish I had a rope. Jeez.*

But if Christophe had done this, I could too. The worst that could happen was a broken leg and a bunch of questions, right?

I'd never broken a bone before. And those questions had teeth. Everything here had teeth.

*This is a stupid idea, Dru.*

But I was going to do it anyway. With someone watching my door, I *had* to. I couldn't take the chance of anyone, friendly or otherwise, following me. And I had to know if it was possible to escape the Schola during the day.

I grabbed the window frame and put my foot up, made sure it was secure, and hauled myself carefully up to stand on the sill. Told myself not to look down, instead studying the stone wall and the roof overhang. It looked like slate tile and the angle would make it tricky. No gutter, either. That was both good—gutters could tear away from the roof—and bad, because I wouldn't have anything to curl my fingers around but the roof's edge.

I turned my back on the dead garden, bracing myself on the sill. Reached up and back with one hand.

*This is a bad idea. Figure something else out.*

The trouble was, there was nothing else. And Christophe had done this. I'd be damned if I didn't at least try. Not to mention that if I pulled this off, I would have an escape route already scoped. And it would be the last path anyone would expect me to take.

Less speed, less strength, less stamina since I hadn't "bloomed." But I'd bet I was outweighing everyone around me in the brain category. It was all I had.

*Then why are you going to do something this stupid?*

I told that voice of reason to take a hike and wrapped my fingers around the edge of the overhang. The angle wasn't really bad, just kind of bad. I shut my eyes and breathed in, out, slate gritty and cold under my hands. The red crisscross slashes on Christophe's hands suddenly made sense now, as I'd known they would.

My other hand found the roof edge too. I played the action over and over in my head, the way Dad taught me to practice rifle shots. *Half of it's in getting it clear inside your noggin, Dru girl, and the body will know what to do when the time comes. See it behind your eyes, feel yourself doing it.*

I'd only have one shot at it. My arms tensed, relaxed, practicing. I stilled the movement of myself inside my skin, focusing inward. Listening.

My heartbeat thudded, a comforting rhythm. My breathing evened out, soft and deep. The wet braid touched my back, moving as my body balanced itself on the sill, weight forward on the ball of my right foot. Heels hung out in space, the cool morning breeze pushing past me into the room.

*Breathe in, breathe out.* Feeling the tingle along my skin. Little tiny muscle movements that make up balance—you never stand completely still. If you did, you'd fall over. Stillness is a constant adjustment, a series of tiny little corrections, like steering a car.

Dad taught me that.

The thought stung, whipped through me, and every muscle fiber tensed. I heard wingbeats, feathers brushing air and whispering against my face. I didn't have to lean back too far; it was almost like pulling myself out of a swimming pool.

The slate edges bit deep into the meat of my hands. I let out a sharp breath, got a knee up. Good thing I was wearing jeans. I found myself scrabbling up the slope of the roof, hunched over and thanking God I'd worn sneakers instead of boots. The soles gripped, and my fingernails splintered on the slate as I drove them in hard.

*Oh crap.* The slope was incredibly sharp, and I made it to the crest and straddled the ridgeline. The big muscles in my legs were shaking. My arms, including the deep bruises on my shoulder, throbbed heavily. I was a song of pain, and the healing capability of the baths wasn't helping as much as I wished it would. My hands cried out, palms full of hot wetness and fingertips scraped raw.

But I got myself arranged so I wouldn't fall off, and I raised my head. The wind hit my face, full of the peculiar smell of being high up, and I saw.

Today there was no fog.

The countryside folded away on all sides, trees choking-close except where two-lane blacktop ribboned in from what I knew from my trip here was a county highway. This was the highest point for a ways around. There was a blue smudge far, far to the south that I thought might be the Alleghenies, but could have been just a fog or cloud.

Down the hill a stream came meandering past, glittering dull silver in the overcast. Clouds were shredding away, and we'd have some full sun before long when they burned off. I saw the boathouse, a run-down shack that didn't look sturdy enough to hold up in a sharp breeze. The Schola turned a cold shoulder to it, its wings raked back like a bird of prey. A gray one with a sharp beak, settled and dozing in its nest.

I couldn't quite see the big circular driveway, but I saw the vine-draped pedestals at the end of it and blinked, rubbing my eyes. I could've sworn there had been stone lions there —

*No,* the voice of instinct whispered. *They were there, but they're not now. For whatever reason.*

I had a sudden, vivid mental image, playing itself inside my head the way a song will get stuck between the ear and the brain.

*Concrete-gray lion padding softly through forest-dappled sun-light, hard muscles under worn-smooth skin. The lion turned its heavy neck and lifted its head, blind stone eyes searching, and its mouth opened. Needle-sharp, slivered teeth packed close, and it exhaled, ruf-*

*fling leaves on the forest floor. It senses eyes upon it, and confusion plucks inside its cold, massive head. The eyes are of a Ruler, but far away, and the stone mane curls upon its shoulders with a sound like wet clay sliding against itself. . . .*

The image faded. I shook my head to clear it. I had to stay sharp, because the roof was steeply pitched all around me, and the slate was damp in places. I could slip and tumble for a long way before falling off the edge, and that wouldn't be any fun for anyone.

I clutched my bleeding hands to my chest and wished I'd thought of gloves. But then I'd lose out on traction. Sometimes you just have to suck up the damage.

I was doing a lot of that lately.

The wind whistled across peaks and valleys of slate tiling. Some tiles were missing, and some sagged, but all in all, the roof looked pretty solid. My hand twitched, and I kept my fingers away from the locket with an effort. I let out another sharp breath, this time in wonder. My heart banged once, twice, settled into a high, hard galloping run. It took a moment of thought before I realized I wasn't scared.

No, the feeling was actually happiness. It swelled behind my pulse and pushed my arms out, fingers spread as a huge disbelieving grin wrinkled up my face. I'm sure I looked like a moron, balancing on a ridgepole and holding my arms out like a circus performer. But here, with the wind keening past me and the trees choking up on the Schola's gray bulk, I felt . . . well, I felt free. For the first time in a long time.

Up here, there was nothing but me and the wind. And a tingling in my teeth, as a feeling I was sure was the aspect blurred through me. This time it was a warm, comforting glow, banishing the pain. My hands stopped bleeding, and when I looked down at them, the ladderlike cuts had scabbed over. The flat-copper smell of my own blood washed away on fresh rainy air, but I thought I caught a thread of warm perfume. When I fisted my hands, lightly, they didn't hurt much and the scabs didn't tear.

*Wow.* I wondered why it didn't work for the bruises and aches inside me. But they were muted now too. The aspect tingled through me, retreated with a sound like owl wings.

*Is this what blooming feels like?* I wished I could ask someone. Gran had told me about The Facts of Life pretty early, and Dad had told me in his gruff way what he thought I should know—which boiled down to *Don't be stupid* and *Don't buy cheap tampons; we've got money.*

This "blooming" thing was like having puberty questions all over again and having nowhere to go to do some, you know, research. Maybe the library had something for curious girl *djamphir.* I laughed, a short disbelieving sound, and felt more like myself than I had for weeks.

After a little while standing there like an idiot, it occurred to me that I'd better start looking for a way down. I had a plan, after all, and it didn't include hanging out up here all day. So I stopped staring at the woods and the sky and breathing in the odd cold rain-soaked happiness. It still stayed with me as I studied the lay of the rooftops, trying to see it like the hollers and ridges around Gran's house. If you could get a vantage point, you could work out your way just about anywhere—with a compass and some common sense, that is. All I'd need up here was the sense.

How much sense I had climbing around on a roof, I don't know. But I took a good look, and the fist inside my head opened up a little, sending out little bits of questing awareness. I waited for the tingle that would tell me it was safe to go, and would also tell me which road to take.

You can't ever rush something like that. It's the same reason why you can't ask a pendulum anything you really, really want to know about. The wanting makes a screen in front of the real answer, which might be something you'd prefer not to hear. So you've got to go still and quiet, as unattached from the answer as possible. It's different from really needing intuition in a pinch, when you have to just shut out the screaming all around you and listen for the still small voice of certainty.

Gran always harped on it, actually, how the pendulum would sometimes tell you just what you wanted to hear, and hang the rest. *Common sense,* she'd say over and over again. *Ha! Common as hen's teeth, maybe. Got to apply that old meat twixt your ears, honey.*

A wave of homesickness crashed into me, so sharp and hot it almost rocked me back on my heels. I longed to be back in Gran's narrow little house up in Appalachians, listening to the whirr and thump of her spinning wheel on a cold evening, smelling whatever she'd cooked for dinner and the floor and window washes she was always using. Yarrow, lavender, wild rose, constant scrubbing. But there was also that time in the evening when it was too dark to work outside, when Gran would spin and I would half-lay on the old love seat and stare at the iron stove. It was warm and safe and I never had to wait for Gran to come get me. She was always there.

The tugging tingle in my solar plexus came. I studied the roof some more and saw the way down. It didn't look like much; I'd have to zag over a couple of sharp slopes, and there was a bit of a drop onto a long, gallery-type roof. I could hop down from there in a protected angle, using a set of—were those dumpsters? Had to be, yeah, that would be right behind the kitchen. Maybe I could even peek in and see who was doing the cooking behind that screen of steam.

*What about getting back up? You're so smart, what about getting back into the Schola?*

Getting in wouldn't be a problem. I'd just bang on the front door for a while. They'd let me in, right?

I thought of the missing stone lions and wasn't too sure. But it was too late to back out now. I'd figure something out.

I checked my scabbed hands one last time and got going.

\* \* \*

It wasn't hard to get into the boathouse. A plain wooden door, a latch that had once probably held a padlock rusted wide open. I looked for any sign of habitation, didn't find it. Pushed the door gingerly with my foot, wincing at the screech of rusted locks, and stepped in. The stiletto had eased itself out of my pocket, and I wished I had a gun instead, to sweep the place.

The entire structure was completely dilapidated. One boat had sunk, rotting, under the glassine water lapping at the central well. Another hung overhead on rusting chains, looking like it hadn't been touched in easily twenty years or so. Holes glared in its sides, and the chains didn't seem too solid.

Coils of rope moldered in the corners. The place smelled like rot and mildew, and the flat iron tang of snowmelt river water. The floor sagged underneath my feet with each cautious step.

And on the other side of the bay where the rowboat wallowed at the sandy bottom under a blanket of clear heavy weight, he just *appeared*.

Christophe stepped out of the shadows, his blue eyes alight. Not a blond-highlighted, expensively cut hair was out of place. His hands dropped down to his sides, as if he'd been holding them up. What had he been planning on doing? Did he think I was an enemy?

Everything boiled up inside of me and I let out a high-pitched, girly sound. The switchblade clicked open at the same time.

*Great. Just great.* All the practicing I'd done for this moment failed me utterly, and I stood there next to a pile of slumping, damp-eaten lumber and stared at him. "You *lied* to me!" I sounded like I'd been punched, hard.

"*Hello* is usually considered a more appropriate greeting." He lifted one shoulder, dropped it. A breath of apples and cinnamon reached me, hit the back of my throat, and tickled the bloodhunger. "And what am I supposed to have lied to you about, Dru?"

Each time I saw him, it was like I'd forgotten how his face worked together, every line and plane proportionate. "A sixteenth, you said! You said you were called a half-breed, but you were technically a sixteenth!"

"What? A lecture on genetics?" But his face clouded. He obviously guessed where this was going.

For one long second I considered how satisfying it would be to hit him, to unleash the ball of rage behind my ribs and see if he could still smack me around so easily. "Sergej." The name sent a glass spike of hatred through my head. "Your *father.*"

Christophe went utterly still, his eyes burning. His thumbs were hooked in his jean pockets, but his hands were tense and his shoulders rigid under the usual black sweater. He stared at me for a little while, his head cocked like he'd just had a good idea and was running it through before he swung into motion.

Finally, he spoke. "Who told you?"

I swallowed hard, lowering the knife. Its blade winked once in the hard, thin light. *Oh God. Did you help kill my mother? Tell me. I have to know. I have to know something, anything, for sure.* "Who? Oh, nobody. Just Anna. Another *svetocha* like me. Was that something you forgot too? She said—"

"Ah. Anna. Spreading her poison." A silent snarl drifted over his face. "I didn't *ask* to be born into my bloodline, Dru. Just like you didn't *ask* to be born *svetocha*." He showed his teeth, blond highlights sliding back through his hair as the aspect folded over him. "You should be grateful, though. My father's strength passed on to me, and it's the reason you're still breathing enough to fling accusations." He straightened. "What are you doing here? Someone should be watching you during the day."

*Yeah, right. Like someone's supposed to watch me when it's Restriction. That's really been working out well.* "I got out of my room. Didn't you leave this?" I dug the note out of my pocket, suddenly wishing I could fold up the knife again. "The night I was . . . attacked?"

"Attacked? And . . . Anna." The aspect kept his hair dark, and his teeth didn't retract. "Tell me."

"I want to know—" My heart was in my throat again.

I didn't even see him move. One moment he was all the way across the boathouse. The next, the silvery screen of water over the sunken rowboat rippled, and he was right in front of me. I jerked back, my shoulders hitting the door, and his nose was inches from mine. His hands thudded onto the wood behind me, his wrists against my abused shoulders. Apple scent drifted around me.

Jesus. He was so *fast*. And his eyes were burning. The aspect retreated, blond sliding in his hair as a stray band of sunlight caressed it. "What do you think you want to know? If I wanted to betray you, *kochana*, I could have. Easily. If I wanted to hurt you, I would have already *done* it. I could have . . ." He paused. His fingers came down, wrapped around my wrist. The knife lifted, and he held it with the point just over the left side of his chest. "There. There's the spot. Between those two ribs and twist, if you can. Don't hesitate, Dru. If you honestly think *I'm* a danger to you, push the knife in. I'll help." His lips skinned back from his teeth, and his fingers tensed on mine. He jerked the knife forward, and I surprised myself by yanking back. I couldn't let go—he was holding it too hard. My scraped fingers gave a flare of red pain, subsided.

He tried again, pulling. The point touched his sweater. The same paper-thin black V-neck he always wore, whether it was hip-deep in snow in the Dakotas, or freezing here. "Go ahead." His breath touched my face. "Every *djamphir* is technically a sixteenth. Any more than that and we're *nosferatu*; any less and we're malformed things, not even human. Something about the gene pairs; I don't claim to be a scientist. It was a joke. But feel free to use your little knife, *kochana*."

I tried uncurling my fingers. He wouldn't let me. We stood like that, him tugging forward and me pulling back, until he let go of my hand. Spread his palms against the wood behind my shoulders and leaned in. "Satisfied?"

My mouth opened. The knife dropped and dangled in my nerveless hand. I couldn't find a damn thing to say. He waited, and the sound of water whispering away under half the boathouse's floor, touching its rotting pilings, was a cold silken whisper.

I dropped my eyes. Looked at his throat. His Adam's apple moved as he swallowed. When he spoke, it was the same businesslike, mocking tone he'd used when I first met him.

"Now, let's talk about something useful. Attacked? When? Tell me about that first. Then Anna." He plucked the note from my nerveless fingers, held it to his nose, and inhaled. But he didn't step back, and the note vanished into his back pocket. Just like that, it was gone. "Ah. Dylan. Sneaky old man. This was our meeting place, once."

"I—what? Jesus." What was *Dylan* doing leaving notes on my pillow? But it solved one riddle.

Christophe leaned back toward me, his hands on either side of my shoulders again. "He's reassuring me of his loyalty. Touching. As well as giving you a reason to slip your leash during the daytime, which I'm not so sure I like. Now start talking. When?"

I told him the whole thing, stealing little glances at his expression. It was a type of relief to spill it all out, like lancing an infection or popping a zit. It's also kind of hard to talk with a *djamphir* staring you in the face. Especially when the aspect keeps flickering through him, and his canines are touching his lower lip, dimpling softly. His entire body tensed when I got to the part about Ash and the sucker. I was busy thinking of what I'd do if he got angry—could I dump him in the water and run for it?

My voice faltered when I got to Ash sniffing me. Just . . . sniffing me. After he'd torn a couple of suckers apart, suckers who said the Master wanted something.

It didn't take a rocket scientist to figure out the "Master" was Sergej. Or to figure out what he wanted with "the little bitch."

"*Mój boże,*" Christophe whispered. "You're certain? *Certain* it was him?"

I nodded. He was so close it was hard to breathe. It was *exactly* like being next to an oven baking a really spicy apple pie. "He bit Graves, I'd know him anywhere—"

"*Mój boże,*" he repeated, then grabbed my shoulders. I was confused, but then I found myself caught in a bear hug, his arms around me and his chin atop my head. He wasn't as tall as Graves, but he was wiry-strong and very warm, burning through his clothes. "He must have killed them all, or Sergej would have sent more. It's only a matter of time now." It sounded like he was talking to himself, and I was frozen. I hadn't been this close to anyone except Graves lately, and there was a weird feeling to it.

A weird, warm feeling. Warm all over, like being dipped in oil. It was kind of like Dad's infrequent hugs when I'd done something really well. But there was something else to it. Dad hadn't smelled like apple pie and he hadn't hugged me so hard my bones creaked, and breathed into my hair. Christophe's breath was a warm spot on my head—he'd tucked his chin to the side now, and his hands spread against my back. The locket, caught between us on my breastbone, was a hard lump of warning.

"Dear God." His arms didn't tighten, but he was still tense. I was trying to figure out what exactly the feeling was.

Then it hit me. It was *safety*. Christophe wasn't about to let anyone hurt me. I don't know when I'd started believing that rather than being afraid of him, but there it was. It was like I felt when I heard Dad's truck rumbling into the driveway in a strange new house, coming back to get me. Like someone was going to Deal With Things, and I could relax a little and just go with it.

Like I knew my place in the world again.

We stood like that for a little while, Christophe and me. I breathed in the smell of apple pies and everything else fell away. The boathouse creaked a little in the thin sunlight, and I couldn't see anything because my face was buried where his neck met his shoulder, my nose in the slight hollow just above his collarbone.

I didn't mind as much as I thought I would.

"Listen to me," he finally said, as if I'd been arguing with him. "Are you listening, little bird?"

My voice wouldn't work right. I made a tiny little nod instead, because—how's this for weird—I didn't want him to let go of me. He'd pulled back a little, just with his lower half, and I was afraid the scorch in my cheeks would set fire to the rest of me, because I had an idea why.

*Wow. Oh wow.*

"I'll take you to a safe entrance. Go back up to your room—don't worry if someone sees you. At this point, it doesn't matter. I have to ask you to wait, Dru. I'll be gone for a day, perhaps as many as three or four; there are arrangements I must make for your escape. Will you trust me?"

You know, if he'd asked me this way the first time—serious instead of mocking, his voice almost breaking—I would have handed over my car keys. Or maybe I was just thinking that now, because he was so close and because he was shaking. We both were. The trembling spilled through me like wind through aspen leaves.

"Anna said you betrayed my mother. Told S-Sergej where to find—" The sentence died because he squeezed me, hard. I was almost afraid my bones would break. The breath huffed out of me, against his neck.

"I would *never*," he snarled, "have done that. Never. Do you *understand* me? God and Hell both damn it, Dru. I couldn't save her, but I'm going to save you. I *swear* it."

And you know, I believed him.

What girl wouldn't?

# CHAPTER 15

**Two hours later,** I eased down the hall. I didn't see anyone outside my room, but I *felt* them there. I made it in and locked, barred, bolted the door. And that, apparently, was that. Christophe told me not to worry about someone seeing me come back—it was getting out without being caught that was the problem.

It reminded me of Dad. Shaking a tail or pursuit was second nature, and it was better for someone to lose you on the way out to a meet so you didn't compromise anyone else. I would have liked to be a fly on the wall when someone told Dylan I'd been spotted coming *back* to my room. It was amusing, in a grim, ironic sort of way.

*Wait*, Christophe had said. *I'll come back for you, as soon as I know . . . when I have a safe place for you. Will you trust me?*

It was just like Dad leaving me a fifty and telling me to do my katas. But scalding flushes kept going through me whenever I thought of Christophe hugging me. I would turn hot, then cold, just like alternating tap water. It lasted all the way through the rest of the sunny day and into nightfall, and I almost didn't hear the bell for wakeup. I was too busy trying to pin down where the hot and cold was coming from. My internal thermostat was way wack.

The lunchroom was a chaos of surf noise. Graves set his tray down. "I've got an idea."

"Oh God." I stared at my plate. Nothing on it looked even remotely appetizing. "What now?"

The cafeteria echoed around us, and he took a good look at my face. "Jesus. You're pale."

*Tell nobody. Not even Dylan. But if there is another attack, try to find him. Don't stay in your room.* Here Christophe had smiled grimly, just a slight curve of lips. *Or if you do, little bird, make certain you bar your door.*

"Just . . . I don't know." Now it was time for a cold flash. I shivered. The entire place was too noisy and bright. Boys kept glancing at me, though once Graves sat down they went back to what they were doing. And only snuck glances at me instead of staring openly. Except for Shanks, who stared at me from under his emo-boy swoop until I locked eyes with him, and he hurriedly looked away. He was all the way across the caf, too.

Dibs hadn't shown up yet. I actually . . . well, kind of missed him. I'd gotten used to that terminal shyness.

"You okay?"

*I saw Christophe again.* The words boiled behind my lips. "Fine." I still felt cold. Even the fact that my hair was behaving couldn't make me happy. I'd braided the whole mess back and forgot about it first thing.

It would figure, the instant I get okay hair I *also* start getting hot flashes. And keeping more secrets than I ever thought possible. Jeez.

"You sure? You look—"

"It's my room." The half-lie felt dirty and left a bad taste in my mouth. "I've been thinking about it. Someone has to have keys. Several someones *could* have the keys. I can't lock the dead bolt unless I'm in there, but someone could have the key for *that* too. There's a bolt and a chain, but they're both old and the door won't stand up to a beating. And warding won't stop *djamphir* or wulfen. It never stopped Christophe."

Saying his name was like a pinch in an already-sore place. *I saw him. He hugged me, and . . . Jesus, Graves. You don't even like me that way, but I can't tell you about Christophe, either.*

"Point." Graves stared at the paper, chewing his lower lip gently with startlingly white teeth. They hadn't been that white before. It was the wulfen dental plan—get bit and never have to worry about your canines again. "You're just frightening yourself, you know."

*Is that all it is? Well, it's working. Spectacularly.* I hunched my shoulders. Waiting for Christophe to come back and collect me was going to wear my nerves down to bare nubs.

"Really," Graves persisted. "You're pretty safe here. If the suckers were planning to kill you, they could do it easier if you were alone and on the run with nobody watching out for you."

"I don't know that anyone's watching out for me here," I mumbled to my plate. "Look at what's happened already."

"Some of *them*—the teachers—must be. And Jesus, Dru, *I'm* watching out for you too." He picked up his burger, took a huge bite. Chewed while examining me, with the air of a man who considered the matter closed.

That only managed to make me feel worse. He'd gotten bit because of me, and he was here because of me—no matter that he thought it was a better place than where he'd been. The Real World was nothing to play with, and he could get killed tomorrow or even tonight if a group of suckers attacked again.

And Christophe. The secret trembled behind my lips again, I swallowed until it sat in my stomach like a stone.

I had to say something about him. Maybe Graves would guess and I wouldn't have to say it out loud. "Why did Christophe send us here?" I picked up my fork and poked at the pile of salad on my plate. I'd dumped some blue-cheese dressing over it, but it still didn't look even remotely appetizing. What I wouldn't have given for Dad's special pancakes, or chili the way he used to make it. Or a good heaping helping of Gran's chicken and dumplings. Or fried chicken and slaw, with biscuits the way she taught me to make them.

"I been thinking about that."

Well, that was good, because I was fresh out of ideas. The secrets hemming me in fought for release, met with the bubble of heat behind my breastbone, and retreated. Even in two hours I hadn't asked Christophe half of what I wanted to. He'd been in a hurry to get me back to the Schola's walls and disappear to *make arrangements*. "And?"

"Maybe he didn't mean to send us *here* in specific. This is a small school. There's got to be others. What if we got put somewhere he didn't plan for?"

I turned it over inside my head. It would make sense, especially if Anna wanted to accuse him of killing my mother. But *why*? Why the cloak-and-dagger? Why all the bullshit?

I didn't have an answer for that one, and pulled myself back to the present with a twitch. "But he found me. Came in right through the window."

"And what if he can't get in again because of the watch the teachers set on the grounds? This place is closed up tighter than Fort Knox. And, well, Dru, he might not have your best interests at heart."

*He's in the boathouse, or he was and said he wouldn't ever . . . and if you'd been there . . .* But the idea of Graves standing there watching while Christophe hugged me made a weird unsteady guilt flood through me. I felt my chin set itself stubbornly. "He saved me from Sergej."

"But he might have done that for a thousand different reasons we don't know about. He called in the Order and said he was a part of them, but there's just as many people here who think he's some sort of traitor. And . . ." But he shut up and took another monstrous bite. He looked hungry, and his shoulders were bulking up. Now he was rangy instead of thin. Like the other wulfen boys, wide-shouldered and narrow-hipped. "Look, I've got an idea."

I hunched my shoulders even further. "You don't understand. I can't even sleep anywhere safe."

"So we steal a solid chair and put it under your doorknob. Even if they have keys, they can't get past that. And it'll brace the door, make it harder to knock down. Right?"

It was such a simple, obvious solution I felt like a moron. "Oh. Yeah." *Unless they hack the door down, but I'm sure I'd wake up for that. And get out the window again. Great.* "I guess."

"All right. So that solves that problem." He gave me a quick sideways glance. "You okay?"

*No, I'm not. Everyone's lying to me, I'm rattled, everything's screwed up all over, and now I feel stupid too. And to top it all off, I feel like I'm lying to you, even.* I flinched away from that thought. Pushed my plate away. "Fine. So what's your big idea?"

He told me, and I was even happier I hadn't eaten. We argued about it until the bell rang, and he went off to his next class.

I went to steal a chair. I was sucking at the attending-classes-every-day thing, but the chair was more important. And if several someones were trying to kill me, a chair would do better than a class would. At least I'd be able to sleep.

While I was at it, I tried to think of how to break into the armory and steal my gun back, too. Once I had a firearm, I'd feel better about a whole lot of things. If more suckers attacked or someone else came after me while Christophe was gone, a gun would do me a lot better than a chair *or* a switchblade.

I carried the chair up the long winding flights of stairs, got it into my room, and stopped two steps inside.

Someone had been in here. I knew it even though nothing was moved. Even the dust was undisturbed, but the room didn't *smell* right.

Cold and heat fought over me. Neither won. I dropped the chair on the faded carpet and reached for the switchblade. My hand stopped halfway. Nobody was in here now; the unloosed fist inside my head stroked the air with sensitive fingers and told me so. I swept the door closed and checked under the bed, pushing aside the dust ruffle.

The *malaika* were still there, oiled wood with its own mellow gleam. So was Dad's billfold. But the lock of Christophe's hair on my nightstand was gone.

My heart leapt into my throat. I stared at the edge of the blue-painted stand, the cold coming back until I had to clench my teeth to keep them from chattering.

There, delicately caught on the grain of the wood, was a single, curling, golden hair. There were a lot of curly-headed blonds at this school—Dibs, Blondie the teacher, Irving . . .

Which one of them would be in my room?

I crouched there for a long time, hugging myself. The cold had finally won, and it didn't go away.

# CHAPTER 16

**did manage to** grab a couple hours of sleep with a wooden chair propped under the doorknob. As soon as I set it there, the feeling of relief was intense, but short-lived. I stumbled over to my bed, fell into it, and only woke up when a bar of weak, cold morning light struggling through fog and the window glass touched the foot of the bed.

My internal clock was all messed up by now, so it didn't seem to matter. Besides, moving around during the day meant there would be no suckers, and most of the teachers would be asleep.

I stood in front of the bathroom mirror and ran through every curse word I knew.

*You can do this*, I told myself for the hundredth time. *Come on. It's no big deal.* Rain-soaked sunlight struggled through the window of the blue room. I checked my sneakers again, scrubbed my hands against my sweater. Paced the whole length of the room, dropped down to my knees to peer under the bed, and saw the glowing curves of wood gathering dust.

When would Christophe come back? As soon as I asked myself, I shoved the question away. There was no reason not to work on trying to find out who was after me, and to do that, I'd need allies. The *djamphir* boys weren't going to be any help. So it was the wulfen, and Graves said—

Just then, there were two taps at the door. I bounded up, raced across the carpet, and jerked it open to find Graves right outside. The hall was shadowed, so his eyes flared green under his messy hair. He shook it back and gave me a fey grin, then laid his finger against his lips.

I nodded. He gave my outfit—jeans, thermal shirt under a big gray wool sweater, sneakers, my mom's locket safely hidden—a critical once-over and shrugged.

I suppose he thought I'd be cold or something, but I knew better. If we were going to do this, I was going to sweat.

*No big deal. Come on, Dru. Buck up.*

Besides, I *was* cold, deep down where no amount of wool was going to warm me up. Who would come into my room and take Christophe's hair, and leave one of his own behind? It was pointless.

Unless it was Blondie the teacher, and he had a reason to tell someone—maybe Anna—that Christophe had been in my room. I didn't know what would happen then, but it would probably be unpleasant.

But I most likely would have been yanked out of bed and questioned by now, wouldn't I? I tried to tell myself to relax, that I'd figure something out. I didn't even buy my own pep talk by now.

And what the hell was I about to do? But I couldn't back out now. And Graves . . .

He beckoned. I stepped out and followed him down the hall. We threaded through the sunlit, sleeping Schola. Every once in a while he'd stop, holding up a hand, and we'd wait for a little bit, or he'd pick an alternate route.

It looked like he'd done a lot of exploring in the last three weeks. But that didn't surprise me. Knowing your ground is good strategic habit, and I had a good idea of the layout too. I should have had a better one, gone exploring instead of standing around in front of the armory or moping in my room.

*Woulda, coulda, shoulda, Dru. Besides, you're not going to be here much longer.* I stepped softly, breathing through my mouth, and we finally ended up in a concrete-floored corridor somewhere in the depths of the building. Graves chose lefts and rights seemingly at random, and we took a right into a dead end, one blank door set in the wall. He reached up, going on tiptoe, and did something to the little plastic box clinging to the wall over it. Wires threaded away, his fingers flicked, and he swept the door open with a grin. Midmorning sunlight burst through, and we stepped out of the Schola.

I took a deep breath. Rotting leaves, wet dirt, rain on the wind that touched the curls springing free of my ponytail. The light felt good, pouring over me. The fog would probably come back around dusk, but for right now we had a clear, pale blue sky and a sun that looked like a yellow-white faraway coin. High horsetails of white cloud brushed what little horizon I could see with the trees pulled so close.

In spring it would probably be pretty here. Too bad I wasn't sticking around to find out.

Graves closed the door with a click. "Come on, we're almost late."

"I am never going to be able to take that route again," I muttered.

"Yeah, well, next time it'll be different. They're watching you pretty close, you know. It's not so bad getting out when it's just me."

"Me being so valuable and all." *And there's another* svetocha. But I still hadn't told him about that either. It seemed like a bad idea. I was struggling with what to tell him about someone stealing Christophe's hair, too.

Two things stopped me. What could he do about it, and if he asked me what Christophe was doing leaving bits of his hair in my room, what would I say?

What *could* I say?

Secrets everywhere, pressing in on me.

I'm good at keeping them. I mean, Jesus, my whole life was nothing *but* secrets from the time Gran died. But it's a whole lot easier to keep them when you've got someone else who knows breathing in the same room. Carrying them alone is like having a huge spiky weight digging into your shoulders and chest, a weight you can't shift even while you're sleeping.

Graves let out a tired sigh. He was almost sounding like Dylan now. "Yeah, well, I'm beginning to think there's something else going on. See, you're supposed to be trained to survive, right? Everyone here is slated for grunt work, infantry. Shock troops. But the instant you show up in a class—except for Kruger's, that is—everything gets dumbed down and the kids get a day off. It's weird. It's like they're waiting for something."

*Kruger? Does he mean Blondie in history class?* It made me feel a little better—if he was honestly trying to teach me, maybe he hadn't come into my room. I ran up against the problem of who could have and threw up my mental hands in despair. "Christophe said I was supposed to be learning and he'll come back." *But he's off making arrangements to spring me from this place.* Something I hadn't considered before hit me: *And where is that going to leave Graves?*

I'd figure it out when the time came. Or so I told myself. But I felt even worse.

"Yeah, well. Christophe's not actually popular around here. Half the teachers hate him, and the wulfen say he's got a long history of being an arrogant jerk. About the only person who's neutral is Dylan, but he's got his own weird thing going on. He's always watching you. It's creepy."

"Yeah. Creep central around here. But we're in a school full of werewolves and part-suckers." I wasn't sure what to think about Dylan either. Everyone was acting weird. Which was probably to be expected in a place where the Real World was taken for granted, but . . .

I was glad to have Graves. And when Christophe came back, I'd argue him into taking Graves with us. He'd agree—he *had* to. And once we were out of here I could tell Graves everything.

As soon as I decided that, the weight on me eased a little bit.

Graves gave a bitter little laugh. "Point. Some of the teachers have something against Dylan, too. Or with him. It's like watching *Wild Kingdom* in here. Much more interesting than high school."

Trust him to put that sort of spin on it. "High school's a jungle too." I followed him up an overgrown path, almost trotting to keep up with his long strides.

He was still in his boots and coat, and there was a bounce to his walk. He was even smiling. "True."

"You're sure this is going to work?" Christ, I even sounded uncertain. Almost wistful.

"You want friends, right? They don't hate you, Dru. This is a good idea. Trust me."

I think it was the first time I ever saw Goth Boy look *happy*. Most of the time he was just kind of dealing with it. But now he looked pretty bright and sunny, his head up and his hair shaken back. The essential difference of skinchanger shone through, subtly different from a wulfen's but miles away from a *djamphir*'s sharp handsomeness.

Happy looked good on him, bringing out the strength instead of the weirdness in the architecture of his face. High cheekbones, big nose, his chin too strong too—but he was looking better these days. Or at least, not so strange.

I was looking at him so intently I almost tripped, had to watch where I was going. I hurried alongside him, brushing past scrubby bushes and trashwood. He took the left fork when the trail divided, and we ended up in a small clearing on the wooded west side of the Schola. Here the forest curved around and hugged the buildings, and there were about fifteen werwulfen gathered.

They all went still when they saw me. Dibs let out a squeak and hunched down. I tried not to stare at his hair. My heart was in my throat.

"What the *fuck* are you doing?" Shanks snarled. Even his emo-boy forehead swoop puffed up.

"She's coming with us." Graves didn't look fazed in the least.

"The Bloodkin watch her." Another boy unfolded himself from the fallen log he was perched on, rising and hopping down to the leaf-littered ground. "And she's slow and clumsy. We're not waiting for anyone."

"I got her out without anyone knowing." Graves folded his arms. "She'll keep up."

"Please. She's one of *them*." Shanks said it like I had some sort of disease.

Graves's upper lip lifted a fraction. "She's with me. You got a problem? Want a girl to kick your ass again?"

I tried to look dangerous. I probably only succeeded in looking thoughtful. Or constipated. But Dibs caught my eye and actually—go figure—*winked* at me. Sunlight ran through his buttery hair, and I caught a flash of an encouraging smile before he looked down at the ground.

Nobody noticed. And I couldn't see Dibs sneaking into my room to steal *anything*.

Shanks's lip lifted in a silent snarl. "If she gets caught out with us, she's not the one they'll punish. You like detention that much? What is *wrong* with you?"

"It's time she started knowing more about this place." Graves didn't look perturbed at all. "If she gets caught, they'll punish me. It was my idea anyway, and whining about detention is for candyasses. Now are we gonna do this, or are you gonna stand around flapping your lips all day?"

"I don't like it." This was from a rangy blond werwulf next to Dibs, one with a thick, corn-fed face and a thatch of golden hair. Straight, not curly. "She's not gonna be able to keep up."

"She'll keep up." Graves sighed and rolled his eyes. "Are we gonna run or not?"

"Let her try." A short, compact wulf with dark stubble all over his pale cheeks spoke up. "If somethin' happens, she's not going to tell on us. Not a squealer, that one."

"That's right." Dibs nodded vigorously, still staring at the ground. "Dru wouldn't squeal on us. She's nice. She's not like *them*. They wouldn't even wipe their boots on us."

Silence. They all stood around, thinking it over. That's the thing about werwulfen—it takes a while for them to do anything. They all have to agree before something happens. Once you think about the fact that they have those teeth and claws, it makes more sense. If they didn't find ways to cooperate, they'd argue each other right into extinction.

Finally, a murmur went through them. I thought about trying to look trustworthy. Considering I was holding a couple of guilty secrets, I guess it was working.

Some essential tension leaked out of Graves. He gave me a sideways look, green eyes glinting. I straightened a little.

It was apparent they'd made their decision.

"Huh. Well." Shanks shrugged. "Fine. It's your ass, anyway. Think you can keep up, little girl?"

*You know, I hate people calling me that.* "I'll do my best." I tried not to sound sarcastic, failed miserably. Graves didn't wince, but he was probably close.

As soon as the words were out of my mouth, an electric current ran through the assembled werwulfen. I glanced at Graves as everyone started getting up, dusting off their clothes, one or two of them bouncing in place. There was a lot of nervous energy in them, crackling just under their skins.

*I am so not ready for this.*

Graves cast me a single look. You know how when you know someone, sometimes all it takes is a meeting of eyes, a slight lift to the eyebrow, a tightening of the lips to speak volumes? It was like that. His green eyes said, *Are you sure?*

My face shifted. *No, I'm not,* it was saying, *but I'm gonna do it.*

He gave me a quirk of a smile, and Shanks rolled his shoulders in their sockets, tilted his head back, and inhaled for a long time, filling his lungs. A crackling, popping sound raced around the clearing, and I caught my own breathing speeding up.

*Just listen for the howl,* Graves had said. *It'll tell you all you need to know. Let it pull you along. I'll be right beside you.*

They began to growl, all of them, the sound rising like steam. Graves was a tense, hurtful silence next to me.

I was really hoping this would work. Then I thought, *Well, if I could handle Christophe hugging me so tight my bones creaked, if I could handle climbing up on the Schola's roof, and if I could handle being nose to nose with Ash, I can probably handle this too.*

*Probably.*

Shanks's head snapped back down, fur swirling up over his

cheekbones, his eyes a hurtful gleam. Seeing them change in full daylight was something else. I lost pretty much all my air as their familiar boy-forms ran like clay underwater, some of them crouched now, knees splayed and hands touching the leafy dirt.

Then, as if on some prearranged signal, they all tossed up their chins and howled.

Hearing wulfen howl is . . . well, it's horrible. The sound is glassy, hovering at the upper ranges of hearing, and it's full of paws on snow and running with the icy wind hitting the back of your throat like stars. Underneath that glassy edge is the song of flesh ripped apart, the sweetness of hot blood, and the savagery of crunching bones with sharp white teeth.

The worst part is how it climbs into your brain, pressing itself like a hard sharpness into the soft folds, and drags open the doors socialization slams shut to keep the howling ravening thing deep inside down and tame.

The thing on four clawed legs that lives in all of us.

A civilized person flinches away from that thing. At the Schola, they called it the Other. Werwulfen use it to violate the laws of thermodynamics and physics, to set the inner beast free. And Graves, a *loup-garou*, uses it in a different way—for mental dominance instead of physical change. I wondered how, and why, and wished they would actually train me instead of dumping me in kindergarten classes.

It didn't matter. I was leaving soon anyway.

Graves's fingers slid through mine, hot and hard. He squeezed my hand, and I flinched. My initial panicked reaction was to curl up more tightly inside my head, squeezing out the little stroking fingers and paws gently tapping at that door in my brain. But the place at the back of my throat where the hunger had blazed through was still raw-sensitive, and the wulfen's cry rasped against it like a cat's tongue.

The cry modulated, ending on a low lonely sound, and the wulfen moved. Graves leapt forward, and I had to go along or get my arm torn off. My feet slipped in leaves and dirt, and the fear arrived, smashing through me and laying copper against my tongue.

Graves dragged me. I had enough to do keeping my feet on the ground. The other wulfen were leaping fluid forms, and I began to get a very, very bad feeling about all this.

We crested a high wooded hill, sloping down a pile of rocks and tree roots, leafless oaks and maples standing wet and secretive, clutching at the ground so they wouldn't slide. Graves yanked me forward, and as we went over the side his fingers loosened and slipped free of mine.

I was falling. My foot hit a rock, the sneakers slipped, and I knew I was going to end up in a heap on the bottom. My heart leapt; I gave a short, blurting scream—

—and the world *snapped* again, hard. My other foot landed squarely on the top of a boulder I hadn't even known was there, and my body woke up, tingling all over. The aspect flooded me like the heat of alcohol on an empty stomach, the Beam and Cokes I used to drink while waiting for Dad to come home and collect me. The heat burst through me, my teeth turned crackling-sensitive, and even my hair tingled as the aspect slid through it. Mom's locket dilated into a point of heat, as if it were melting against my chest.

Have you ever run so hard you thought your heart would burst? There's just you and your legs and the sound of wind in your ears mixing with the pounding of your pulse. The endorphins kick in if you can do it long enough, and all of a sudden you're not thinking. Your body's doing all the thinking for you. It leaps like a gazelle, it dances like a star, and the only thought on your mind is *God, keep going, don't let this slow down, don't let it ever stop.*

Running. With werwulfen. Their shapes blurred around me, the high unearthly howls distorted because of the speed, splashes of sunlight on fur and bright eyes as we moved in a mass. They spread out around me like a cat's cradle, and if I'd had time I might've wondered who was picking the direction. But it was enough to just run. If I just *ran*, nothing else mattered, and I didn't have to think about Mom or Dad or Gran or Christophe or any other hundred things crawling through my cluttered head. I could just *be*. It was like that place in the middle of tai chi where the world faded and there was just the movement, force and reaction spilling through arms and legs, hands like birds and feet like horse's hooves.

We crested another hill. The world was spinning underneath me, I didn't even have to move forward, just put my feet down every now and again to touch it. I heard the muffled wingbeats of Gran's owl, and a fierce joy flushed through me, a cleaner feeling than the rage of the bloodhunger. I was clear. I was see-through, I was a girl made of crystal, and this was the best thing in the world.

I don't know how long it lasted, but the force bled away. It got harder and harder to keep up with the world, but I was doing my best when someone grabbed my arm and everything came to a tumbling, spinning halt.

I landed hard on my knees, jarring, and retched. Someone dropped down beside me and patted my back. A couple other kids were coughing too.

"Jesus *Christ*," someone gasped, a high boyish voice. Someone else laughed, a high, unsteady sound, and the hilarity spilled through the rest of them. It bubbled up in my own mouth between the retches, my stomach informing me that *oh holy God, you should not have done that*.

My legs were on fire. All of me was burning and my back was a solid bar of pain. But it didn't matter.

What mattered was Graves next to me, also rubbing my back and laughing like he'd just found Christmas in his pants. Dibs was on my other side, on his knees and leaning against me, coughing. His eyes were bright with the tears that trickled down his cheeks, but he didn't look sad in the least.

Then Shanks squatted easily in front of me, flushed and windswept, leaves caught in his thick dark hair. "Well. You kept up." For once, he didn't sound supercilious. "Never had *that* happen before."

"Told you." Graves was breathless. A hiccupping laugh interrupted the words. "It's in the books. *Svetocha* can keep up."

"Huh." The taller boy eyed me. I tried not to puke on him. No wonder Graves had told me not to eat anything beforehand.

*But God.* I managed to get some breath back. "When . . . can we . . . do that . . . again?"

At that, everyone burst into laughter. Some of us were still retching, but the merriment kind of canceled that out. It didn't matter how much I hurt or how my heart felt like it was trying to climb out my windpipe. It didn't matter that everything was fucked up beyond repair and I was stumbling blindly around in the middle of a game that was way too big for me.

All that mattered was the sun on my shoulders, the wulfen gathered around me, and the way every one of them suddenly looked like . . . yes. Like a friend. And Graves right beside me, his hand making little circles on my back, his face all alight. It was like standing on the Schola's roof and seeing the world spread out underneath me, but not nearly so lonely.

It was the best I'd felt since my world fell apart and a zombie smashed through my kitchen door.

Hey, you take what you can get.

# CHAPTER 17

The disused classroom was in the bowels of the Schola, and it had an empty chalkboard on the curved wall. When filled with wulfen, the entire room had a nervous, fidgeting feel to it.

"So they're not teaching you anything." Shanks nodded. "Yeah, we wondered about that."

What else had they wondered about me? "I, uh, just don't go. It's all remedial shit I could get in normal high school."

Graves shook his head. "Skipping isn't allowed for anyone else. It's a trip to detention, and who wants that? So why let *you* do it? I mean, you're special and all"—he ignored Shanks's snicker—"but it don't make sense, and putting you in remedial classes doesn't make sense either. Especially with the chance of you-know-who finding out you're here—they should want you trained and trained *hard*, so you have a better chance of surviving."

"And then there's Christophe." Shanks was settled on a dusty brown couch, taking up most of it with his long legs. A ripple ran through the rest of the wulfen at the name. "He hasn't been around for years, but they're scared of him."

"Wouldn't you be?" Dibs piped up. "He's *dangerous*. Just look at his kill record. He's never wanted to make himself liked, either."

"Well, people have been calling him a traitor for a long time, but never to his face." Shanks shrugged. He'd picked most of the leaves out of his hair. "And he did bring her in. I know Juan's cousin—I talked to him last week during phonetime. When Christophe was tryin' to save your asses, someone was tryin' to kill him. The battle-group got a directive to kill a *nosferat*, and he didn't realize it wasn't a *wampyr* but Christophe until the guy had held off every one of them and had plenty of chances to kill 'im but didn't, and he was *djamphir* to boot. And he fucked up *you-know-who* but good, to rescue her."

A hot flush went through me. Did they know about Christophe and Sergej? And now that I'd gotten some sleep and run until I was close to a cardiac arrest, I felt like I was thinking clearly. If Dylan thought Anna was right, why would he be telling me Christophe was going to train me? If he didn't, why did he stay quiet when she accused him?

Why did he say he was on my side? And what was Anna's whole game with the file and the pictures of the house my mother had died in front of?

I didn't remember enough about the night Mom died. I didn't *want* to remember about that night. I was five years old, for chrissake.

I tried working it out again inside my head. Christophe said Dylan was loyal. I'd carried that note between them like a message, and Dylan was supposed to find me if there was another vampire attack. But I wasn't supposed to tell anyone, even Dylan, that I'd seen Christophe.

That didn't make sense either. But I'd been so confused from the heat of Christophe's body against mine. . . .

*Don't think about that, Dru. Jesus.* But what else was there to think of? The single blond hair caught on my nightstand? Other secrets, other lies, all pressing down on me?

"Something's off," another wulfen said. "They just watch her. And then there was the other night."

"Yeah." Graves leaned forward next to me. He still hadn't taken his coat off, and I understood why. It was chilly in the classroom, especially with sweat drying on my skin. "Nobody came to pick her up from the classroom and get her to her room. Isn't that a little suspicious, given how they're watching her?"

I stared at the cracked chalkboard. How long had it been since I'd seen an actual *chalk*board? Most schools had whiteboards nowadays. "Dylan said he didn't know who was supposed to be watching me. The duty roster disappeared, and—" I stopped short. I could have gone on, but I was taking Dylan's word for an awful lot, and I couldn't say any more without explaining the whole Anna thing.

I was pretty sure talking about another *svetocha* wasn't a good idea, if she was supposed to be a big secret.

But it didn't look like *I* was such a big secret, maybe. Had Ash killed every sucker there? If they were from Sergej and none of them came back, he wouldn't know for sure I was here—unless the traitor, whoever it was, could manage to tell him. Or a sucker could survive the next attack and go tell him.

The pieces fit together inside my head. Christophe must have realized this—it was why he was coming back to get me out.

It was anyone's guess whether he'd get back in time. My mouth was dry and my heart was still thumping along.

"Shit." Shanks rubbed at his chin. "I didn't know that." His dark eyes rested on me for a long moment. "That true?"

I nodded. "Someone was supposed to come and get me, or the teacher's supposed to take me to my room. That's what happened every other time. But that time Blondie vanished as soon as class was out. And nobody else came."

"Blondie?" Someone chuckled. "Oh wow."

"Kruger." Shanks didn't look amused. "And his helpful lectures. So how did you get out of there?"

"I saw . . ." The usual habit of keeping the woo-woo a secret made me pause. I plunged ahead. This, at least, was one secret I could get off my chest. "I saw an owl. My grandmother's owl. Whenever there's trouble, it shows up and tells me to get out." I took a deep breath. "And so I ran. But when I was outside . . . I saw a wulfen."

"Who?" Shanks could really bore a hole in someone with those eyes. He leaned forward, tense and expectant, like I was going to produce something he could chase down and bite.

"His name's Ash. He's got a streak on his head—"

"He's a Broken," someone supplied. "The last Silverhead. You-know-who's wulf."

Shanks waved a hand. "Yeah, I know about the Silverhead. You saw him?"

"I didn't just *see* him. He killed the suckers chasing me. He was pretty beat up afterward. He sniffed me, but he didn't hurt me." It wasn't coming out right. "I mean—"

"He sniffed you?" They were peppering me with questions now, one after another.

"How did he sniff you?"

"How close was he?"

"Was he bleeding?"

Shanks held up a hand. "Slow *down*, everyone. Jesus. First things first, okay?" He looked at me speculatively for a long, tense-ticking twenty seconds. "Dru." It was the first time he'd said my name without sneering. "Do you have any idea why you're here and not at the main Schola? Or even a big Schola?"

"The main . . ." I sounded as blank as I must've looked. "Isn't this, like, *a* main Schola? A big one?"

"Shit, no." He laughed, and some of the other older boys did too. It wasn't nice laughter, but it wasn't pointed at me, either. "This is like reform school. We're the troublemakers, the retards. The actual Schola for *this* district, the first Schola ever made, is in the Big Apple. Down over the state line. I wondered why you were way the hell out here."

*Oh.* "Nobody . . ." It made sense now. And of course Anna would have been coming from a bigger city, right? It was all over her.

"Nobody said to your face that you were on the short bus?" He shrugged. "That's interesting. But you shouldn't trust what they tell you even if they open up their mouths. *Nosferatu* lie, and half-vamps are right behind them sometimes. We're just dumb muscle and they're supplying the *tactics*, they say. So they get to order us around."

"But we're surviving now," Dibs piped up. "Not like it was. My grandfather told me about the Dark Times. They aren't so far away." A murmur of assent greeted the words.

"Dark Times, man." Another dark wulfen shuddered. "At least we're not slaves now."

"Yeah, well." Shanks shrugged. "They still treat us like shit even if they don't murder and enslave us. It's not a huge step up, but I'll take it. Most of the time."

"That always bothered me," I had to tell Graves. "The way Christophe treated you." The other, more tremendous secret swelled behind my ribs. I pushed it down. *Tell nobody*, he'd said. And they didn't need to know I was leaving soon anyway, did they?

Graves shook his head, black hair falling in his glowing eyes. The restlessness in him was evident. "This really isn't getting us anywhere."

"Patience," a lean lanky wulf with broad shoulders and a blond buzz-cut said. His hair wasn't long enough for me to stare at him. "This is how consensus works."

"What exactly are we discussing here?" I wanted to know. I was tired of stumbling around and having people drop information on me. I wanted to *do* something.

Shanks held up a finger. "You're at a small satellite full of delinquents instead of the main Schola. Could be to throw people off the scent, but"—another finger—"Ash knows you're here. Which means you-know-who could know. He killed the *nosferatu* who attacked last time—but we don't know if he killed *all* of them." One more finger, the nail chewed all the way down. "They're lying to you about a whole hell of a lot, and refusing to train you."

"Christophe said there was a traitor in the Order," I said, slowly.

Shanks nodded. "Whoever signed the directive to send Juan and his pack after him, right? Okay. Huh."

Everyone thought this over. At least, I was thinking furiously, and everyone around me had a creased forehead. Graves fidgeted a little, then a little more. He opened his mouth, closed it, and stared at me.

"What?" I sounded more irritated than I really was. "What are you sitting on?"

"You're bait." The words came out flat and sharp. "Christophe wants to know who the traitor is, so he's dangling you out in front of someone. You were his bait for Sergej, too. Maybe he *did* specifically send you here."

The room went cold when he said *Sergej*, and several of the wulfen shivered. It wasn't like Christophe saying it, with the tinge of hatred instead of outright fear. It still sent a glass spike of pain through my head.

Graves didn't seem to notice. "He was all over getting you out of town once he realized the bad guy knew where you were, but before that? He was just hanging around, waiting for something before he'd make his move. Your dad had his phone number. They talked at least *once*. And the teachers here, some of them might be wanting to train you, but they've gotten orders not to, probably from . . ." He trailed off. "I don't have that part of it yet. I don't know why they wouldn't be training you even if you are supposed to be just dangled out in front of the suckers. But I'd bet my last smoke you're bait, Dru."

*Stay here, Dru. Trust me.* Everything fell into place. As hard as I tried, I couldn't find a flaw in that logic. "It would explain a lot. But what about Ash?"

"What about him? Just be grateful he didn't open your guts up." Shanks laughed, a cold sound.

"What if he needs help?" I persisted. "I've been thinking about it, and I—"

"You want to help a Broken? You want to help *Ash*? He was probably confused, or he didn't want to kill you just yet because you-know-who wants the pleasure."

"But when he was after me before he damn well wanted to kill me!" I was shouting before I realized it. My chest ached with the enormity of the confusion. "He *saved my life* the other night—there's got to be a reason!"

Graves grabbed my shoulder. "Calm down."

Calm *down*? He wanted me to calm *down*? Oh, *hell* no.

I was about ready to explode. "All this talking doesn't get any-thing *done*! What if we could find Ash? We could try to help him, and then we'd have a chance of finding something, *anything* else out."

"Why are you so set on this?" Shanks wanted to know. "You were poking pretty hard about saving a Broken in class the other day, too."

*Right before we got into it and I kicked your ass.* I went cold all over, goose bumps standing up on my skin. *Right before I wanted to drink blood. Just like a sucker.* "You didn't see his eyes." Almost defeated, I slumped back into the couch. "You just didn't. I want to help him."

"He's been you-know-who's wulf for a long time. Since the Dark Times, when you-know-who used him for hunting his kin. There aren't any other Silverheads left, just Ash." Dibs shivered. His tone was soft, scared, and terribly sad.

My hands were fists. I took a deep breath. "But he didn't hurt me. And he killed how many suckers? This wouldn't be a bad thing on our side."

A ripple ran through them, like ink threading into water, and I knew I'd said the wrong thing.

"Sides. You *djamphir* are all the same. Sooner or later you start talking about sides." Shanks's lip curled up. "Then it's time for wulfen to do the dirty work while you lay back and—"

The ball of fury inside my chest swelled. My teeth tingled, and I felt something sharp touching my lower lip on each side. I rocketed up to my feet. "*Fuck* you."

"Let's just calm down—" Graves began.

"Calm down my *ass*! I almost died, and this asshole's acting like everything's *my* fault!" Frustration boiled sharply under my skin, prickles and pokings. Every secret I was keeping jostling for release. "If we're gonna start the *you're just like the rest of them* shit, then how about finding someone else to pick on? I didn't ask to be born part sucker! I didn't fucking know until everyone was trying to *kill* me and my dad never came *back!*" I had to stop to take a deep breath. Everyone was staring at me. "Now nobody will tell me what the fuck is going on, and I'm sick of it! I'm sick of feeling like I've done something wrong just by *breathing*! I didn't *ask* for this!"

"Nobody's saying you—" Graves started. To give him some credit, he was trying to smooth the ruffled waters, or something. But I was done with being soothed.

"Yes they *are!*" I jabbed an accusing finger at Shanks. "That's *exactly* what he's saying! That I deserve all this shit somehow because of what I was born like!"

The air changed just as I ran out of breath, and a ripple ran through the room again. This one was cold, a breath of warning. Graves grabbed for my shoulder, but I ducked away from him. If anyone touched me right now I was going to go absolutely postal.

The bloodhunger was a roiling ball of fury inside my chest, and it was hard to push it down and lock it away. Did all the other *djamphir* feel like this? All the time, or just when the aspect came over them?

How did they stand it? How could *anyone* stand it?

"Oh Jesus." A wulfen in a crouch by the door lifted his head and sniffed. "*Djamphir* on the way. Must be a teacher."

"Crap." Shanks bounded to his feet. "We'll have to split up. If they catch us out here with *her*—"

"Don't worry about it." I had already spun on my heel and was headed for the door.

He let out a snorting laugh. "What are you gonna do, tell on us?"

"I should," I tossed over my shoulder, picking up my weary feet. "But I'm not like *you* assholes. My dad raised me right, dammit. I'm going to draw whoever it is off so you can go back to the dorms and fuck yourselves."

I hit the hall at a run and plunged into the corridor. Here in this wing it was cold, and my shoes were wet and covered in dirt. I made a lot of noise, feet slapping, yelling anything that came into my head—usually four-letter words, bouncing back eerily at me from the stone and paneling.

That, at least, would distract any teacher coming down here. The wulfen of them could go back to the dorms and play pinochle or spin the bottle or whatever, for all I cared.

I burst out into the lunchroom. Which was strangely deserted, sunlight falling from the high windows. The chairs were all stacked on the tables, and I picked one stack and pulled it down with a bouncing clatter. *That ought to bring someone out.* My heart pounded, and the sheer injustice of it all rose up to choke me. The ball of fury behind my ribs smoked and boiled so hard my eyes leaked heat and water.

"FUCK THIS PLACE!" I yelled. "I WANT SOME ANSWERS!"

"You don't need to scream," someone said behind me, and I whirled. Dylan stepped out of the shadows with a creak of leather, stopping just short of a bar of heavy yellow sunlight. "You should be more careful. If I can catch you out during the day, so can someone else."

It took a couple seconds for my heart to climb down out of my throat. "Jesus Christ!"

"Nope. Just me." A crooked smile lifted the corners of his lips. But his dark eyes were serious, and there were bruised-looking rings underneath them. "We don't have much time, Dru. Come on."

You know, any other day I probably just would have gone with him. But not today. I was tired of following people around, tired of being led by the nose. "Where? Does what's-her-face want to see me again?"

Dylan sighed, an aggravated, familiar sound. The sleepless rings under his eyes matched the tension around his mouth, and his hair was messy too. "You should hope not. Come *on*, Dru. Please. I've got something to show you."

I folded my arms and refused to budge. "Why should I hope not?"

"Because I'm not so sure Milady can be trusted." He stepped back, retreating from the sunlight. "Are you coming, or do I have to wait for another time when I'm on duty to watch you?"

"You were on duty?"

He shrugged. "Why do you think I let you out with your little friend? At least I'm sure he and his wulfen won't kill you, even if they are delinquents and thieves." Another two steps back. Dylan's eyes glittered, the aspect sliding over him and retreating in waves, sending fingers of ebony highlighting through his hair. "Dru. Believe me. You want to see this, and it's not safe to talk up here."

*Up here?* I sighed. It was what everyone said: *Trust me, Dru. Believe me, Dru. Let me do what I want, Dru.*

I was helpless, the way I'd been all along. And the idea that Christophe maybe wasn't coming back for me, that he was using me as bait, that I might be stuck here for a while—it was enough to take the fight right out of anyone.

My shoulders slumped. The dampness on my cheeks clung to my fingers as I scrubbed at it.

I followed.

**was spending a** lot of time following boys through stone-walled halls. Dylan didn't speak for a long time, just took me into the north wing. He moved soundlessly in his heavy engineer boots, with the peculiar grace of the Kouroi. I got the idea his jacket only creaked for effect, too.

I finally had to open my mouth. "The wulfen. They're not going to get in trouble, are they?"

"Of course not. I'm not one of the proud." He unlocked a wooden door and paused for a moment, breathing in deeply. "There's so much more than you've been told. I wondered why they sent you here, and I wondered even more when the directive came that you needed 'time to recover' and shouldn't be held to a teaching schedule, and that no allotment would be made for tutors or bodyguards this quarter." His tone turned bitter. "Then Milady started meddling even further. And when Milady meddles, beware."

*Milady?* "You mean the chick who was here the other day." *The one who thinks it's really important that I hate Christophe. He called her that, too.*

"That 'chick' is the queen of the Order, Dru, and the head of the Council. *Svetocha* are precious. Milady was saved from the *nosferatu* about fifteen years before your mother was, and I think those years gave her a taste of ambition. I wonder . . ." Maddeningly, he stopped short, so I didn't get to hear what he wondered. "At the main Schola, you would be given everything your heart desired. Here we've had to make do because of funding restrictions. I thought you'd be sent downstate as soon as arrangements could be made. I *thought* you'd at least have a battery of tutors, not to mention a bodyguard or five like Milady herself. But it would draw too much attention, the directive said. You were better protected when you were less protected, because it wouldn't bring attention to your survival, and Sergej would be looking for traces."

When he said it, the name didn't make the air turn chill and unwelcoming. But it still sent a bolt of almost-pain through my head. *That doesn't make much sense.* "That doesn't make any sense at all."

He bared his white *djamphir* teeth in a wide, mirthless smile. "That's what I thought. But I've already been demoted to running a tiny little reform school for cannon fodder out here in the sticks. Mine is not to question why, Dru."

*Oh, comforting. Not.* "Wait a second—"

A shrug and a quick motion, brushing the past away. His leather jacket creaked. "When you bring in the fact that Christophe found you, there's also the question of his loyalty. And the fact that you are . . . who you are." He pushed the door open and motioned me through. "I've been stuck here for a long time. My own loyalty, to your mother and to Christophe, was professionally expensive, to say the least."

"So—" I wanted to get a word in edgewise. Unfortunately, I had no word to get in. I tried again. "Okay. Can you do me a favor and start from the beginning? What the hell *am* I doing here?" *Am I bait?*

But I felt the heat of Christophe's body against mine again, and didn't believe it. Couldn't believe it. No matter how much sense it made.

The room was long and low, windowless, and full of metal racks with boxes stacked on them. It went back for a long while, and the only light came from bulbs in thick, wire-crossed glass shields wrapped with cobwebs. It looked like an abandoned bomb shelter, and the rows of shelves receded to infinity.

"I think you're here because someone is biding their time. It's the oddest thing, but I can't get through to any of my regular contacts over the state line. This entire node is being held as a blackout zone. Now, that *could* be to protect you. But it's looking more and more like *nobody even knows you're here.* Nobody at the main Schola, nobody in the Order except Augustine and Milady, and nobody's heard from August recently. He's missed his last two call-ins with his handler—who is, incidentally, one of my friends." Dylan swung the door shut, turning back to face me as I edged nervously away. "And Christophe is unreachable too." His eyes asked a question; did he suspect I'd taken his note to Christophe?

He *had* to suspect it. Which meant he was playing a game too. Just what kind of game I couldn't guess yet.

"August is missing?" My throat was closing down to a pinhole, I had trouble getting the words out. Augie was Dad's friend from way back—and the person I'd called to verify Christophe's story. Right before everything went to hell with the dreamstealer, the sky turning dark in the middle of the day, and Sergej.

I shivered. The sweat dried on my skin itched and reeked. It was a sour scent I was pretty used to by now.

It was fear.

I didn't even remember what it was like not to be terrified anymore. Dylan examined me for a long ten seconds or so, and I was suddenly, scorchingly aware that I was down here alone. Nobody knew where I was. And he was telling me an awful lot of stuff about how I wouldn't be missed by anyone who had the power to do something about it if I just up and disappeared.

But Christophe had told me to go find Dylan if there was another attack. He'd said Dylan was loyal. He'd told me he was coming back for me, too, and if I doubted that there were all sorts of things I could doubt.

*Oh crap. I don't trust anyone anymore. Not even myself.*

"I've stolen this from the armory." Dylan's hand made a small movement, and I stared at the gun. It was reversed, the butt offered to me. It was the nine-millimeter I'd handed over when the helicopter landed in the snow, to take me to the Schola and what I thought was safety. My heart pounded high and hard in my throat. "If what I suspect is true, you're not safe here. You're not safe *anywhere*, but especially not here."

I reached out. Heavy metal, cold against my fingers. My hand closed around the gun. I popped the clip out and checked it, habitually. Still loaded with Dad's silver-coated bullets. "So what am I supposed to do now?"

"Come take a look at this. Do you have a holster for that thing?"

I shrugged. *Um, no. I can't sign weapons out in the armory; all my stuff is in the truck—which Christophe's hidden. And I have no way of contacting him.* "How about I hide it in my bra?"

I didn't mean to sound so sarcastic. But Jesus. And I felt a lot better with the gun in my hand.

Ridiculously better.

He sighed, a regular vintage Dylan sigh. "We'll figure that out in a little bit. This way."

I followed him between two rows of bookshelves, the gun kept carefully pointed at the floor. "What am I supposed to be taking a look at?"

His shoulders came up a little. "Something I've been sitting on for a while. The transcript Milady was talking about exists, but the one she showed me was heavily redacted. I have the original."

All the breath left me in a whoosh. "Whoa. You've got it?"

"See? I told you you'd want to see this. The agent who transcribed the call was a friend of mine and a good Kouroi." He hunched even further, as if the weight of the world was bearing down directly on him. "He died alone, in terrible pain. He was betrayed. I didn't believe him when he gave me the envelope and told me not to share it with anyone unless it was an emergency."

"So it's an emergency now?"

"I certainly think this qualifies, Dru." Dylan took a sharp right at the end of the row of bookcases and kept going until we ended up at a heavy wooden door set in the stone wall. "I thought I would give this to Christophe. But you'll probably see him before I do. If he's still alive." He gave me an odd look, his eyes shadowed.

The urge to tell him that I'd already seen Christophe fought with the reasonable caution to keep my mouth shut. Everyone was lying, for God's sake. Next I was going to find out that even Graves was fucking around with me.

*No. Not him. You know better.* But Graves was okay hanging out with his wulfen buddies. They didn't seem like bad kids to me, just stupid and aggressive. Hey, that's boys for you.

And if nobody was supposed to know I was here, where did that leave them?

Dylan unlocked the door with a heavy iron key. "We've got about two hours until Kruger's on duty to stand guard. I want to get you back in your room before then."

"Sounds like a plan." The weird spinning sensation had filled up my chest again. *God, I wish Dad was here. Or August. Or even Christophe. Just someone else to deal with this.*

I closed that thought away for the hundredth time, and followed Dylan through the door.

* * *

I watched the sunset spill orange and gold through my bedroom window. The gun was on the bedside table, pointed carefully toward the blind corner behind the door. A copy of the transcript—three and a half pages covered in single-space typing—sat obediently near my bare feet.

The date and time were military; I could tell just by looking. Strings of numbers marched across the top and bottom of each page. The text in the middle was even and close, little black ants marching on white paper.

SFR-1: *The information is well guarded.*

SFR-2: *That's none of your concern. Where is she? We are prepared to pay for the information.*

SFR-1: *Keep your money. I just want the bitch dead.*

SFR-2: *I can arrange that.*

It was my *mother* they were talking about. Calmly discussing killing her, like her death was just one more item on a grocery list. There was a mention of Dad, too—"the husband." Nothing about me.

Of course, according to the date, I would have been about five years old. Was I my mother's secret?

I squeezed my eyes shut so hard phantom yellow fireworks

splashed in the darkness behind my lids. It was the most hurtful memory of all, even worse than Dad's eyes, the whites rotting and the blue irises clouded as his dead body chewed at the air and shambled straight for me.

This memory lay at the very bottom of a deep well inside my head, and dragging it out made my entire body shake just a little.

"Dru," she says, softly but urgently. "Get up."

I rub my eyes and yawn. "Mommy?" My voice is muffled. Sometimes it's the voice of a two-year-old, sometimes it's older. But always, it's wondering and quiet, sleepy.

"Come on, Dru." She puts her hands down and picks me up, with a slight oof! as if she can't believe how much I've grown. I'm a big girl now, and I don't need her to carry me, but I'm so tired I don't protest. I cuddle into her warmth and feel the hummingbird beat of her heart. "I love you, baby," she whispers into my hair. She smells of fresh cookies and warm perfume, and it is here the dream starts to fray. Because I hear something like footsteps, or a pulse. It is quiet at first, but it gets louder and more rapid with each beat. "I love you so much."

"Mommy . . ." I put my head on her shoulder. I know I am heavy, but she is carrying me, and when she sets me down to open a door I protest only a little.

It is the closet downstairs. Just how I know it's downstairs I'm not sure. There is something in the floor she pulls up, and some of my stuffed animals have been jammed into the square hole, along with blankets and a pillow from her and Daddy's bed. She scoops me up again and settles me in the hole, and I begin to feel faintly alarmed. "Mommy?"

"We're going to play the game, Dru. You hide here and wait for Daddy to come home from work."

This is all wrong. Sometimes I hide in the closet to scare Daddy, but *never in the middle of the night. And never in a hole in the floor—a hole I didn't even know was there. "I don't wanna," I say, and try to get up.*

*"Dru." She grabs my arm, and it hurts for a second before her grip gentles. "It's important, baby. This is a special game. Hide in the closet, and when Daddy comes home, he'll find you. Lie down now. Be a good girl."*

*I protest, I whine a little. "I don't wanna." But I am a good girl. I snuggle down into the hole, because it's dark and warm and I'm tired, and the shadow on Mommy's face gets deeper. Only her eyes glitter, glowing summer-blue. She covers me up with a blanket and smiles at me until I close my eyes. Sleep isn't far behind, but as I go down I hear something, and I understand she's fitted the cover over the hole, and I am in the dark. But it smells like her, and I am so tired.*

*I hear, very faint and far away, the closet door close, and a scratching sound. And just before the dream ends, I hear a long, low, chilling laugh, like someone trying to speak with a mouthful of razor blades, and I know my mother is somewhere close, and she is desperate, and something very bad is about to happen.*

My eyes flew open. Sunlight poured in a flood through the window, past the curtains.

Things don't just go wrong once. They go wrong far enough and then they explode and it's impossible to put everything back together. If I was with Dad down South right now, we'd be either getting ready to go out and deal with something—poltergeist infestation, hex trouble, cockroach or gator spirits, you name it. Or he'd be getting ready to go out and I'd be cooking dinner, moving around the kitchen while he loaded clips or filled holy-water ampoules, and sometimes played Twenty Hunter Questions with me. He'd pop the questions and I'd answer, usually correctly. Each right answer would get me a smile and a *Good girl, Dru. Now here's another one for you.*

Everything from *How do you take apart a poltergeist?* to *What are the rules in a bar full of Others?* And if it took me more than thirty seconds of thinking, he wouldn't let me flounder. He would jump right in and explain. Not like so many others who liked to call themselves teachers.

*Say it, Dru. Say it out loud.*

"No." My own voice startled me. Here I was, sitting up here in this bedroom that was kind of pretty, yeah, but it was also cold and soulless and there was no safety in it. Dylan had just brought me back and plopped me down in here with the gun and the transcript, and a warning.

*Don't trust anyone. If we're attacked again, hide. Don't let anyone know where you're hiding until the all-clear sounds. Take the gun with you, and for God's sake keep it hidden.*

And the point to this whole thing, delivered just before he closed my door.

*I'm going to try to find Christophe. He needs to know that this is a blackout zone, and that* wampyr *attacks have been increasing. We need to get you out of here.*

There I was, throwing a distraction across my own brain. *Say it, Dru. You might as well.*

"He's gone," I whispered.

Gran had pretty much raised me, until she let go and I was in free fall for that one awful night before Dad showed up to sign all the papers and collect me. I never knew how he'd known, but then again, she'd raised him, too. He hadn't put much credence to "that backwoods foolishness," but he still tossed salt over his shoulder when it spilled.

You'd be a fool not to, when you're hunting the things that go bump in the night.

And he'd still sometimes known things. He didn't laugh when people talked about intuition. He also never really doubted mine.

"He's really gone." It sounded even worse when I repeated it. It was like I had just fully realized I wasn't dreaming, that I wouldn't wake up from this and find him in the kitchen loading bullets in clips, or in his camp chair in front of the TV, or . . .

No more driving with the windows down and the atlas in my lap, navigating him to where he needed to go. No more handing ammunition in through the broken windows while things skittered and leapt for him. No more playing the guessing game, figuring out which part of the Real World we were up against this time.

No more listening to someone else breathing in the house in the middle of the night. No more seeing him slumped in his chair in front of the television, no more of his special pancakes on Sunday mornings or the immediate call when he stamped in the door. *Dru? Dru, honey, you there?*

No more chili nights or warm arms over my shoulder, no more reassurance in the middle of the night when I woke up screaming—it didn't happen often after I was about fourteen, but it was nice to know he was there, you know?

He was really, truly gone. I was all alone here, and what I thought would be a safe place was turning out to be a snakes' nest. Like that little store we'd been in before heading to the Dakotas. The one with the copperheads and cottonmouths in glass aquariums, stinking and making that awful ratcheting noise.

Cottonmouths are mean, too. They'll jump you with no warning. They hit the sides of the aquariums with dry thumps the entire time I was in there, while Dad was closeted with the owner.

Had he been getting Christophe's phone number? What else had he been doing?

I rubbed at my wet cheeks. I hate crying. It fills up your head with stupid and makes your entire face hurt. I folded up the transcript, leaving damp tear marks on the edges of the paper.

The *malaika* were still under my bed. Right next to them were Dad's billfold and a blot of darkness I grabbed and pulled out. It was my black canvas bag, still dirty from the snowy mess of the Dakotas. I'd packed it carefully while Graves and I were clearing out the house and Christophe was on the phone, arguing with someone about coming to pick me up.

That felt like a lifetime ago. Back when I'd still been thinking things could be fixed, maybe, if I just coped hard enough.

Cash, both in my wallet and in the little space under the flap at the bottom of the bag, a sort of secret compartment Dad had shown me how to sew in and use. ID, both in the wallet and under the flap. A fresh clip of nine-millimeter ammo under the flap. ChapStick, my Yoda notebook, a comb, two pens, a handkerchief, a clean pair of underwear and a bra, and a small bar of hotel soap.

Hey, you never know.

The black book with Dad's contacts, because I'd thought it would be a good idea to keep it with me. But if August had disappeared, who else could I call? And it wasn't like there was a phone here. I hadn't even seen one in Dylan's office. Shanks had talked about phonetime, but I had no idea where to even find a line to the outside world.

I was as isolated as a prisoner.

Compass, road map for Florida, and another for North and South Dakota. Neither map would do me any good, but the compass would be useful. Mini flashlight—I flicked it on and off, checked for the extra batteries. It still worked. Those were good things to have.

Travel-size bottle of ibuprofen, small bottle of holy water, bottle of salt. I slid the switchblade in one of the smaller pockets sewn along the back of the bag. It rattled against two large silver dollars and four or five iron nails. Well, they're steel, actually, but the iron content makes them a good defense against all sorts of things. Revenants, some apparitions, fairies—you name it.

I shivered, thinking of fairies. People who think they're all sweetness and wings should pray they never run across a sidhe with a bad temper and the ability to steal years from your life. And pray that they never hear silver horns in the dead of night, echoing against the hills as hoofbeats rattle on a lonely stretch of road and the Wild Hunt looks for a victim. Gran taught me about never, ever messing with fairies.

I was even scaring myself at this point, but it felt good to be doing something. To be planning, instead of just being buffeted along with what everyone else wanted me to do. This preparation was something I could have done in my sleep.

Dad's billfold went in the secret compartment under the flap. I folded the transcript one more time and slid it into Dad's little black book. Then I picked up the nine-millimeter and checked the clip once more. It was habit. I tore up a pillowcase from the blue bed and wrapped the gun, so something couldn't press against the trigger. I put the wrapped gun in the bag and wished I did indeed have a holster.

Wishing wouldn't get me one, though.

*Come on, Dru. Think. Think hard, and think fast. How would Dad put it? Think logically.*

My logic-thingy wasn't working too well lately. But I'd give it the old college try.

Anna wanted me to think Christophe had betrayed my mother. But he'd saved me, so that didn't make much sense. She *also* thought

I was stupid. Just showing me two pictures of the house we'd lived in Before wasn't going to make me not trust Christophe.

Unless . . .

Things exploded behind my eyes, my brain finally making some connections. *Oh shit.*

My hands were shaking. I held up one of them. Even my fingers were jittering. I grabbed for the locket and rubbed it with my thumb, hard, like I could polish away the fear.

Showing me two pictures was useless. Unless she wanted to find out what I remembered about that house. She'd been watching me very carefully while trying not to look directly at me.

And why the hell would she come all the way up here herself, especially since it was so dangerous for a *svetocha*? Bodyguards and tutors, and here I was locked in a room for them to decide what to do with me.

For Anna to decide? Or for Sergej to decide? Did it matter?

*Well, Dru, there're two words that apply.* Fuck that. *That about covers it.*

But what about Ash? And what about Christophe, asking me to wait? Could I depend on him to come back for me?

*It doesn't matter. You can't help either of them if you're dead. Blondie's on duty to watch you at the moment, but as soon as it's dark it'll be time for the first class of the evening and he'll be gone. You'll have a chance.*

A chance to do *what*, though? What could I do? I wasn't about to go crawling around the roofs at night.

At least I knew Christophe was alive. I could be the only person that did know that for sure—and still, anything could happen to him in the next few days.

And there was the fact that Christophe could be using me for bait. Everything inside me rose up in revolt at the notion, because every time I thought of him I felt his warmth against me and smelled a ghost of his apple-pie self. Maybe I *should* just wait around for—

*Dru, you're counting on other people to save you. That's not going to happen.* I let out a shaking breath. *This one's all about you.*

But what about Graves?

*Shit. That's the only hole in this plan.* But if I wasn't around, would he be so much in danger? And he was happy here, even if it was a reform school. Graves was just peachy hanging out with his hairy friends.

His hairy friends who liked blaming me for even being born. Jesus.

A band of shadow was moving up the window as the sun sank, the light taking on that golden-honey cast of the best hour to capture it, if you could. I'd never been much into photography, but I remembered drawing in this light while Gran spun thread or finished dinner, sometimes singing in her queer atonal way, other times muttering imprecations at chicken broth or vegetables. I missed both things—her singing, and the steady hiss-thump of the antique spinning wheel. It was probably sitting under a dust cloth in the corner near the fireplace right where she'd left it. The house, mine under the terms of the trust, was closed up nice and tight, and I had the keys right on my key ring—that was still probably with the truck Christophe had hidden.

But there was another key ring, and I knew exactly where it was. In a metal box buried under the north side of a big granite boulder, the one Gran poured fresh milk over every new moon.

She also bolted the door every new moon. They left her house alone. That's another reason why I always shiver when I think about fairies.

There's nothing like waiting for the night to make you really nervous. The plan came together inside my head, and I was really wishing I had access to a car, any car. How did the food get to the school? Who did all the laundry?

It was a fine time to wish I'd been looking around instead of moping up here in my room or skipping classes. Then again, I wouldn't have been taught anything worthwhile if I'd attended class, now would I. They were actively trying to prevent me from learning something.

So. No car, just me. There was one lonely country road dipping away from the school, hitching up with the county highway a good distance away. Far enough away that I hadn't seen it from the roof of the Schola.

Two unpainted lanes of blacktop, with a deep ditch on either side, ribboning through the woods and occasional fields. It joined up just north of the town the wulfen were always running to. I could buy a map there and . . .

*Then what? You don't know anyone around here, and anyone you contact is going to be a question mark. If August was a part of the Order, maybe some more of Dad's friends were too. And if he's vanished, what's to say the others won't as soon as you call them for help?*

My head hurt trying to think about all of it. But the absolutely essential first step was getting *out* of here. Once I was on the move, I could figure everything else out.

Graves and Christophe had both pointed out it was easier for the vampires to kill me when I was away from a Schola, even a small one.

But they'd have to *find* me first.

I got up, left the bag on the bed. What do you wear when you're running for your life? Layers, boots because your feet are your lifeline and sneakers are too flimsy, and wool. Graves's shirt had vanished in the laundry. It gave me a funny feeling to think about it.

I felt like I'd just woken up after a long winter's nap, but I couldn't stop shaking.

# CHAPTER 19

I t got dark early, heavy overcast coming in from the northeast. The sky turned steel-indigo, and thunder rumbled in the distance. Fog didn't rise, and that was odd. I was used to the whole place being wrapped up in cotton wool. It felt oddly naked, and I didn't like it.

I also didn't like the clouds. They just didn't *look* right, thick dark blankets boiling lower and lower until they seemed to press the treetops in some weird way. It reminded me of the iron-gray sheet of the sky back in the Dakotas, the day I'd come face-to-face with Sergej.

Unusual weather. Vampire weather.

I stayed at the window, rubbing at the locket and watching the shadows stretch through the ruined garden below. The Schola woke up, a subliminal buzz just under the surface of the silence. It was the same as every other night. Except this night I was cold even through three sweater-layers, jeans, and a pair of almost-new boots. I had my bag on, strap snugged diagonally across my body. After some thought, I slid the switchblade in my left ass pocket. Now if I could just remember to dig it—or the gun—out when someone was trying to kill me, I'd be all set.

I ran over it again in my head. Down the stairs once the bell for first classes rang, through the halls, and into the night. Now was my chance.

I gave the room one last glance, from the pile of clothes I'd tossed in front of the closet to the rucked-up bed. I was getting sloppy and not taking care of my space. It would have gotten me another Lecture from Dad.

Christ. I was even missing his lectures about *Cleaning Up So You Can Find What You Need When You're Under Fire, Dru, and That's Going to Save Your Ass.*

Loneliness rose in a wave that tasted like acid. I paused by the door, closed my eyes, and *listened*, unloosing the fist Gran had taught me to make inside my head. That clenched-tight feeling is necessary if you don't want to end up saying the wrong thing, or repeating people's thoughts back to them. Plus, it's hard to concentrate on your own business if you're busy listening to everyone else's, as Gran told me until she was blue in the face.

Gran was big on concentrating on your own business. I wondered what she would make of all this, and missing her was a stone in my throat.

There was definitely a sense of *presence* in the hall outside my room. I suddenly wished I'd gone up and out of the window again, but the thought of doing that so close to dark made my knees feel kind of funny. Once was enough. Besides, the whole point of this was getting out before it was an emergency.

I waited, barely breathing. The presence slowly slid away, just in time for the first bell. It tinkled sweetly all through the halls, muffled by the door. Time for breakfast. Or dinner, whatever way you wanted to look at it. The boys would be getting up, getting dressed, and getting to the caf.

I took a deep breath, twisted the knob, and stepped out into the hall. It was empty. The whole place seethed quietly. Was it just me, or was there an odd note in the seething? Something feverish?

*It's just you, Dru. Focus on what you've got in front of you.*

Still, I hesitated. What about Graves?

*The farther you get from him, the safer he probably is. The wulfen will look after him. They won't do a damn thing to help you, though, so get your ass moving.*

The door clicked shut behind me. I took two steps and froze again, because a new sound filtered through the air.

It was the Restriction bell, its high hard tones cutting through the silence like a hot knife through butter. I could tell this wasn't a drill, too. The awareness of danger prickled all over me with little diamond claws.

The Schola took a deep breath, bracing itself, and just as the tones of the bell died away I set off down the hall, my jaw firming and my hands turning into fists.

I would never have a better chance to escape.

\* \* \*

Even the best-laid plans have holes in them. My beautiful little plan was to get downstairs and to the intersecting halls, where I could take a hard right and have a clear shot at a gallery with doors on either side. Half those doors led to a courtyard garden; the other half opened up to a crumbling playground with swings and foursquare courts, quietly rusting away. From there I had a chance to get to a belt of shrubbery, and once there—

Well, anyway, I didn't get that far. I took the hard right, and as soon as I did my head pounded with approaching footsteps. They were running, and each step landed too hard to be human. I backed up, buttonhooked around the corner back into the hall I'd just left, and cast around for cover.

Nothing. Carpeted floor, industrial lighting, bare walls. Locked, empty classrooms on either side, other halls opening up to go down to the caf, two janitors' closets.

*Janitors' closets. Great.* One was locked. The other wasn't, and I lunged in, pulled the door to, and crouched in the darkness. My hip hit something metallic; I grabbed and stopped it from falling over. It was a metal bucket. I let out a soft, wincing breath and hoped they'd be making too much noise to hear me.

The footsteps ran in lockstep, hard metal sounds like iron poles hitting frozen earth. The taste of rusty blood and wax oranges burst over my tongue in a rotten flood, and the weird places on the back of my palate both opened up like flowers. My teeth ached, even the pressure of my tongue and lips against them agonizing. Little cold prickles raced up my arms and legs.

The steps were going pretty fast, and I shivered when they echoed on the winding stair up into the tower room.

The secret was out. They knew I was here now. A wounded vampire from last time had escaped to tell Sergej so, or the traitor had managed to tell him I was here, all wrapped up in a nice little blue room like a TV dinner in foil.

*Holy shit. I . . . holy shit.* The shaking had me by my scruff like I was a puppy, pitching me back and forth. Something crumpled in my left hand, the metallic thing I'd hit on the way down into a crouch making an odd soft sound as it bent.

*They're going up to your room,* Dad's voice said inside my head, pitilessly. *Move your ass, girl!*

I slid out of the closet on noodle-soft legs, shut it as quietly as

I could, and set off down the hall as fast as my protesting muscles would allow. Everything in me wanted to go back and cower in the dark, waiting for someone to find me.

*That's rabbit talk, Dru. Move it along.*

Down the side of the hall, hard right. There was my shot at the next part of the plan, and I took it, much faster than I should have been able to. My boots made odd scuffing sounds on the short carpet as I bolted into the gallery. Now the darkness pressed against the windows and glass parts of the door, and I'd forgotten I'd be clearly visible to anyone watching from outside.

*Shit. Shitshitshit!* No help for it now, nothing to do but to go flat-out toward the door I'd chosen and hope nobody was watching. Maybe they would all be too busy with—

An enormous crashing jolt shook everything around me. The fabric of the Schola rippled like a bedsheet given a good hard shake, and the glass broke with tinkling, pretty sounds, a shower of crystalline snow. It actually knocked me off my feet, tossing me into the side of the hall, directly against the stone facing. My shoulder flared with red pain, I went down in a heap, and it was a good thing too. Because then the screaming started, and I huddled against the wall with my head in my hands, trying to shut it *out*. It went on and on, scraping against the sensitive inside of my skull without pausing for breath. I clapped my hands over my ears, uselessly, and screamed as well. Hate exploded behind my eyes, fear and pain smashing bright fireworks through the map of my nervous system.

It was a struggle to pull myself back *into* myself. A thin thread of something warm trickled down from my nose, caressing my upper lip with a tiny wet finger. I licked without thinking, and a warm copper taste coated the inside of my mouth, reached down, and woke up the hunger.

My teeth hurt, a sharp piercing pain. Two pinpricks touched my lower lip, and I pushed myself forward on hands and knees, crawling. *Outside. Get outside.*

The bloodhunger set me on fire with thirst, but it also smacked the screaming away from the inside of my head and gave me a chance to make myself a fist again. The sheer hatred in that sound tore against my skin, rubbing like a wire brush. Broken glass littered the floor. I scrambled to my feet as cold air poured up the hall, whistling.

I hit the door in a mad tangle of arms and legs and dove into a bath of frigid air. It was a clear night, the stars coming up in small hard diamond-points of useless light, and I took off for the playground as fast as I could stumble. The swings that weren't broken moved gently, back and forth, and my boot soles slapped crumbling concrete.

The scream behind me ended, and another glassy cry split the air from the other side of the Schola. It was then I realized the entire place was lit up too bright to be night, and when I snapped a look over my shoulder I found out why.

The school was burning. You wouldn't think there would be a lot in a stone building to burn, but wet orange flames with blue wires in their centers leapt and crawled through the turrets, shone out through broken windows, and turned the night into flickering shadows. Those flames were wrong, and the snapping crackling hate in them told me what I needed to know—that this was something *nosferat*-based. There was nothing natural about the flames, just like there was nothing natural about suckers.

The fire shaded into regular orange with no blue threads out toward its edges. But that didn't make it look less freaky.

*Wow.* I stared. *If that reaches the library, fat chance studying afterward. Holy crap.* Another grinding crash rocked the building, and I heard more screaming.

This time the voices were young, and human. Well, mostly. Human at the bottom, even if there was growling over the top.

*Oh no.* I skidded to a stop. *Oh, shit no. Fuck. No, no, no.*

There were kids in there. I *knew* them. Cody and Shanks and Dibs and—

And oh holy God, Graves was in there and it was *burning*.

*Stick with the plan, Dru. It's a good plan, and it'll let you live.*

I hung there for a few moments, sick with indecision, the pinpricks against my lower lip turning more definite as half of me ached to bolt for the belt of scrub brush at the edge of the playground. The other half told me in no uncertain terms to turn right back around and tear the whole place apart until I found Graves. I had a gun, an extra clip, and a knife. That had to be enough.

*But—*

*But nothing!* This time it was Gran's voice, and it spoke up loud and clear. *You get your ass in there and you find that boy! He never would leave you behind!*

He wouldn't. I knew he wouldn't. But hadn't I been planning on doing just that to him?

*He's already left you behind! He's always playing with his happy shaggy friends! Get going, Dru!*

They were fighting over me, the two voices, and I had no idea who would win. But my stupid body turned itself around and started running straight for the burning building and certain death.

I really don't know why.

# CHAPTER 20

**ran along the** side of the gallery. *He'd be in the caf or the dorms; it wasn't time for class yet. So if they—*

Another big ripping sound. Jesus. Had they brought supernatural dynamite in to tear the whole place apart? Blue-flaming stuff fell, hitting the ground less than three feet away and hissing like a rattlesnake. I leapt back and found that I'd stopped shaking. I was too busy, and it was too warm. Sweat sprang up in the curve of my lower back and the hollows under my arms. It was like standing in front of an oven, heat radiating in every direction. Mom's locket was a chip of ice against my skin.

I made it around the corner of the building, skipped over more hiss-burning debris, and decided maybe I shouldn't run right next to the wall. Shapes flew like wet ink over the big lawn in front of the school, the wide circular driveway painted with leaping shadows and lurid orange light. The concrete lions watching the entrance to the driveway seemed to shift, raising their heads and baring their teeth as I skidded to a stop. My heels dug in, and I stared with a dropping jaw.

It was a war zone.

The wide circular paved expanse ran with lean hairy forms. The wulfen leapt and circled, teams of them peeling away to dash in, clustering dark forms with shining eyes and inhuman speed. There were *djamphir* there too, a line of defense in front of the massive steps I'd struggled up the day we arrived. One of them had long slender blades that didn't gleam in the light.

One of them had the wooden swords. *Malaika.* It was Blondie, his curls glistening in the flickering light as he lifted his chin and yelled something. The *djamphir* shifted their collective weight.

My knees went squooshy. I couldn't see Graves, and I swayed drunkenly for a moment. Another explosion ripped the air, and the breeze veered. Thick smoke wandered across the open space, threading between the motionless and moving forms like questing fingers.

The wulfen gave ground, falling back, and the *djamphir* on the defense line bunched up a little. It was confusing, everything moving so fast, and I hesitated, unsure what to do.

Dad never said anything about charging into a pitched battle.

I was still standing there like an idiot, staring at the chaos, when another unearthly howl split the night behind me. A breath of air touched the back of my neck under my braid, and I spun, throwing myself aside and down. The world slowed again, and this time I actually felt the muscle inside my head flexing to encase everything in clear Lucite. It hurt a little, like when you've pulled something and haven't slowed down enough to let it heal.

The wulf hung over me, firelight glittering in the white streak down one side of his head. All the breath whooshed out of me and I rolled, gravel scraping the back of my sweater. The firelight twisted in weird ways, refracting around him, and he landed in a scrabble just as I realized he hadn't been aiming for me at all.

*Oh crap.* I scrambled to my feet, right-hand fingers fumbling at the flap on my bag. It was time to get the gun out, because everyone fighting in front of the school had seen us.

Ash hunched in front of me, snarling. Little strings of spittle dripped as he snapped, twice, white teeth clicking. I let out a choked sound, my feet threatening to tangle as I backed up in a hell of a hurry.

He snapped again, and the mad gleam in his eyes was like the unearthly firelight. Another explosion shook the school, and the wall nearest me started to crumble. The noise was immense, and Ash dashed forward a couple of steps.

I half-screamed again and backed up, realized he wasn't attacking. He was just snapping at me, like a sheepdog.

*Herding* me. And when I glanced up, I could guess why.

Because every vampire who had been trying to get into the front door of the school was now looking at me. The fire lit them all in weird stasis, wulfen forms tumbling in the air, the *djamphir* on the steps — I saw Kruger, his jaw dropping — all staring at me with various horrified expressions.

"Svetosssssssssssha!" The cry lifted on the night wind, and their faces blurred into caricatures of hate and sharp teeth. "Svetossssssssssssha!"

*Oh shit.*

The *nosferat* broke and wheeled at once, blurring toward me. Ash lunged again, desperately, the white stripe on his head actually leaving a blurring trail, like a sparkler waved in the dark. It shook me out of shock and I whirled, my braid flying out in an arc, and took off around the side of the burning school again.

I wasn't going to make it, I could just tell. It was pretty clear now why they were attacking the school. And now, again, I was running for my life.

Just before I reached the corner, I heard the cries behind me—the wulfen's rising chill and glassy, the *djamphir*'s a shrill piercing ululation, and the vampires' a weird deadly scream lodging in the brain like crystal splinters. They made a weird three-part harmony, and if you ever recorded that sound, you could stop someone's heart just by playing it loud enough. The locket bounced against my breastbone, trapped in a fold of cloth and so cold it stung.

My teeth filled with aching, and if I'd had enough breath I would've screamed too. There was no time for it, because the footsteps behind me shook the earth, so I did the only thing I could do.

It wasn't a great idea, but it was all I had.

I ran along the side of the school, fists pumping and bag slapping against my hip, and as soon as the gallery loomed ahead of me I jagged for the biggest hole I could find, braced myself as best I could, and hurled myself forward into the unnatural flames.

* * *

Burning. Smoke choking the air. I reached the end of the hall and dropped to my hands and knees, crawled forward in a blur. Glass glittered, crunched under my jean-clad knees, and I hoped I wasn't about to flay my hands. My mouth ran with wax and rotten oranges. I spat and heard sizzling. The heat was like oil, my skin tight and shiny. The fire turned weirder—blue wires in the middle of orange flames, crawling through the stone walls like veins and spreading oven heat. Still, a circle of orange moved with me, the blue fading out of the flames as they drew closer.

Screaming behind me. If you've never heard a vampire die in battle, you can count yourself lucky. They don't just scream with their mouths—the sound goes on and on inside your head, bouncing off the inside of your skull and burrowing under your sanity until you want to scream yourself, until the edge of the world peels up and you can sense the nasty things that lie underneath regular waking consciousness. I scrambled through the burning gallery, carpet melting under and sticking to my fingers, until I spilled out another broken door into the courtyard garden. It was pure instinct, a draft of cooler air pulling me out.

Coughing, retching, I scrambled toward the middle of the garden. Smoke belched. Burning things fell like meteors, crashing to the ground.

*Well, Dru, this was not your best idea.* I almost pitched headfirst into the gravel path, snapped a terrified glance over my shoulder. There was a wall of orange flame and black smoke, but no vampires yet. Their keening soaked the air, fueling the flames. It was pure hate, rolled in agony and set alight, just like the Schola itself. I tried to shut out the noise again, failed, gasped and choked, and tried again while I crawled.

The bushes were burning out here too. I made it to the middle of the courtyard—there were stone benches with wooden slats, the paint on the wood smoking. I made myself as small as I could, knees up, my back braced against a bench's legs. I dug in my bag, got the gun out, and the tears rolling down my cheeks weren't from pain or fear. It was the smoke crawling around me, thick greasy fingers pressing behind my eyes. Coughing shook me in great racking bursts.

I'd thought I could break through the gallery and maybe find a flame-free part of the school to hide in. Now I was trapped. The vampires couldn't come in here and get me, but the fire might do their job for them. Still, I'd take being roasted alive over getting ripped to shreds by suckers any day.

Or would I? It was getting awful hard to breathe. I hunched

down further, trying for usable air close to the ground. The locket was still oddly cold and buzzing against my chest. Steam rose from my sweater, and the smoking paint on the bench wasn't too happy either, adding a weird pungent note to the thick vapor. A dead-looking rosebush in one corner of the courtyard blossomed into flame.

*Oh wow.* I stared at the thin thorny sticks, now alive with crawling orange flowers that fizzed and crackled. The gun dipped. Everything was a wall of flame, and I was beginning to feel lightheaded.

"*DRUUUUUUUUUUU!*" A long-drawn-out howl. I didn't recognize the voice, and it shook the streaming flames. I coughed steadily now, choking on the smoke. Everything blurred, the blue wires threading through the stone of the courtyard pressing against the circle of orange around me. The bench was getting awful hot, and I had a sudden terrible mental vision of the gun blowing up in my hand. Ammo could do that, if it got too hot. Dad had told me.

*Really not your best idea, Dru,* I thought, right before I slid over to the side, my fingers cramping on the gun. A black blot dilated in the middle of the flames. "DRUUUUU!"

I coughed again, scouring my lungs. There was nothing to breathe; it was all smoke. Haziness filled my eyes.

Someone was cursing steadily. At least, it sounded like cursing, but the words were put together funny. They sounded foreign. Fingers bit my shoulder and I was dragged up. I fought feebly, the gun loosened from my fingers. Something pressed itself against my cheek, hard little divots and something softer. Then, movement. The world fell away underneath me.

Falling. A jarring through my entire body. Splintering glass and a roar, and I was on fire, burning, flesh crisping and peeling before we burst out into cooler air and rolled, steam rising in waves, a hissing sound and a scream of pain. Then, more chaos.

*"Get the goddamn oxygen!"* someone screamed. Hands grabbed me and I fought back wildly, coughing and retching as I struck out with fists and feet.

*"Calm down!"* Another yell, this one I recognized. *"Goddammit, Dru, we're trying to help!"*

*Graves?* I tried to say his name, choked, tried again. My eyes wouldn't work right. My skin was still on fire, and I starfished again, throwing out my arms and legs as I tried to breathe. That was my last hurrah. All the fight just spilled out of me.

Something wet and cold wiped at my face. It felt good.

More coughing. They rolled me on my side, I choked up a thick mass of burning snot and spat. Someone caught my head, something was jammed in my nose, and a flood of something cool hit my burning lungs.

I collapsed again onto cold, hard ground, wet grass poking at my hands. My arms and legs refused to work properly. Someone had their arms around me, and I blinked, gritty stuff filling my eyes the tears flooded.

"Jesus Christ," Graves whispered brokenly. Someone else was coughing and cursing There was a crash and a snarl. "Leave him alone, he dragged her *out!* Leave him *alone!*"

The last three words hit that rolling-thunder-under-the-surface tone again, and the noise subsided except for the roar of the burning.

"I'll take care of the oxygen," I heard Dibs say. "Dial it up as high as it'll go. She's almost cyanotic."

"Never seen a Burner before. I thought they died out years ago." Someone coughed, a deep racking sound.

"Well, they found one." It was Shanks. I barely recognized his voice without all the mockery. "Guess they had to, with a *svetocha* here. Jesus."

"You're in my way." Dibs had lost the squeaking, terrified tone; his voice was cool and professional. "Give me that, you're not a medic."

"Can you carry her?" Shanks sounded deathly tired. "They're going to come back as soon as they regroup."

"I'll carry her," Graves answered grimly. "You okay?"

"Had better days." Shanks coughed weakly. "I'll do. Come on."

"What about him?" someone else asked. "He's one of *them*."

"Bring him," Graves said immediately. He sounded like he was getting used to this answering-questions thing. "They'll kill him if we leave him here. Let's go."

I was dragged, then. I was too busy breathing to really care. Blessedly cool air touched my soot-stained cheeks, and my feet padded at the ground uselessly. I kept blinking, hoping my eyesight would come back. The whole world was black with smudges of gray. My head lolled drunkenly.

"Is she all right?" A hoarse rasp of a voice, one I should've recognized. "Is she?"

I choked, spat another gob of stuff. It splattered dully. *Ewwww. Gross.* The song of pain that was my entire body hitched up another notch, a choir of pulled muscles and still-burning skin. I couldn't feel Mom's locket, and it disturbed me until I retched again and had other things to worry about until the nausea retreated a little.

"She's fine. Probably a bit stunned." Graves sounded worried. I was jostled as well as dragged now, one of my arms over someone's shoulders, the other over someone else. I hung between them like a scarecrow. "She's still breathing, at least."

"Let me see. Let me *see* her." A scuffing, footsteps. The movement halted, and someone let out a sharp, pained sound. A light feathering touch along my forehead, grit scraping lightly against the skin. A gusty sigh. "God in Heaven, *dziękuję*. Thank you."

"Can we move it along?" Shanks sounded irritated. "I would really *hate* to fight another pitched battle with vampire shock troops *and* a Burner."

"They've probably set up a cordon." The husky voice was so familiar—I couldn't place it though. "Do we have any water?"

Shanks actually sighed, an aggrieved sound. "Dylan broke out to the west. They're going fast and loud to draw attention away from us. Let's *go*." A sloshing sound. "Drink while we run. Can you keep up?"

"The day I can't is the day I turn in my blades."

I finally placed the husky, sour voice. My heart leapt inside my chest.

I had to cough and spit again before I could rasp, "Christophe?" The word was a husk of itself, scarring my throat. *You came back.* Intense relief warred with the fact that I really, truly was not feeling very good.

The person holding up my right side stiffened just a little.

"Right here, *malutka*." He coughed again, a deep racking that ended on a choke. "Keep breathing. We'll handle the rest."

*He sounds really sure.* "I've g-g-g—" My lips refused to work right. My entire brain had seized up. There was so much to tell him. And so many questions to ask.

But he'd come back. For me.

"Later, *moj mały ptaszku*. Later. Focus on breathing for right now." There was a crackle of undergrowth. We started moving again. "Your guardian angel is here, Dru. Don't fear."

# CHAPTER 21

**M**y vision returned in fits and starts, and a little while later I could walk. The stuff jammed in my nose was clear tubing attached to an oxygen canister slung over Dibs's shoulder as he braced me on my left side. Graves was on my right, his hair wildly mussed and his coat singed. Blood painted the right side of his face, and his jaw was set.

My heart almost burst. My arm tightened, and he gave me a sideways look. "Hey," he said, quietly. "How you, kiddo?"

My mouth was full of poison. I spat again to clear it, and Dibs giggled, a high, nervous sound. "Peachy," I managed. "Wha' happen?"

"All hell broke loose." Graves barely looked where he was going. Trees pressed close, the night like a wet washcloth over the eyes. I wasn't blind; it was just *dark*. Country-dark. There was a sense of stealthy movement, and the glitters and lamps of eyes around me told me I was in the middle of a group of wulfen. "They got into the school. There was a vampire with red hair, she just looked at things and they started exploding. Shanks and Dylan—"

"Save your breath," came Christophe's harsh voice. "We're not free yet."

"Christophe?" I had to know. "Where *were* you? I thought—"

"Around and about. Be quiet now." He didn't bother sugarcoating the command, but then his tone softened. "You seem to delight in doing the worst, most dangerous thing possible. Try to restrain yourself for a day or two, hmm?"

*I'm just trying to stay alive, Christophe. Thanks.* I wished I could put my head down on Graves's shoulder, settled for putting one foot in front of the other. I was reeling, step to side-step. The oxygen felt good and cool on my burning throat. My teeth weren't aching anymore. Much.

My head dropped forward. I sighed. Coughed again, trying to do it quietly. There was a pause, all the wulfen stopping at once.

A howl lifted in the distance. *Vampire.* The hatred in it scraped inside my skull, the taste of wax oranges on my tongue over the foulness, and I found out I was shaking again. I didn't have the energy to pull myself up inside my head and block it out.

"God and Hell both *damn* it," Christophe said quietly, but with a coldness to the words that turned the darkness into danger.

"Shit." Shanks sounded like he seconded that emotion. "Let's hurry it up, people."

"What happened?" I whispered. Graves just shook his head. His arm tightened around me, like he wanted to pull me away from Dibs. The small blond werwulf was quivering too. I couldn't tell whether I was shaking him or he was as scared as I was.

"Someone just died. We can hope it was the Burner—she would be a high-priority target. Without her, the *nosferatu* are merely dangerous, not overwhelming," Christophe said softly. "Just breathe, Dru. Do we have another oxygen tank?"

"Just the one." Shanks moved away. They glided noiselessly through the forest. My eyes were doing funny things, piercing the gloom one moment and showing me moving shapes, sticks, and the texture of bark. My teeth would give a sudden burst of pain; then the darkness would return.

All the questions I couldn't ask swirled around inside my head. My right arm tightened over Graves's shoulders. "I thought you were inside." My voice was a harsh croak. "God."

"Is that why you ran into a burning building?" He sounded shocked. Go figure.

*I thought I could throw the vampires off my trail.* It was too hard to explain and I didn't have the breath. I tried anyway. "Well, yeah. That, and—"

"Quiet." Christophe was a deeper shadow, his eyes glowing weirdly blue. Most of the wulfen's eyes just glimmered dully. Shanks's were actually yellow, and I could tell whenever Graves blinked because the green gleams next to me would vanish for a moment and my heart would stop again.

The motion suddenly halted. Everyone froze. I leaned on Graves. His hand, spread against my sore ribs on my left side, tensed just a little, fingers gone hard. I tried not to breathe too loudly. The oxygen bottle made a small sound, and I winced. Dibs and I shook together, my teeth clenched to stop their chattering.

Little noises filled the woods around us. I couldn't tell if they were the regular cacophony of the woods at night—because it's rarely ever silent out in the country—or if it was *something else*. I felt very small, and very soft and pink in the middle of the wulfen.

"We need cover," Shanks mouthed. He leaned toward the shape that was Christophe, their eyes glowing at each other. "How drained are you?"

Christophe blinked, slowly, deliberately. The blue glow of his eyes came back, settled on me. "And I thought you would take convincing."

A movement that could have been a shrug. "I don't want to die. And I'm responsible for them."

"Granted." The single word had sharp edges. "I'll need to drink."

The four words fell like a stone into a glassy pool and vanished without a trace. There was a collective sharp inhale among the wulfen.

"Wait a second." Graves sounded like he was having trouble with this. I tried to hold my head up. It dipped forward. Curls had come free of my braid and bobbled in front of my face. "What are we talking about here?"

Shanks didn't even bother to listen. "You can't take it from one of mine. So it's me, or . . ."

A sliding motion. Graves sucked in a sharp breath, and Christophe was suddenly right in front of me.

"Dru," he said softly. The hurtfulness was gone from his voice. "I need your help."

I swallowed. My throat was full of smoky acid. "Yeah. Sure. What?"

Christophe moved in closer, but not as close as he had been before. Still, I could feel his heat. "Give me your hand."

"Oh *hell* no." Graves shifted his weight, like he was going to pull me back and away.

I stayed where I was, digging my feet into the ground. "What are you going to do?"

"I need to borrow something of yours. It will come back, I promise. It will save all of us." Those blue eyes held mine, glowing in the darkness. Was it just me, or were they not quite as cold as they used to be? He smelled like smoke too, and under it was the edge of apple pies—spice and goodness. Jesus. Even after all that he smelled like a bakery. "You're going to have to give me the keys this time, Dru."

It wouldn't make sense to anyone other than Graves and me. I'd refused to trust him once before, and it had ended up with Sergej almost having me for lunch. Now we were out in the middle of the woods with vampires looking for us, and there were a bunch of terrified kids here in the dark.

Kids who had done their best to save me. Kids who would be in the cafeteria or heading for their first classes right now if not for me.

*Way to go, Dru. You just get everyone in trouble, don't you?*

I licked my dry, smoke-tarnished lips. "It'll get them out of here?"

"All of us." Christophe sounded utterly sure. "I just need to borrow something of yours."

*What, the wooden swords? I left them behind, couldn't carry them.* "All right. What?" My throat was full of something. Graves shifted again, but I stayed where I was.

"You don't have to," Dibs whispered. He sounded scared to death. "Dru . . ."

"Give me your hand," Christophe repeated. "Either one."

I slid my heavy left arm free of Dibs's shoulders. Blindly stuck my left hand out in his general direction. "I don't know what you're gonna do, but do it." I leaned into Graves, who was shaking now too. I couldn't tell if it was the stress of holding me up or something else. "They're getting closer." I didn't know how I knew. The sounds in the woods drew close, nasty tittering laughter and the padding of booted feet.

Warm fingers clasped my wrist. Christophe ran his fingertips down the center of my palm, and a weird feeling shot up my arm.

I had to know. "Christophe?"

He went utterly still. "What, *skowroneczo moja?*"

"Where were you?" *Was I bait? What were you doing? You said you'd be gone, but here you are.*

"I was making arrangements to come collect my little bird." His fingers bit in, and he raised my hand, palm up. "You don't think I'd leave you, do you?" There was a gleam of teeth under the lamps of his eyes, and all of a sudden I knew what he was going to do. The knowledge sprang full-blown into my head, and if I hadn't been so scared, exhausted, lonely, pained—you name it— I might have tried to backpedal. Graves let out another strangled sound, his arm tightening as I lost all the strength left in my legs.

And Christophe drove his fangs into my wrist, just where the radial pulse beats. It was like rusty spikes spearing through my arm, the pain branching up nerves to detonate in my head, and a horrible *draining* sensation spilled through me.

It hurt. Have you ever been so sick dying seems like an okay thing because it will make the feeling *stop?* Have you ever felt something inside you—something you never noticed before, something rooted deep in your chest—getting ripped up inch by inch? Stubbornly resisting, something twined around your ribs and internal organs being torn free.

I collapsed. A wave of coldness dilated around my mother's locket, held trapped against my skin.

Graves made a soft, hurt little sound, holding me up. "Dru—" he whispered.

The drawing pull came again. This time it stretched up into my brain, a bony hand digging clawed fingers up my throat and into my skull the hard way, squeezing the tender meat I thought with. Memories splashed and whirled, draining away.

Graves was holding me up now. I was trying to scream, but I couldn't. My voice box had frozen up. Everything about me had frozen. One thought managed to escape the relentless, digging agony.

*—please don't please don't not again please don'tdon'tdon't—*

But it came one more time, and this time was the worst because the digging, awful fingers weren't pulling at anything physical. Instead they were scraping and burrowing and twisting into *me*. The part of me that wasn't anything but me, the invisible core of what I was.

I'd call it the soul, but I don't think the word fits. It's as close as I can get.

Digging scraping pulling tearing *ripping*, invisible things inside me being pulled away, and something left me in a huge gush. My head tipped back, breath locked in my throat. Graves made another small horrified sound and tried to pull me away.

Christophe jerked his head back, fangs sliding free of my flesh, and something wrapped itself tightly around my wrist, below his bruising-hard grip on my forearm. He exhaled, shuddering, and Graves tried to pull me away again. My arm stretched like Silly Putty between them, my shoulder screaming, and I couldn't make a sound.

The winter-blue of Christophe's irises clouded, dark striations like food coloring dropped in water threading through the light. They still glowed even more intensely, in a way that shouldn't have made sense. "Sweet," he hissed, and made an odd hitching movement. His chin dipped, and his fingers tightened bruising-hard on my wrist, like he was going to do that again.

I wanted to scream, couldn't. Nothing worked. My body just hung there, frozen and unresponsive.

"Christophe." Shanks sounded nervous. "Um, Christophe?"

The world trembled on a knife edge. Blackness crowded in around the corners. My head tipped further back. Graves held me up, both arms around me now. I was so tired it was work to breathe. In, out, in, out, my ribs almost refused to rise. There was air outside my face, but it was just so hard to bring it in. Instead, the sea of atmosphere pushed down on me, crushing.

"Jesus," Graves whispered. "What did you do to her?"

Another gleam of teeth below Christophe's darkened eyes. "I just *borrowed* her for a while, dogboy." The casual, hurtful edge to the words abraded the inside of my head like an ice scraper against a windshield. I flinched. "Don't worry. I'm not about to let one of *them* get their ugly fangs in *moja księżniczko.*"

Pain and dragging weariness pulled on every nerve and muscle in my body. Behind us, another chilling howl lifted into the night.

"We need cover," Shanks said urgently. "And—"

"I know what you need. Shut up." Christophe touched my face, stepping close and sliding his fingertips against my dirty cheek. I flinched. Graves dragged me back, and how weird was it that he stepped silently? All around us, the woods creaked and sighed in the darkness. The snarl running under the surface of Graves's skin bounced around, echoing, inside my skull.

They faced each other, the two boys, and I was suddenly very sure something bad was about to happen. The moment hung, suspended in the cold night air.

"They're getting closer," someone whispered.

Christophe laughed. It was a bitter little sound, not unlike Graves's sarcastic, pained bark. "I'm not saving *you*," he said, very quietly. "I'm saving *her.* Remember that."

He turned and literally vanished. The air made a weird popping sound, collapsing where he'd stood, and one of the wulfen sniffed deeply. Shanks cursed, but softly. Thick white wetness boiled in the air, rising from the ground where Christophe had stood. It rose in veiny, ropy fingers, curls of it touching my legs.

The touch made my skin crawl. It was exactly the kind of greasy fog the suckers had shown up in. *Wait a minute. What did he just do?*

"Bloodfog," one of them said. "It'll cover us, and he'll hunt *them*. Let's go."

At that point everything just turned weird and soupy gray. Dibs helped Graves heft me up on his back like I was a little kid getting piggybacks. I tried to say I was sorry, but the words wouldn't come.

They started moving through the forest, everything blurring together. My head bobbled and joggled against Graves's shoulder, and I heard him cursing steadily under his breath. The places inside me where everything had been ripped up twinged and settled, throbbing like a sore tooth. It was like a headache, only not in my head. In the invisible places where I lived that weren't connected with any muscle or bone.

"Graves . . ." I whispered against his shoulder. Then the darkness swallowed me, and everything inside me still hurt. I fell down into the hole where things had been ripped free, and small chill voices laughed while I did.

# CHAPTER 22

**came back to** myself slowly, in fits and starts. First there was gray light, coming through two horizontal cracks. A single spot of warmth against my chest, like someone had breathed on me. Voices—Shanks and Graves, mostly.

"She still out?" Grudging concern. The tall werwulf didn't sound happy.

"Like a light. I can't believe you suggested that." Graves, tired and unhappy too. The movement under me hadn't stopped. Wind touched my hair. For the first time I smelled something other than smoke. Leaf sludge, fresh air, the iron smell of very early or very, very late.

"We had to. Jesus Christ." Feet hitting the ground. "All right, everyone. Let's get moving."

The horizontal slices of light thinned and vanished. I drowned in blackness again. Something inside me felt different, but I couldn't figure out what.

A sound like feathers surrounded me. I waited for the owl, but it didn't show up. Its wings beat frantically, a muffled heartbeat. The horizontal bars of light dawned again, and I realized they were my eyelids opening a little to let in morning.

Voices, arguing. I felt like I'd been ripped apart and put back together wrong. My arms were around something, and a tree trunk was braced against my back. My feet dangled. I hitched in a breath. It was a relief to find that breathing wasn't a huge struggle anymore. My lungs and ribs had decided to work together, and the air was no longer heavy as lead.

"The *wampyr* have gone to earth—if Reynard left any alive. We have to move *now*, and get to a safe place."

"Like where? And Shanks is half-dead. We can't leave him."

"You're not in charge. We're already carrying *her*. You gonna carry him too?"

"Fuck you I'm not in charge. We're not leaving anyone behind." It was Graves, like I'd never heard him. Angry, determined—and with that growl under the edge of the words. He sounded like he knew what he was talking about, and he wasn't about to take any shit.

I realized my mouth was open, dry, and tasted like something had died in it. I closed it and tried an experimental movement. The haze of light coming in through my eyelids sharpened.

"Please. Who do you think you're kidding? The *djamphir* might think you're gonna control us, but you're not."

Movement. I was shifted to the side. A small sound escaped me, like I was caught in a nightmare.

Go figure.

"Let's get this figured out right now," Graves said, quietly. The growl turned into a sharp crackling, as if bones under plastic wrap were snapping into dust.

*Oh boy.* The thought was sharp and clear, and it was another relief. A little bit of warmth stole back into me, the locket oddly heavy under my shirt. The ripped-up places inside me quivered like scabs. With thought came being again. I *was*.

*Dru. I'm Dru. And that's Graves.*

Life, color, and sound all rushed back into me. I opened my eyes and found out I was slumped against Dibs, who had gone pale, his eyes wide. He stared at the clearing, which was ringed by wulfen in various hunching poses. Some of them even lay stretched flat on the forest floor. Oily-white, almost-glowing fog drifted cotton-packed between the trees, and birds were calling uncertainly. It even smelled like dawn—if you've ever been out when the sun comes up, you know what I mean. It's the metallic scent of sunlight hitting the atmosphere and everyone needing a good shot of caffeine.

Graves and another black-haired boy were the only ones standing up in the middle of the clearing. Beads of water touched Graves's messy hair. The fog was so thick it was like being caught in a bubble, swallowing the rest of the world.

The shape at my feet was Shanks, stretched out at full-length, dried blood in a shocking spill down the side of his face. His clothes were ripped to shreds, and more blood—black and still-smoking as well as red and human—crusted him. He looked like he was in bad shape, cheese-pale and with his sides heaving as he breathed in shallow gasps.

Graves leaned forward. The other boy—slim, black hair cut short, big dark eyes almost glowing with anger—rocked back on his heels as if he'd been punched. The invisible tension between them boiled like heat-haze above pavement on a tar-melting-hot day.

"Don't fucking mess with me right now, man." Graves said every word very slowly and very clearly, his lips moving as he enunciated. He had to, because his jaw was shifting. Still, the command-voice came out clean and clear. The other boy rocked back even further on his heels, dropping his shoulders and dipping his chin.

"We'll all die," the other kid whined, but all the starch had gone out of him. "You're not ready."

"Not ready my *ass*," Graves snapped. "I was born ready, dick-wipe. You want to test me now, you go ahead, but it'll waste valuable time. We get caught, you'll die just like the rest of us. So *stop* being an asshole and *shut* the fuck up."

Silence, as ticking-tense as the moment between stepping off a diving board and the instant you hit the water. I leaned against Dibs and looked down at Shanks. His eyes were half-closed, little gleams peeking out from under the eyelids. There was no sign of iris or pupil, just blind white.

Something was wrong. The world looked flat, oddly two-dimensional. I tilted my head back, trying to hear something, anything, with the touch. Trying to unloose the fist and send little questing fingers out to take in the world.

My pulse leapt up, hard and high in my throat. There was nothing there.

*Stop it. You're just tired.* God knew I was exhausted. But it was like being blind. I'd never realized before how the *touch* lay under every thought, bubbling and boiling and showing me the depths of things.

It was gone, and I was blind. I hated the feeling.

I found I could stand on my own two feet. Dibs still clutched at me, though. His skin was hot against mine, and he smelled just like a regular boy, without the undertone of cold fur and danger.

*Is this what it's like to be normal?* Shaking spilled through me. The trees looked dead. The fog was flat. And Graves and the rest—

No, wait. Graves looked normal. He stared at the other boy, green eyes piercing and a high blush of color on his cheekbones, the slight suggestion of epicanthic folds vanishing as his face shifted to more hawklike than half-Asian. Other than that, he looked just the same as usual, except a little more unwashed. His coat was singed and plastered with mud up the side, his hair was wildly mussed, and a bolt of something hot and hard went through my chest as the other black-haired boy dropped his eyes. Graves kept staring until the kid actually crouched, as if the green gaze was a heavy weight.

It looked like a grainy color film I'd seen on late-night cable in a weird little motel outside a teensy town named Zavalla in Texas. It was a nature special on satellite cable about wolf packs, and all about how wolves will give in and give up so the more dominant wolf keeps his position and the less dominant one doesn't get killed. There was a lot of snapping and snarling, but killing everyone who wanted to maybe get a little higher on the ladder was bad evolutionary logic.

I blinked. My eyes were full of crusty stuff. And Graves really did look like the only real 3-D human being standing there. Even with his hair in messy strings and his coat singed, he looked . . .

I don't have a word for the way he looked. Solid. Comforting. Like he was the one piece of the world that was holding the whole damn thing up. I let out a small sipping breath, trying not to taste the smoke smell rising up all around me or the stink of danger in the air. And that was another thing too—everything smelled washed out. Insipid. Not as real and true as it should have.

There was that spot of warmth against my chest, though. That was comforting.

"Now," Graves finally said, "anyone else want to piss me off? Anyone else think this is a goddamn *democracy*?"

I swallowed, hard. My throat clicked, but nobody paid any attention. He'd drawn himself up to his full height, and turned slowly in a circle, looking at everyone.

"We're a *pack*." He halted once he'd made a full circle, and looked down at the kid in front of him. It might've looked weird anywhere else, but here in the woods surrounded by fog it looked perfectly normal.

Well, not *normal*. But natural. It looked like he belonged here, splashed with mud and scorch, his eyes burning and his coat straining across shoulders that had grown broader. It was the *loup-garou* burning in him, turning him into something other than the weirdo bird-thin Goth Boy hiding in the corners of your average school.

His hands were whiteknuckle fists. "We don't leave someone behind. We've all been left behind one way or another, we ain't gonna do it to nobody else. Anyone got a *problem* with that?"

Seconds ticked away. The tension went out of the air, but Graves tilted his head. A few of the boys sat up, and the black-haired boy made a quick inquiring movement.

"You hear that?" Dibs whispered. Either his skin was burning hot or mine was ice cold. I wasn't sure which. "Choppers. Again."

"What if it's the Order?" someone wanted to know. "I mean, coming to get us?"

"Too fucking late," the black-haired boy muttered. *Peter*, my weary brain finally whispered. *That's his name.*

Graves scrubbed at his chin with long fingers. "We'll move as far as we can under the fog. We can't trust that it might be the right kind of people up there looking for us."

"Are we on our own, now? No more Order?" Dibs piped up. He was dirty and disheveled as the rest of us, his round blond face creased with worry. But he didn't look as scared as he'd always looked in the cafeteria.

"Don't know yet." Graves sighed. "We'll move as long as we have cover, then hide until nightfall. By then Christophe will be around again."

"So will the *nosferatu*." This boy, long and brown-haired, lay on his back with an arm over his face. He wore a flannel shirt that had seen better days and a messy bandage tied around his head, a dark bloody patch over his left temple. "I got an idea."

"Shoot," Graves said immediately.

"I've got family around here—not kincousins, my aunts married into them. Maybe we should go to ground. It's a short shot from the last town we passed. We're all exhausted, the girl don't smell like herself, and if we dive now, we'll have a better chance of running at full strength tonight—or even better, tomorrow when the sun rises."

Graves half-turned and looked across the clearing, straight at me. I looked back, as steadily as I could while hanging onto Dibs and sandwiched against a tree trunk.

He was looking to me for direction, I realized. Back in his snow-piled hometown, I'd been the one who knew what to do when it all went sideways. At least, I'd known what to do when the burning dog and the streak-headed werwulf tried to kill us. I'd gotten Graves to my house. I'd been the one who had the books and the guns and the knowledge, however patchy.

We looked at each other. *What the fuck do we do now?* he was asking.

I tried to think. "What do we have?" My throat was sore, and the words didn't have the weight I was used to hearing behind them. They were made of paper. "In the way of supplies."

Because I knew how to do this. It didn't depend on the touch or the aspect or anything else. It was just doing what I'd been taught. We were in hostile territory, and we had an objective—the objective was not dying.

*First you find out what you have,* Dad would say. *Then you figure out how to make it work for what you need, 'cause you don't get what you want. You get just what you have and no more.*

It turned out to be a load of cash, my bag, the clothes on our backs, some switchblades, the oxygen tank, a medikit Dibs was carrying as well, and two packs of cigarettes. Shanks lay on the ground, breathing shallowly. He didn't look good.

It was a relief to have my brain working again. Every muscle I had hurt like hell, and the weird two-dimensionality of the world was new and awful. My head ached, but I'd done this sort of thing a lot with Dad—him throwing scenarios at me, teaching me how to plan.

"We didn't have enough time to get to the armory." Peter very carefully slid his switchblade back in his pocket. "They hit us so fast. And a Burner. Jesus."

*At least we've got money.* I leaned against the tree instead of Dibs. My left wrist was wrapped in a very capable pressure bandage. Shut my eyes, squeezing out the light, and took a deep breath. *Come on, Dru. You know how to do this.* "So our choices are to run on the money we've got and try to make the city tonight with the wounded, or hide at Andy's family's house until tomorrow." I paused. "Do we even know where to go once we get to the city limits?"

"Shanks knows." Andy had sat up, and he was looking at me like I'd grown a new head. "My aunts are loyal. They'd hide us even if it was the Dark Times."

"I'm just not sure we won't bring them trouble." I blinked again, tried to focus. The world still didn't look right, and a funny quivering feeling was pushing its way up through my chest. I didn't need a dictionary to know it was called fear. A whole new brand of being afraid, an unsteady heat like indigestion underneath the warm spot of Mom's locket. I was beginning to realize there were shades of fear just like on a color wheel, all of them slightly different but still awful. I looked up at Graves again. "You're not going to like this."

"What?" He leaned on the other side of the tree I was holding onto, his messy hair shaken down over his eyes again. Goth Boy was back on display. His earring winked once, silver shining.

"My dad trained me for this type of thing. I can hit the next town and find some transportation. I can vanish, and that means they won't have a reason to chase—"

"No." Graves shook his head. "Hell no."

"Let her finish." Peter crouched next to Shanks. His face twisted up bitterly as he looked down at the other boy.

Graves stiffened. "*You* shut up. They'll chase us whether you're with us or not, Dru, and what part of this do you not *understand?* I'm *not leaving you.*"

"If vampires will attack a whole school full of people trained to fight them to kill me, what makes you think they won't attack a wulfen's house? And . . . Sergej . . . might be on his way too. Come on." I braced myself against the tree. No spike of pain went through my head, but several of the wulfen shivered at the name.

"It's a compound," Andy piped up. "The kin, they believe in the old ways. There's my aunts and the uncles, grandparents, my cousins—"

*Great. More people to die.* "It's a better idea if I just go it alone. I can make it to the next town, get some food and some wheels, and—"

Graves made a spitting sound of annoyance. "Add carjacking or theft to your list of things to do today? No dice, Dru. Look at you, you can't even stand up."

He was right. I held onto the tree. "I could kick *your* ass." But it was bravado. We both knew it, and he shook his hair back and gave me a fey toothy grin. In a couple years that smile would be a heart-stopper.

Who was I kidding? He was a heart-stopper now. Why hadn't I seen it before? Or had it been hiding in him, just waiting to come out?

"Anytime you think you're man enough, sweetheart." He shook himself all over, let go of the tree, and I wondered where the scared kid had gone. The one who had hugged me on the cold stairs while something awful knocked at my front door—something old, and foul, and smelling of rusty blood. "All right, Andy. Lead the way. Tony, Beau, you two carry Shanks. Does he need another shot, Dibs?"

"Can't." The blond boy shook his head. "If I give him more sedative he might get too tired to breathe *or* heal."

The fog pressed close, as if it was listening. It reflected the sunlight oddly, shapes moving in its curtained depths. The wulfen started moving. Graves stepped around the tree and looked down at me. He looked taller, or maybe it was because I was so goddamn tired even though I was awake and mostly upright. The light had grown stronger, and the thopping sound of helicopters faded into the distance. I didn't even know which direction we were going, or where we were.

Two of the wulfen heaved Shanks up. He looked pretty bad. Graves stepped close to me, picked up my left arm, and ducked so it settled across his shoulders. "I'm not leaving anyone behind," he said, fierce and low. "Not anyone. Not anymore."

"I'm sorry." I tried to pitch it low, too. "If I hadn't—"

"Shut up." He took a few experimental steps. Once I let go of the tree, the ground swayed drunkenly underfoot. "Come on."

"Aye-aye, Captain," someone said, and I surprised myself by giggling. The sound was very small and lonely, but Graves looked at me, and the corner of his mouth tilted up a little. Just a little.

The empty places inside me didn't feel quite so big after that.

*I need to borrow something. . . . It will come back, I promise.*

I didn't ask where Christophe was. I was too busy trying to keep upright. And besides, if I had to really admit the truth, I didn't want to know. Not while my wrist pulsed, hot and sore. Not while the world looked like a paper cutout and the space inside my head where the touch should be was glaringly empty. Not while I was still scared, and hungry, and smelling of smoke.

It was better to lean in close to Graves and smell whatever shampoo he'd used before everything went bad. A breath of it clung to him under the smell of outdoors, smoke, and healthy young male who needs his daily shower.

We moved into the weird fog, steadying each other. And vanished like ghosts.

# CHAPTER 23

The woods were a dripping, treacherous wonderland. It got a little warmer, and the trees ran with fat drops of sweat from all the moisture in the air. I wondered about that, but it meant that the helicopters passing over were nothing more than sounds. They got awful close and circled for a while, but faded away as we moved down wooded slopes, over small streams trickling with black water under ice, and slogged through slippery mud.

"At least it's not raining," someone said once.

Someone else snorted. *"Djamphir,"* he said, as if it explained everything.

Maybe it did. How was Christophe doing this?

I hung onto Graves, and slowly I realized the fog—or whoever was behind the fog, keeping us under a curtain of vapor—was watching us.

If I hadn't been so tired and drained I might've seen it sooner. The empty place inside me started feeling a little bit more normal, three-dimensionality returning to the world, and I began to see faces peeking out of the thick white vapor. They were thin, sexless faces with burning deep-socketed eyes and mouths that hung ajar just enough that you could see the fangs.

Just after mid-morning it got pretty bad. No matter how many times I blinked, the faces wouldn't go away. I could walk on my own now, a kind of lurching. There was a whispered conference about what to do with the oxygen tank. I just slung it on my own shoulder and kept carrying it. *Leave no traces*, that was the first rule of being on the run in hostile territory.

One of the boys—Beau, the slim quick redhead—had a package of beef jerky, and we shared that out equally at one stop. Everyone took a small piece and we walked while chewing. The salt in it stung my smoke-rough throat, but a couple of the boys had water bottles and we each got a swallow or two as we walked. It made the jerky into a flavorless cud of salt and ick, but I kept chewing. I was too hungry not to.

Graves had held me up until I could walk on my own. But I veered around so drunkenly he reached down and took my hand, warm fingers slipping through my cold, wet ones. I was worried about my sweating, filthy fingers for about half a second, until my legs made me veer again. I couldn't find my bearings with the world looking as paper-flat as it did. And I was so tired. My head felt like a pumpkin balanced on a stem.

But it was better with him holding my hand.

The faces crowded around. The better I felt, the more the world started looking normal again, the more they clustered around us, their mouths open as they stared at me. Some moved their lips; others vanished into thinning smoke as the sun climbed toward noon.

Yeah. Some normal. Why was it that I only felt like myself when the weirdest shit was happening?

"Fog's thinning," Peter remarked.

This got Shanks's attention. He sucked in a deep, sharp breath, raising his shaggy head a bit. He looked like death warmed over, but at least the blood sticking to him was dried instead of fresh. Terrific bruises swarmed across his face, one eye puffed almost shut. And his eyes were there, not just the whites glaring between his bruised eyelids. "Noon. Sun at its highest."

"Which means Christophe might not be able to cover us from wherever he's hiding during daylight." Graves said it quietly, as if he was just talking to me.

*Oh. That makes sense. Kind of.* My wrist throbbed. I didn't want to peel the bandage back. I didn't want to even look at it, because the thought of that pulling against everything inside me was too horrible. It made me sweat under my four layers and coating of dirt and soot. I itched all over, miserably, but it was a better feeling than the dragging drunken pain *or* the sense of the world having been drained of its entire third dimension.

"I didn't know a *djamphir* could do this." Dibs scrubbed at his cheeks with both hands. He had a little bit of peach-fuzz stubble. A smudge of dirt wandered across his forehead.

"They usually can't, and now he's pretty much crippled until sunset." Peter hopped up on a fallen tree, its moss gleaming with fat pearls of moisture, and glanced back over his shoulder at me. "How much did he take?"

*He means me. How much of* me *did Christophe take?* A wave of dizziness passed through me, hit my heels, and rebounded hard enough to bring bile up into my throat. The remnants of beef jerky clung to my tongue.

Underneath that was the real thought.

*He means how much of my blood.* "I don't know." I had to pack my cheek with chewed beef jerky like a Bible Belt farmer sucking on a wad of tobacco. "It was . . . it was horrible."

"Well, no shit. It's not a pleasant thing to get bit by a sucker of any stripe." Peter hopped down. The rest of them drew closer as the fog thinned. For a group of teenage boys wandering through the woods, they were remarkably quiet. Not a leaf stirred or a stick crackled underneath, unless I stumbled and Graves didn't give me a quick jerk on the hand to bring me back on my keel. "But seriously. How many gulps did he get down?"

*Jesus Christ.* "Th-three. I think." The strange unsteady feeling under my heart was better than the emptiness, too. It was a relief to feel anything other than that soul-destroying numbness.

"That's good, right?" Dibs looked up anxiously. "More than that and you'd be at risk of bonding and the blood-da—"

"Shh!" Peter stopped. Everyone froze. Graves actually stepped close to me before going absolutely still, most of the boys with one ear cocked. Wulfen never look particularly canine unless they've *changed*, but seeing them all holding their heads that way made me think of the RCA dog on some of Gran's old records. A rancid laugh bubbled up inside me. I listened just like they did, blood pounding in my ears, and the sound of another helicopter split the eerie silence.

A nasty little thought came padding into my head on little cat feet.

*A sucker of any stripe, huh? I didn't know djamphir drank blood. I suppose that's what the hunger was about. If I drank someone's blood, would I be able to do . . . something? Whatever it is Christophe did? Or what we're guessing he did, since this fog is nowhere near normal?*

Sergej had made the weather change too. He'd made it as dark as night during the day, called up a huge snowstorm. And Christophe was his son.

The whole line of thought made me feel queasy. It was one thing to have something inside yourself ripped out by the roots. It was another thing entirely to think of doing that to someone else. I mean, that made me one of the things from the Real World, all right.

It made me one of those things that my dad would have loaded up his guns and gone hunting after.

*Oh God.* I shivered. Graves squeezed my cold, limp, sweating fingers. The weighted whir of the helicopter sounded different than all the other ones that had passed since morning. Just how I couldn't say, but—

I smelled dirt, a thread of warm perfume, and the colorless fume of violence approaching. A tingling touched my chest, as if the locket was vibrating again. "They're looking for us," I whispered, not knowing I was going to say it until the words slipped free of my lips. "And they're not friendly."

Graves glanced down at me, his mouth opening as if he wanted to ask how I knew. Dibs slid down into a crouch, and before I knew it the rest of them had crouched too, except Graves and me. We stood, and if my knees hadn't been desperately locked trying to keep me upright, I would have fallen down in a heap. Something slid through my head, broken glass and cigarette ash scraping through tender places I hadn't even known were sore, and I flinched, driving my shoulder into his. He didn't move, solid as a rock, and his head tipped up. The fog was thinning in curlicues of steam, and I suddenly smelled a thread of apples and spice mixed with rotting dirt. The scent came in waves, flaring and fading, trying to draw a covering over us.

"Will the bloodfog hold?" Dibs whispered. He looked up at me like I should know, and my throat closed up. I didn't know what to tell him, and the touch quivered inside my head.

The thopping sound got closer. It was hard to tell because of the fog, but it was circling. I could feel it like a sore tooth, nagging inside me.

It was a relief to feel the *touch* throbbing inside me again. I never thought I'd be happy to have that place on my palate open up again. I never thought I'd be so happy to have the thing that made me unable to fit in anywhere coming back.

My teeth turned aching-sensitive inside my salt-dry mouth. My hair tingled, and warmth spilled down my skin.

The fog thinned further. Sunlight intensified, glaring through like a bulb shining through wax paper. *Oh shit.*

"Dru—" Graves's voice cracked. He was staring at me like I'd grown another head.

The aspect flooded me. I took a deep breath, the locket heating up as if held near a candle flame. Had it done this for Dad too? Or just for me? What did it mean?

There was no time to ask, even if there was anyone around who could tell me. The copter's sound grew nearer. A shadow loomed through the membrane of water vapor keeping us safe.

*Come on, Dru. Do something, anything!*

The raw places inside me twitched and twisted. I pulled on them, something that should have been easy as breathing suddenly like lifting a Buick with my bare hands. Blue sky peeped through the shredding fog, and the shape of the copter loomed darker, its downdraft swishing the fog around in vapor trails.

It built up around my hands, my canines sliding free and touching my lower lip. The wad of jerky in my mouth turned into an irritation of salt, but I couldn't worry about that. My belly buzzed, and the smell of spiced apples bloomed around me. Only it was deeper, with an edge of familiar, warm perfume.

The woods around me smelled suddenly like my mother, and

memory crashed inside my head. Memory and new certainty.

*We're going to play a game, Dru.*

"What the fuck—" Peter rose halfway from his crouch.

I jabbed my free hand up, letting out a short cry lost in the sound of the helicopter. The hex—just like the one I'd thrown at a teacher in the Dakotas, a bolt of intent—flew free, sparking and fizzing, and arrowed toward the mechanical shadow. Graves caught me as my legs buckled, and my heart labored in my ears. My ribs flickered, fast shallow breaths, and for a moment the sharp divots of canine teeth touching my lower lip dug in. Warm trickles slid down my chin, and Graves went to his knees trying to hold me up.

There was a weird pinging sound, and the copter veered off, its shark-shadow slicing through the naked tree limbs and thinning vapor. A screech of metal twisting and shearing, and Graves came up in a rush, hauling me with him.

Helicopters are very complex machines. And if you throw one little bit of that complexity off, bad things can happen. It was a tiny hex, barely even worth the name, but Dad would've been proud. *Easy to bring a copter down,* he told me a couple times. *You just remember that, Dru. One little thing goes haywire and alla sudden, whammo!*

Had he known somehow?

My heart hurt at the thought. I would've given just about anything to have him back and dealing with this. He would have sorted this right out.

"Whammo," I whispered, and sagged against Graves. It was only the second hex I'd actually *thrown* in my life. The first one had been a few weeks ago, and I'd almost killed Bletchley, my American history teacher. She'd deserved it, but still.

What was I turning into?

"Jesus." Peter's soft, awestruck whisper. A deep rumble sounded in the distance—thunder, swallowing the screeching sound the copter was making.

*That can't be good for anyone in it.* The smell of rain suddenly rose from the ground, thick and wet, and a huge grinding noise screeched through the clearing. A deep, coughing explosion.

"Ouch," I said, and pressed every muscle down against a retch. The beef jerky was having a hell of a time staying in my mouth. My bones felt floppy. The world receded on a tide of gray shot through with little spangles of blue sky and Graves's voice saying something.

A rending, crashing noise snapped the grayness. Everything got confused, my hands and arms flopping like a rag doll's. My stomach hurt—someone's shoulder was in it, and the world was jouncing up and down.

"Whammo," I whispered again, and the grayness swallowed me whole.

*I think I shouldn't have done that,* I thought hazily, and then I thought no more.

# CHAPTER 24

**I came to in** bits and pieces. And I felt like shit. My entire body hurt, my head worst of all. I groaned a little, and sheets shifted. The sound of hard rain on a roof filled up my head, and a crack of thunder made me wince. For a weird vertiginous second I thought I was back in the blue bedroom during the day while rain splashed the windows and the Schola slept.

Then a cool hard hand touched my forehead. "Shhh, *milna*. All's well."

My left wrist gave a little pinging flare of heat and I opened my eyes. For a moment I couldn't see anything and I thought I was blind, but then something clicked. A nightlight near a door-shape went on. It seared through my pupils, and tears welled up. I flinched.

The light clicked off. My wrist turned hot again, two pinpricks of fire. Thunder cracked and boomed overhead again.

"Your head will be sensitive for a little while. Just rest." Gentle words, like I was really sick and he was trying not to upset me.

My mouth was dry. I'd lost the beef jerky somewhere. When I tensed my arms and legs I could feel the bed under me, and pain like a river over my skin. "The others?"

"Safe and sound. Even your *loup-garou*." A glitter of blue eyes showed in the darkness. Christophe's irises were glowing faintly.

"Good . . ." Relief filled me, warred with the pain, and retreated. I exhaled. His hand touched my forehead again, fingertips skating the curve of skull under skin. Then I remembered what he'd done, and tensed even further.

He laughed. It was a small sound, as bitter as Graves's scornful little bark. "More than you bargained for, hm? I'm sorry, I know it hurt. But I only borrowed; I didn't *take*. Remember that."

*Yeah, I don't think I'll ever forget, Christophe.* I sighed and moved my head away from his touch. He leaned back a little, and I heard a creak. A chair by the side of the bed—I *felt* it there without seeing it, hard to describe. My throat was sore, and the locket wasn't doing anything weird. Thank God.

At least the *touch* was still working. I felt like myself again. Beat up and pulled apart, but still me. "Where?"

Like, *Where am I?* Yeah, a totally cliché question, but it was reasonable.

He seemed to understand. "One of the wulfen—Andrew—has kin here. You're in the safest part of the compound. It's night now; by morning you should be all right to travel. Especially with me around."

*Oh, good. But I feel like sleeping in.* "Travel?"

"Your *loup-garou* made a persuasive case for reaching the safety of the city. I'll be able to bear the sun after tonight, when the aura-dark fades." He let out a sharp sigh. The glimmer of his eyes vanished, and the shape of him slumped. "I thought Dylan, at least, would explain a little."

*I think he probably had other things on his mind, Christophe. And I think the history teacher was trying, too.* "Tried. He tried. Look—" There was so much to tell him.

"Sleep." He moved again, and I heard cloth sliding and the creak of the chair again. A breath of apple-scented spice blew across my face. "It's the best thing for you now."

It sounded like a good idea, but I wanted something else. "Graves." I swallowed. My dry throat clicked. At least my mouth wasn't tingling, and my teeth were regular and blunt when I ran my dry rasping tongue across them.

"I told you, he's fine. The prince of the house, here." Christophe's eyes opened again. "You could ask me how I'm feeling. I've had a hard few days too."

*You know, when you put it like that I couldn't care less.* "Go. Away."

"Charming as ever. I'm sorry, Dru."

Then I felt like a bitch. He'd saved my life, hadn't he? Run right into a burning building to get me out. And the fog, that had been him too. And the heat of him against me, a shameful memory that would have made me squirm if I hadn't been so exhausted. "Don't worry about it." I coughed a little. The words scraped hard coming out.

"You think you want water, but it will only make it worse." His tone was very soft. "Nothing will take it away, not even wine. It will fade in a little bit."

The burning in my throat got a little worse. "Do you . . ."

"Me? Always, little bird." Another small laugh. It sounded like it hurt him. "The stronger the *nosferat* strain in your blood, the stronger the bloodhunger. And if a Kouroi ever gives in to it . . ."

I waited. My heart beat hard, in my wrists and my throat. It was really dark in here, and I wondered whose bed I was lying on. We'd made it to safety. A wulfen house.

"If you ever give in, it becomes much harder to control. And if you're raised to give it full rein, *kochana*. . . ." He sighed again. The chair creaked a little as he rose and pushed it back. I saw the shadows of posters hanging on the wall, no windows, and the suggestion of a half-open closet sketched in charcoal. It was deathly quiet. "My father raised me to be a scourge instead of a Kouroi." His eyes winked out, and I half-sensed him rubbing at his face. "Dylan brought me to the light, but it was your mother who ensured I stayed. If you don't have a reason to fight it, the hunger will make you an animal worse than the ones we exterminate. Because we are born to be so much more." The vague outline of the door was blacked by his darker shadow. "I'll send in your *loup-garou*."

He sounded so . . . sad.

"Christophe." I couldn't even prop myself up on my elbows. "Wait."

The sense of movement faded. He stood in the door for a long second, then turned. The apple-scented breeze filled my face. He bent down, and the sudden irrational fear that he might bite me again stopped my breathing. His fingertips rested against the locket's warm curve. I felt their weight.

Something soft and warm pressed itself against my mouth. It stayed there for a few seconds, my nose full of pie-smell. Before it even registered, he'd straightened and stepped back. His eyes glowed now, an unholy blue. "If I need a reason now, Dru, it will have to be you."

The door filled up with his shadow, drained away. I moved fretfully. I couldn't even begin to figure this one out. Sleeping sounded really good.

I closed my heavy eyelids again and was gone.

* * *

When I surfaced again it was even quieter and someone lay next to me. He was warm, and took up most of the bed, and I knew who it was even before I accidentally elbowed him and he lunged into wakefulness. He jerked like a fish on a line, half-sitting up and only relaxing once he figured out where he was.

"Jesus—" The word died. "Dru? You okay?"

I coughed. My skin crawled. "Peachy." The starch had come back into my bones, and I felt a million percent better. Best of all, the empty riven places inside my head were no longer throbbing like something had been yanked out. I had a slight headache and I was still god-awful thirsty, but the world was back together again. "Hey."

"There's the floor." He curled up to sit, and blankets moved. Sleeping in clothes always makes you feel bunched-up when morning comes. "If you, you know—"

"Why?" I pushed myself up on my elbows. It was a relief to be able to move. "I mean, we're okay, right? Unless you feel weird about sleeping in the same bed as . . ."

*Oh shit.* I went from feeling pretty okay to feeling totally stupid.

"I thought you'd feel weird about it." But he settled back down. There was only one pillow, and it was scrunched between us. "But, you know."

"Yeah." I didn't, but I was okay with it. "How's Shanks? And everyone?"

"They fixed Shanks up. He just needs some sleep now. It's . . . weird here. Anyway. How are you really?"

I cleared my throat. He was still fully dressed, and I tried to push the pillow over to him but he was having none of it. We settled down, finally, and I breathed him in. Cigarette smoke, healthy young male, the smell that was uniquely his. I needed a shower and my teeth really wanted a good scrubbing, and I was suddenly afraid I had dragonbreath. So I stayed where I was, on my side with my arm under my head, trying not to breathe on him. We were quiet for a little while. The thunder was retreating.

"Some storm," I finally whispered.

"Yeah. Christophe said it was because of messing with the weather system." Graves moved a little bit, lacing his fingers under his head. He was tall enough that I had my face almost in his armpit. It wasn't optimal, but at least he smelled clean and I wouldn't be breathing anywhere he could get a faceful of it. "You should get some more sleep. We're leaving in the morning."

"We?" Meaning, *Who's this we?*

"I'm going with you." Almost sullen. He sighed. "Look, Dru—"

"I hoped you were coming along. Where are we going?" I edged a little bit closer to him. He didn't move away. It was a relief.

"The city. Christophe thinks that if we get you to the central Schola, whoever's trying to double-cross and kill you won't be able to. Dru, I want to ask you something."

The tension came back. "Okay."

I expected something like, *What was it like when he drank your blood?* or *What did you do to that helicopter?* or even . . . I don't know. Something about *djamphir* or wulfen. Something complex.

"Do you like Christophe?" It came out in a whisper. "I mean, really *like* him?"

It took me a second to figure out what he was really asking. *Oh God. Awkward.* "Not, like, *that* way. Jesus. No."

As soon as I said it, I felt like I was lying. Christophe's arms around me, his body hot through his clothes, the spiced-apple smell surrounding me. The broken roughness of his voice as he hugged me, and my lips burning because he'd pressed his mouth against mine.

*If I need a reason, Dru, it will have to be you.*

But there was also his teeth in my wrist, and his scary speed, and the mockery under every word. I was glad it was dark. My cheeks were on fire again, the flush turning my whole body into a lamp in the dark.

I couldn't like Christophe that way, could I? I mean, he'd known my *mother*. And—

"Oh." Did Graves actually sound *relieved*? Thunder rumbled, dissatisfied, in the distance.

"I mean, he knew my mother." I meant to say something different. Like, *He scares me*. But that would be a real blow to my tough-girl image, wouldn't it. And that image was taking a hell of a beating lately.

And if I said it out loud I might say other things. Like, *He doesn't feel like you do when he hugs me*. That would just open up a huge can of worms, wouldn't it?

No. I didn't like Christophe. Not the way he was asking.

At least, I didn't want to. And Graves never had to know about the boathouse, or about anything else. I'd made up my mind.

I was still blushing. Scalding hot.

"Yeah." Quiet agreement. "Can I ask you something else?"

My heart leapt. He sounded serious. "You just did. But go ahead." A slight huff of breath told me he was smiling, and I half-smiled too, in the dark. I waited. Silence stretched out. I finally moved, restlessly. "Are you asleep?"

"No." He moved too, pulling his knees up and turning on his side to present me with his back. "Never mind. It's nothing."

*Oh, dammit*. My heart crashed. Stupid boy. Was he going to ask me if there was someone else I liked?

I lay there in the dark, working up to it. My clothes were irritating, but if I took any of them off nothing would go right. When I edged a little bit closer and slid an arm over him, he stiffened again. I snuggled up close and fit my knees behind his. He was in a T-shirt, so when I breathed out it was a pocket of warmth between his bony shoulder blades.

It felt right. His hair touched mine, and I inhaled. Tucked my arm under my head. It was a little uncomfortable, with my clothes all rucked up and sweat dried on my skin and everything else going on. Still, with the rain on the roof and the way I felt warm inside instead of cold and hurting, I figured I could deal.

It wasn't the scary, fiery warmth of blushing around Christophe. This was a gentler feeling. It was like sitting just the right distance from a campfire, so it warmed you perfectly but not too much. Less hurtful.

Less intense.

I searched for words. "No, I don't *like* Christophe. I'm holding out for someone else."

All the tension went out of us both. He relaxed all at once like a cat, and I felt even warmer inside. Almost gooey.

"Someone else?" His whisper cracked in the middle and I had to smother a laugh.

*Someone who doesn't scare me the way Christophe does. Someone I can count on.* "Yeah. He's a dipshit, but I like him."

"Not that much of a dipshit if you like him that much," he muttered, but I could tell he was smiling.

I yawned hugely. Breathed out, making a spot of heat on his back. The burning in my cheeks and throat, I told myself, would fade. It was dark. He never had to know I was blushing. "No problem, Goth Boy. First one's free."

He snorted a little laugh, and I smiled again. It felt good. My heart went from a shriveled pea to something more, well, heart-size, knocking against my ribs. And I lay there listening to the rain and him breathing for a little while before I fell back into a dark well of sleep.

The flushing heat didn't go away. It followed me down into the dark. But when I woke up in the morning, it was gone.

# CHAPTER 25

The "compound" was three long double-storied log cabins built around a wide paved driveway, a huge garage set behind one of them, and a whole bunch of wulfen running around.

I found out I'd been in one of the "cub bedrooms," in the central log cabin. Sleeping arrangements in a wulfen compound are kind of odd—pretty much everyone sleeps where they get tired, and bedrooms are for when you need some privacy. When I woke up in the morning, Graves wasn't there, but he showed up as soon as I found the hall outside the bedroom door leading to a bathroom and four more bedrooms.

"I got you some clean clothes." His hair was wildly mussed, and he smelled like rain, fresh air, and cigarette smoke. His earring twinkled cheerily at me. "You probably want to get cleaned up."

I rubbed sleep-crusties out of my eyes, made a face. "I probably stink."

"Nah. You smell like you." He grinned, green eyes almost twinkling. "Bathroom's in there. Use any toothbrush, they say. There's breakfast when you're ready."

"What time is it?" There weren't any windows, but the sound of rain hadn't gone away. It tapped and slithered against the roof.

He shoved a pile of clothing into my arms. "About seven. You're up early."

"My sleep schedule's all messed up. We leaving soon?" I swallowed a yawn with the last three words, and his grin broadened. Goth Boy looked pretty bouncy, all things considered. "And is there any coffee?"

"Yes, and yes. Christophe sent me to wake you up and get you going. We're leaving in half an hour or so, soon's you're ready and the sun's really up."

I suppressed the urge to ask more questions. "Okay." I pushed hair out of my face. Curls clung to my fingers. I probably looked like the Bride of Frankenstein. "I'll hurry, then."

His hands dropped back down to his sides. He looked at me, I looked at him, and a big stupid grin spread over my face to answer his. "What?" I sounded more aggravated than I really was.

The aggravation only made him grin more broadly. Boys are like that. "Nothing." He turned on his heel, the long dark coat flaring sharply, and all but skipped away.

The bathroom was clean, and I felt squidgy about using someone else's toothbrush, but when your mouth feels like something died in it and you could probably kill a cactus with your breath at twenty paces, it puts a different shine on the sanctity of personal hygiene products. The hot water felt so good on my back I almost cried, and the interesting crop of new bruises and scrapes stung a little. They were healing up more quickly, I thought. But there were so many of them. I looked like a pinto horse.

The new clothes did fit, amazingly. Jeans, panties, two T-shirts—one blue, one gray—and a blue sweater that looked hand-knit. No socks, no bra, and my boots were filthy. But it felt so good to be in clean clothes again I hardly cared, even if the clothes had the odd feeling of being someone else's.

One of the things about dressing in layers is that you almost always have some of your own clothes to put on after a bad night. Unfortunately, mine reeked of smoke and blood and terror, not to mention dirt and sweat. I could almost see the stink lines rising off them. My bag was gone and I wondered where it was.

The question was answered when I opened the bathroom door, an armful of my stinking but neatly folded clothes clutched to my chest, and found Christophe leaning against the wall down the hall. He dangled my bag loosely from one hand and smiled at me, blue eyes glinting. "You can leave those. They're probably ruined."

His gaze dropped down, but I'd tucked the locket away under my shirts. It made me feel better to have it against my skin, even if it was doing some funky stuff lately.

"They'll be fine with some washing." *Besides, I don't have that many clothes left.* I tried not to stare at my bag. My hair was a heavy weight. I'd squeezed all the water I could out of it. "Can I have that, please?"

"Of course." He handed it over and subtracted the pile of clothes from me. "I'll put this in the car, then. You need to eat. Follow me." He set off down the hall toward a door and a set of stairs washed with pearly rainy-morning light.

At least I wasn't blushing. I tried not to think about it. It helped that he was all business. "Why aren't there any windows down here?" I asked his back, bending down to grab my boots.

He didn't even break stride. "The *nosferatu* find it harder to get in. And it means the parents and uncles and aunts can defend the little ones. Come along, Dru."

The kitchen was wide, spacious, filled with light and wulfen. It was a crowd, and I saw my first female wulfen. They moved around the kitchen in perfectly choreographed waves, and some of the boys and girls were carrying plates and platters of food out to a huge dining room with three tables that looked easily fifteen feet long apiece.

"Good morning!" A tall, slim brunette woman wearing an apron over her jeans and sweater stepped out of the bustle. Christophe had disappeared in the chaos. "You must be Dru. It's a pleasure to meet you." She seized my free hand and shook it, took in my bare feet and dirt-clomped boots with one swift look. "I'm Amelia. Welcome to our den."

"Um." The noise and activity were enough to make me blink. "Hello. Hi." Coffee. Eggs sizzling in a pan. Bacon. The good sound of pancakes hitting a hot griddle. And was that orange juice I smelled, and jalapeños? Cheddar cheese?

"Must be overwhelming. This way." She swept back a sheaf of glossy dark-brown hair and pulled me toward the dining room, gracefully avoiding the kids scrambling back and forth. "Oh, good, those fit you! I thought you were just about Danica's size. We'll have some socks around here somewhere, too, don't you worry." She halted and glanced over her shoulder. "We're glad you're here. And we're glad you brought Andy and the young ones."

"I didn't do much bringing," I managed awkwardly. My hair was dripping on the sweater, curls beginning to develop out of the mass. "I was mostly out of it. Graves was—"

"He said it was all you." Her laugh was like bells. "Thanks for bringing Andy to us, and for trusting us. We're loyal."

The way she said it, maybe anxiously, rang a wrong bell in my head. Yesterday was a collage of weird snapshots and disembodied voices, confusing if I thought about it too much. "That's what he—Andy—said. I, um, thanks for letting us sleep here. I—"

How do you tell someone, *Gee thanks for letting us crash, we're probably being chased by mad vampires and a traitor in the Order and you're pretty much risking your lives*? I couldn't figure out the words and something blundered against my knees. When I looked down, a smiling toddler in pajamas over a sagging diaper grinned up at me, her dark eyes merry and her thatch of brown hair rumpled. She grabbed my knee and shrieked.

"Bella!" Amelia scooped her up. "Good God, who's supposed to be watching her?"

"Not me." A passing wulfen girl in a wide broomstick skirt and a yellow sweater deftly took the baby. "But I'll figure something out."

"Bless you, Imogen. Come, *svetocha*, let's get you something to eat. You're not vegan, are you?"

*What?* "No." I watched as the teenager stuck the baby on her hip and plunged into the chaos of the kitchen. The noise level was incredible. "I grew up in Appalachia."

I don't know why I said that.

"Oh, really? That must be where your accent's from." She led me into the dining room proper and smartly rapped an older boy on the head. He let out a yelp. "Get your fingers out of that sugar bowl and finish your eggs! You there, stop torturing your niece. And you, go back and scrub those paws!"

It was like seeing a battlefield general make order out of chaos through sheer force of bellowing. It reminded me of Dad, in a weird way, and my eyes stung. I didn't tell her that whatever accent I had was probably from years spent below the Mason-Dixon line, hunting with Dad.

And I don't think I have an accent, for the record. Everyone up North just talks funny.

She plopped me down at a long table between Graves and Shanks, who was munching on a stack of flapjacks as tall as my hand. Shanks nodded, the blood scrubbed off him and the bruises on his face just faint shadows.

"Jesus, you look better," I blurted.

"Damn straight." He shoveled in a huge bite of syrup-drenched pancakes and Graves slid a plate in front of me.

Eggs. Crispy bacon. Three pancakes. Two wedges of buttered homemade-bread toast. A glass of orange juice, and a big pottery mug of coffee appeared too.

"Eat." Graves's shoulder bumped mine. "It's rude if you don't."

Everyone was showered, in clean clothes, and talking up a storm. It was like lunch at the Schola, only with everyone acting nice instead of the *djamphir* and wulfen growling at each other. The older wulfen ate fast, catcalling and talking back and forth, then picked up their plates and cleaned off a slice of table, taking everything to the kitchen in time for a new person to come in, sit down, and start shoveling in food. Everything ran like clockwork—even the cleanup when a whole jug of syrup got upended somehow. It was incredible to watch, and Graves kept elbowing me and telling me to eat.

I did. I was starving, and the sight of food made me suddenly aware of it. I started eating, and I didn't realize I was gulping down the food until I took a long draft of orange juice and almost choked. My cheeks were wet. Graves handed me a napkin and pointedly didn't look.

I saw Dibs, his head down and his shoulders hunched, and a few of the other boys I knew. Peter was all the way across the room, scowling while he put away a small mountain of grits. He had a fresh black eye. I wondered how he'd gotten it.

There were two more babies, both old enough to sit in high chairs. I saw the one who'd grabbed my knees as she was swiftly buckled in and started chowing down on chopped-up bits of pancake. She grinned and crowed, mashing her baby spoon onto her plate. The other two were babbling, and whoever was closest kept an eye on them and rescued their flung silverware and sippy cups.

Was this what families were like? Or was it just wulfen who ate this way? I liked it better than the Schola, but it was so *noisy*. I wiggled my toes in my boots—Amelia had given me a pair of white tube socks. It was almost pathetic, how much more human a pair of freaking *socks* made me feel. I found myself rubbing at the lump of the locket under my sweater, and made myself put my hand down in my lap like a proper-mannered girl.

I ate until I couldn't hold any more, then sat with my coffee mug and mopped at my cheeks. The tears weren't bad, just hot and embarrassing. I didn't even know why I was leaking. But it was loud and comforting and nobody paid much attention. Shanks was still putting it away at a steady rate—a huge bowl of oatmeal, a mountain of eggs, a generous handful of bacon, and a few more slices of toast.

He saw me watching and swallowed hastily, grinned. "Got to heal up," he said, when he had his mouth clear. "Going with you."

"Oh." I nodded, took a scalding gulp of coffee.

"Stupid asshole thinks he owes me," Graves called in my ear.

"Peter would've left me behind, the bastard," Shanks cheerfully yelled back. "That's why he's all the way over there. I beat him up this morning."

I believed it.

One table freed up and was cleaned with incredible speed, just in time for a group of hard-faced boy wulfen, some of them with wet hair and damp clothes, to come trooping in. All of them looked young, from their early teens to mid-twenties, but you could tell the older ones. It was something subtle—how they moved, or how their eyes were calm instead of dancing with excitement. I couldn't figure it out but I didn't want to stare. Maybe if I had a pad of paper and a pencil I could do a few sketches and find out what it was.

For the first time in two weeks my hands itched to draw, a sudden fierce need. I rubbed my right-hand fingers against the coffee mug, trying to scratch out the sensation.

"They were on watch, running through the woods," Graves yelled in my ear. "They're on vacation from the Schola downstate. Nobody there even *knows* about you."

My stomach closed itself like a fist, and Christophe appeared in the door to the kitchen. An odd almost-silence spread from the table ends nearest him, and Amelia appeared, leaning in and talking intently to him.

It was funny. Even the obviously adult wulfen looked just slightly older than the *djamphir*. Nobody here looked a day over twenty-five, except for around the eyes a bit. I hadn't realized how quickly I'd grown used to being surrounded by teenagers.

I would have wondered where the adults to handle this sort of thing were, but they were here. Just in young-looking bodies.

Christophe nodded, his blond-streaked hair falling carelessly into his eyes. Jewels of water clung to the strands and dewed his face. I dug in my bag and found the transcript, pushing my plate away. The paper crinkled.

I couldn't pull it out here. Jeez.

"Aren't you going to eat more?" Graves almost elbowed me, glanced up to see what I was looking at.

"Full," I said, but my voice wouldn't work quite right. I had to clear my throat and try again. "I'm full."

"Eat while you can." Shanks shoveled in another heaping fork-ful. "Might not get a chance later."

It was good advice, I'd heard Dad say it before. But my stomach had closed down, and I *was* full. Christophe glanced across the room, saw me, and nodded slightly. His expression didn't change. He said something else to Amelia, who pushed her hair out of her face and untied her apron.

Christophe vanished again, and Amelia started across the dining room for us, her forehead furrowed. I pushed my chair back and stood up, scooping up my boots and grabbing my bag. After a few startled seconds, Shanks and Graves did too.

I know that look on an adult's face. It means it's time to go.

# CHAPTER 26

The car was long, lean, and dark blue, older than me but in excellent shape. Dad would've liked it, and I suppressed a desire to pop the hood, because a dark slight wulfen had just slammed it shut and turned on his heel, taking in all of us with a swift glance. His mouth turned down when he saw Christophe, but he covered it well.

"This is Corey. He's our mechanic." Amelia looked proud. "Anything he touches runs like a dream."

The boy wulfen rolled his eyes. "Mom. Jeez."

"It's true," she insisted, and she looked seven different flavors of proud. She hooked an arm over his shoulders and gave him a squeeze. He wriggled away after a few seconds and blushed. You could see he was secretly pleased.

My heart hurt. I took a deep breath and shoved the feeling away.

He wiped his calloused fingers with an oil-stained rag and indicated the car with a short, graceful gesture. "'74 Dodge Dart. She's a good car. Old American heavy metal, run until the doors fall off. Just had a tune-up and an oil change, checked the lights and everything this morning. Fresh tabs, too. So everything's good."

"Very good. I can barely believe it's the same vehicle." Christophe nodded, examining the paint job like he wanted to find rust flakes in it. "We should get going. The longer we stay here, the more dangerous for you."

Amelia shrugged. "The woods are set with traps and we have warning. Other than the Broken"—her mouth firmed up and her eyes turned cold—"nothing's moved all night, and we're well prepared should they find your trail."

*The Broken?* "Ash? He's here?" My heart leapt up into my throat and I pushed down the urge to find a safe place to hide. "Where?"

"He's been following us." Shanks folded his arms. "Cagey little bastard. Slips right through every net."

"He saved my life." I hitched my bag higher up on my shoulder. "Twice, even."

"Nobody's disputing that," Christophe chimed in, darkly. "But it's best not to keep him wandering around here. Let's go, children. Keys?"

Corey tossed them over. "She accelerates well, and the brakes grab. Go easy on them."

Christophe nodded, plucking the keys out of the air and glancing at me. "Good work. Dru, you're in the front seat. You two—"

"Wait a second!" A blond streak crashed out of the rain outside the open garage door and almost plowed into Shanks, who stepped nimbly aside. It was Dibs, his backpack bouncing, shaking the water off in spatters. "Wait for me! I'm coming too!"

"No room." Christophe stalked around the front of the car.

"I'm coming." Dibs glared at him, then darted a quick little glance at me. "Tell him, Dru. I'm going with you. You need us."

"Jesus, Dibs—" Shanks didn't sound like he thought much of the notion.

Graves just looked at me. I raised an eyebrow; he shrugged and dug a pack of cigarettes out of his pocket. His coat was freshly washed, and it looked like someone had ironed it, too. Wonders never ceased.

"We're leaving." Christophe opened the driver's door. "Everyone in."

"Please, Dru." Dibs hopped from foot to foot. He looked as much like a bird as it was possible for a wulf to look. "Please."

Why the hell was he asking me? But since he was, I was going to make the call. I didn't have too many friends, and he'd sat beside me in the lunchroom. "Get in," I told him. "You guys too."

"Three wulfen in the backseat," Christophe muttered. "What are you *thinking*?"

"He's got medical training." I hitched my bag up again. *And he carried me halfway across the state. At least, I think he did.* "He's my friend."

Graves gave me an indecipherable look, and Shanks laughed. I was getting kind of tired of boys treating me like I'd lost my mind. Dibs piled into the car and scooted into the middle of the backseat, where he sat and clutched his backpack protectively.

"Let's *go*." Irritation edged each word. Christophe dropped into the driver's seat and a moment later the engine roused, purring loudly.

"Thank you very much." I sounded really prim. "For everything." *I hope the vampires don't find you.*

Amelia's grin broke out over her face like sunlight, her velvety brown eyes lighting up. Corey stepped back, his gaze running over the car like he wanted a few more hours to tinker with it.

"It is our honor," Amelia said, and it was the weirdest thing—it sounded like she really meant it. People don't often say exactly what they really mean. "Go quickly, and be safe."

I dropped into the front passenger seat. The car was a boat, and Christophe nosed it gently forward into the silver curtain of rain. I waved at Amelia, who hooked her arm over Corey's shoulders and hugged him despite his *"Awwww, Mom!"* wriggling away. Something hot and nameless boiled up in my throat. I swallowed hard twice, tasted pancakes when I burped, and dug in my bag for a piece of gum. I didn't have any, and when I looked up again we had slid smoothly between two of the buildings and were on the paved drive. The place looked deserted, all the windows dark. I wondered if it was intentional.

Christophe muttered something, the car eased through the rain, and the windshield wipers started.

"I hope they'll be okay." I had to fumble with the seat belt. Old seat belts are cranky sometimes. The defroster was on, and the whole car smelled like engine oil and the healthy dry smell of wulfen. And a thin thread of apple pies, blowing in my face when Christophe leaned forward to twist the radio knob.

"I've done what I can to confuse our trail. And to make certain none of *his* trackers survived to report in." His face settled against itself as we threaded down a long single-lane strip of paving starred with unevenly fixed potholes.

"Do you think the vampires will find them?" I twisted to look into the backseat. Dibs sat bolt-upright, blinking owlishly. Shanks had settled back and closed his eyes. Graves stared out his window, his jaw clenched.

"It's not the vampires I'm worried about," Christophe said darkly. The radio crackled. "Find me some music, Dru. We've got a long drive ahead of us."

# CHAPTER 27

**A**fter so long walking it was weird to see the road slipping smoothly away underneath the car. The windshield wipers marked off time, back and forth, and Christophe hummed along with the classic rock station I'd found. He drove the speed limit, too—not a hair over or under. Shanks was breathing softly with his eyes closed, his mouth hanging open a little; Graves stared out the window. Dibs bounced up and down every once in a while, but otherwise kept quiet.

It was, in other words, completely awkward.

Christophe also stuck to the less-traveled roads, not even glancing at a map. If it had been Dad driving, I would've been navigating him. Instead, I sat there uselessly, clutching my bag and staring at the wet world outside the window. Naked trees pressed close to the blacktop, their bare arms reaching out to clutch empty air. Water gleamed on the road, the tires made wet shushing sounds, and Christophe kept turning the radio up in tiny increments when music was on, then turning it down when advertising took over.

Lunch was in a small town on the far end of the county, a pizza place that looked like it had seen better days. All three of the boys in the backseat headed straight for the bathroom as soon as we got a table, which meant I could fish the paper out of my bag as Christophe motioned me into the red vinyl booth.

"Unless you need the facilities too, *kochana*." He ran a hand back through his hair, shaking random drops of rain out.

"I have to talk to you." I dropped down, then handed the sheets of paper over. It all came out in a rush while he looked at me, blue eyes narrowing. "Dylan gave me this, right before everything . . . well, it's important. When Anna showed me the transcript of the call, she wanted me to think you made it. And it was an edited version." I felt like I wasn't making any sense. "She wanted to find out what I knew, too. Dylan said this was the original version of the call. When someone gave my mother's location."

Christophe lowered himself down next to me in the booth and scanned the paper. His mouth turned itself upside-down, the corners pulling toward his jaw. "He gave this to you?" For a moment I thought I saw something close to his true age, eerie on his unlined face.

"When he told me to hide the next time the Restriction bell rang." It was a relief to tell someone, to get at least one secret out of my chest. "It's a good thing he did, too, or they would have caught me in my room."

"They?" His aspect slid over him, his hair sleeking down and turning darker. His fangs peeped out. He took a deep breath and they retreated. I stared at his profile, fascinated.

"Well, the bell for first classes rang. Then, a little while later, the Restriction bell. I hid in a closet and heard them running by. They had to have been *nosferatu*." The word felt strange in my mouth. Even now I was half-lying, keeping a secret.

"Were you going to class like a good girl?"

*No, I was heading for the hills. Why does that even matter?* "I was out of my room. It was like a tomb in there."

The two sheets of paper rustled a bit. His hand was shaking. "Anna." Slowly, thoughtfully. Like the word had a bad taste. He folded the papers back together and handed them to me. "Hm."

"She said you . . ." I swallowed. My throat was dry. "She said you were the one who made that call. I think she wanted me not to trust you."

Christophe stiffened. His fangs peeped out again, retreated. "I would *never*—" he began.

I hurried to cut him off. The flush threatened to rise up my neck again, and I didn't want that. "I already told you I didn't believe her. She wanted me to, and she wanted to know what I knew. If I suspected something, if I'd seen you."

The emotion submerged. It was eerie to watch, his face smoothing out and the blond streaking back into his hair. "So. Milady is meddling."

*Dylan said that too.* "I want to know what's going on."

He opened his mouth, but Dibs appeared at the booth, smoothing his damp hair down. "Can we get pepperoni?"

Christophe dug in his pocket, pulled out three twenty-dollar bills. "Get one meat pizza and one vegetarian, no onions or olives. And five drinks. Off with you."

Dibs took the money and bounded away. Christophe's hand turned into a fist, resting on the table, then relaxed with an effort. The difference between his smoothed-out face and the way he had to force his fingers out and loose was jarring. "Keep this secret. We'll talk later."

It was hard to look tough when my heart was thundering and

I was sweating. I folded my arms and stared at him, uncomfortably wedged in the booth and suddenly aware he was between me and any possible escape. "I want to know *now*."

"I don't know enough myself to tell you anything useful. There is a traitor in the Order. We know that much. Now we know that the traitor is highly placed, and that I wasn't the target. I haven't *been* the target so far, just incidental damage." He ran his tongue along his teeth, and the aspect retreated even further. His eyes were still cold. I wondered why I'd ever thought they could warm up.

"How do you know?" The edge of warmth I felt from him was the uncomfortable sterile heat of the blue-threaded flames. I shivered.

"This is a vendetta. The sins of the parents visited on the children—though your mother was blameless. You have my word on that, at least." In one quick, economical movement, he slid out of the booth. He wasn't looking at my face; he was looking at my chest. At the tiny lump under my sweater. "Put that away. Don't speak of it where others can hear. And for God's sake, Dru . . ."

I waited, but he didn't finish. Instead he stalked away to the counter, where Dibs was all but hopping with impatience and the bored woman working behind the register was punching buttons too slowly.

The aroma of crust and tomato sauce, baking cheese, and the sticky smell that always fills a pizza parlor closed around me. I slid the transcript back in my bag and found out my hands were shaking too.

*Go to the Schola*, he'd said. *You'll be safe there.*

But I wasn't safe anywhere, was I? And I didn't even know *why*. Because someone in the Order had hated my mother enough to want to kill her? And, years later, kill *me*?

Jesus. How could you hate someone that much and still be human? Or even just better than a sucker?

Graves dropped into the booth right next to me. "Hey." He'd

slicked his hair back behind his ears and his face was still dewed with rain from outside. "You okay? You look a little pale."

*Oh, I'm just fine. Not.* I reached down under the table and grabbed his hand, slipping my fingers through his. His skin was warm, and my heart took off pounding in an entirely new way.

"Everything's all wrong." I squeezed his fingers hard. "It's fucking awful."

He squeezed back. A flush crept up into his sallow cheeks. Under the Asian coloring he could really change it up. "Not everything. We're here, right? And we're safe during the day."

"Yeah." A million questions boiled up inside me. Everything from *Do you mind that I ruined your life?* to *Can you imagine hating someone so much you sell them to a sucker?*

"Hey. Whoa." His grip intensified, stopped just short of pain. "Everything's gonna be okay, Dru. It's gonna work out."

"I don't know." I stared at the fake wood of the tabletop, its plastic topping peeling up. "We haven't seen any of the *djamphir* from the school."

"Yeah, I been thinking about that." His tone dropped confidentially. A trickle of customers had started in through the swinging glass door. "Dru, if things happen . . ."

"What kind of things?"

"You know what I'm talking about. If it gets bad, Dru, I'm going with you."

My hand cramped a little. Neither of us let go. He took a deep breath and his eyes met mine squarely, the green circles around his pupils glowing even with the electric lights in here. Rain coated the front window of the pizza parlor, shadows moving like weeds underwater.

"I . . ." Words failed me.

"'Cause I've been thinking. You had your bag and you had three sweaters on. You were heading out."

*Oh Christ.* I opened my mouth. Shut it.

"See, normally I'd get upset about that. But I think you thought you were going to help me out by leaving me someplace you thought was safer for me than you. Right?"

My head fell down into a nod. I picked it back up. My mouth felt like it was hanging open.

"Don't do that." He leaned a little closer, and the rest of the world went away. "Okay? Don't leave me behind."

"They're looking to kill me," I whispered. "You don't get that. It's for real. It's—"

"What do you think I was doing at school, playing footsie?" Irritation made his matching whisper sharp. "You've got a better chance with me, Dru. Don't do something stupid again. If something happens, it's you and me against the world. Got it?"

I was saved by Dibs showing back up at the table. "You're supposed to get your own drinks." He popped a stack of red plastic cups on the table. "I think this is the only place in three states that serves Mr. Pibb. Awesome, huh?"

"Completely." Graves gave my hand another meaningful squeeze under the table, then slid out and grabbed two cups. "Whaddaya want, Dru?"

"Um. Coke. Pepsi. Whatever."

"Not diet?" Dibs wanted to know.

"Are you kidding?" Graves bumped him with a shoulder, but gently. "That shit'll kill you. Back in a flash."

\* \* \*

Dinner was fast food in another weird little town, and the light was failing when Christophe finally found a freeway he liked. "No smoking in the car," he said for the fifteenth time.

I'd kept count.

"Do you really want to see me in nicotine withdrawal?" Graves flicked the lighter, inhaled, and exhaled. His window was down and the sound of wet tires on the road melded with the hum of the engine and the back-and-forth of the windshield wipers, and the Rolling Stones singing about a beast of burden on the radio. "Tell him, Dru."

I rolled my eyes. None of them would see it, but it made me feel better. "Since when was I appointed referee? I hate to ask, Christophe, but how much longer?"

"We're almost to a safe location. Or what passes for one." He rolled his window down a little and wrinkled his nose, and I took a pull off my vanilla milkshake. "Moving after dark isn't a good idea."

"Because that's when the vampires are out," Shanks chimed in, a singsong that managed to be creepy and sarcastic all at once. "And they like to eat little *svetocha*."

"Blow me." I propped one boot on the dashboard. It wasn't like a trip with Dad. He and I could go just about forever without talking, with only my brief comments to navigate him through tangles of overpasses and surface streets.

"Don't make me stop this car." Christophe turned the radio up a little. The Stones faded and the Beach Boys started singing about California girls.

Shanks made a retching noise. "God, when are you going to play some decent music?"

"What's wrong with the Beach Boys? Brian Wilson was a genius." I tapped my foot to the beat.

"Amen," Christophe muttered, and twisted the radio dial another increment. "Now everyone shut up, I have to find this place."

"If you had a map, I could help." I wasn't liking this not-know-ing-where-we-were thing, but Christophe had refused to buy a map when we stopped at a gas station, and I had to save my cash.

I didn't know when I'd need it.

"No need." He slowed down, hit the blinker, cut left across two lanes of traffic, and zoomed us onto a side street. Horns blared be-hind us, and I almost dropped my milkshake. "We're here."

"*Goddam*mit!" I clutched at my waxed-paper cup. "What the *hell* is wrong with you?"

The boys in the back were laughing, troll-like snickers and chuck-les. We turned right, then left, and plunged under a canopy of bare branches. It looked like this street had been paved sometime back in the '50s, and the trees marching down either side were wet and black and naked under the iron-gray sky. Dark was approaching.

"Was that *really* necessary?" I popped the top back on my milk-shake—I'd crumpled the cup, dammit. "I mean, really?"

"Streets change." Christophe cut the steering wheel hard again and bumped us up into an overgrown driveway. "I actually wasn't sure until I saw that water tower. All right, kids. Everyone out, and you'll find the garage unlocked. Bobby, open it, if you please."

The boys in back scrambled out in a trice, and I reached for my door handle. The house was narrow and dark, white siding and a peaked roof. It had a glassed-in storm porch, and dead leaves covered the postage-stamp-size front yard. The street was quiet and had the air of genteel shabbiness most really old, expensive neighborhoods do. I'd bet the neighborhood association really went overboard for Christmas and probably held meetings when someone didn't rake their leaves. They must have righteous fits over this place.

"Dru." Christophe reached over and grabbed my wrist. His fingers were warm and very hard, just short of bruising. The milkshake teetered. "You stay."

A slice of darkness opened, Shanks hefting the garage door like it weighed nothing. The car nosed forward as he made little shooing movements with his free hand. He grinned, white teeth flashing.

When the engine shut off, the silence was deafening. It was a familiar silence, though, one I heard every time Dad shut off the car someplace that was supposed to be our new temporary home.

"I think it's best you ward your room tonight. Since you can." Christophe pulled the keys free of the ignition. "And sleep in your clothes."

*I was planning on that anyway.* "Yeah."

"I'll sleep at your door." He gave me a sideways glance, blue eyes firing in the gloom as Shanks pulled the garage door down. There was barely enough room to get the car doors open, and the entire cube of concrete-floored space was empty and bare. "Do you understand?"

*I wouldn't bet a penny on me understanding anything right about now.* I was tired, my entire body ached from all the excitement and sitting in a car for hours and hours, and my stomach was unhappy with the fast food. I never thought I'd be missing school food *or* having to cook my own damn meals, but there it was. "I guess so." I pulled against his hand. "Let go."

"Not until I'm sure you understand. I did not betray your mother, Dru. It . . . it just isn't possible."

Oh. Was *that* what he was talking about? "Yeah, Christophe. At this point, I'm pretty sure it wasn't you."

Graves tapped at the half-open driver's window. "Hey, Christophe. Pop the trunk, will you?"

Christophe let go of me reluctantly, and I yanked the door handle. Dibs already had the door open into something that looked like a utility room, and warm electric light flooded out when he flicked the switch.

"Smells all right." The blond wulf half-turned. "Like nobody's been here in a while, but the lights are on."

"Check every room." Christophe rose out of the car gracefully, and I wrestled my bag out and slammed my door. "Robert?"

"On it." Shanks bounded up the steps and pushed past Dibs. "Stay back, Dibby. Let the professionals work."

Dibs snorted. "Just tell me when I can pee."

I seconded that emotion, and headed for the bright opening. "When will we get to the Schola? I mean, the other Schola?"

"Tomorrow, a little after noon. I want to do it in broad daylight, and I want everyone to be able to see you. That way, you're safer." Christophe took a step forward, and the hot tension invading the air made me stop and look back over my shoulder.

Graves stood near the back of the car, hands in the pockets of his long dark coat. He wasn't looking at Christophe, though. He had his chin tilted up, and he was staring straight at me. His irises were rings of green fire, the pupils reflecting an odd gold-green tint. Like a cat's eyes at night.

Christophe's shoulders stiffened as he stepped forward, right over the barrier between "space" and "someone's personal space." Graves didn't move.

Christophe took another half-step. "You'll have to get out of the way." His tone was deceptively mild, but I've seen so many shoving matches erupt in school hallways. All the signs were there.

Graves lowered his head a little. He stared directly at the *djam-phir* for just two seconds longer than he would have if he was being polite, but just a second less than an actual challenge. "Close quarters. Hey, Dru. Wait for me."

I ducked through my bag strap, settling it across my body. "Hurry up, will you?" My voice cracked. For some reason, I didn't want to see the two of them get into the same stupid petty grandstanding I'd seen a million times.

Graves was *loup-garou*, and Christophe was *djamphir*. Werwulfen and *djamphir* pushing each other, the violence and disdain boiling just under the surface. Like jocks and nerds—no, that wasn't quite right. Like two sets of jocks, each with a reason to hate the other. And I didn't so much blame the wulfen. The way the *djamphir* treated them wasn't quite a crime, but it was close.

There was something else between these two boys, though. Something vicious and snarling just under the surface.

It probably had to do with the heat rising up in me, staining my cheeks with fire. I took a deep sharp breath.

Graves turned on his heel. His back was presented like an insult, and he skirted the rest of the car. I stood, watching. When he got to me, he reached down and grabbed my hand. His fingers were warm too, but they didn't hurt.

The sound of the trunk opening was very loud, but when I glanced back, Christophe's head was down. "Samuel. Come help."

*Samuel?* I blinked.

Dibs twitched. "Right. Sure." He hopped past us. The car dripped, its hood ticking as the engine started cooling down, and I decided I really needed to be somewhere else. Rain swept restlessly against the roof.

I pulled Graves up the two steps into the utility room. There was an ugly avocado-green washer and dryer, a big utility sink, and not much more. The kitchen past it was likewise bare, and I felt more than heard Shanks prowling the house.

"What did you do that for?" I whispered, but Graves just grinned.

Not his usual pained half-smile, and not the wide-open sunny grin I liked best on him. No, this was a wide, wolfish grimace, showing every centimeter of tooth he could dredge up.

"Just so he knows, Dru. I'm gonna go help Bobby. Stay here, right?" And he slipped through my fingers and was gone.

*Oh, for the love of—* I couldn't even finish the sentence mentally, it was so ridiculous. Dad used to time me while I swept every new house we moved into; he and I also practiced doing it as a team. Graves was getting all he-man, when a couple months ago he hadn't even known the Real World *existed.*

Yeah, things were changing all right.

I stood in the middle of a kitchen that looked like it had last seen a meal cooked back in the '70s, breathing and listening to the house creak. The windows were full of the bruised, fading light of dusk. I could hear all of them, wulfen and *djamphir* alike.

And I still felt completely alone.

* * *

*The Schola burned around me as I ran, my arms and legs too heavy. It was like running through molasses—not the clear Lucite the world turned into when the muscle inside my head flexed, but a brown-tinged tide of terror dragging at every inch of flesh.*

*They were behind me. I could hear them howling, something between a vampire's glassy, hateful cry and the screams of an enraged werwulf. They ran in lockstep, boots hitting the ground in parade cadence, and the walls cringed and burned away from the sound.*

*There were doors on either side of the hall. I blundered into them, tugging at the knobs, but they were all locked. My fingers scorched, and as I rattled each door I could hear the boys behind them scream-*

*ing. The smoke stung my eyes and filled my nose. And it was my fault they were there, because the things that were after me didn't care who they hurt.*

*It was all my fault, just like Dad. He was dead because I hadn't told him about Gran's owl, and Gran was dead because I was just a kid and couldn't save her, and Mom was dead too because—*

"Dru!" A fierce whisper.

*It was because of me, all because of me, and the growls and shrieks rose as the hallway stretched out into infinity and the jackbooted footsteps got closer. There was no turn in the corridor, and any moment they would be able to see me. The flames hissed and whispered, cackling in dirty little voices that reached inside my head and scraped the curves of my skull dry.*

"Dru! Wake up!" Someone shaking me.

I sat bolt-upright, clawing at empty air, and swallowed a scream. Graves had my shoulder, his fingers biting in as he avoided my thrashing. The mattress in here was thin and cold, set on the empty floor, but it was better than downstairs—at least the bedrooms were carpeted.

"Hey." Graves's eyes gleamed. The blinds on the window weren't tilted up or down, and thin moonlight shone through, fighting with streetlamp light. The rain had stopped. "You were dreaming."

I grabbed for him. He put his arms around me and squeezed. My heart pounded so hard it threatened to come out my throat. He'd unzipped the two sleeping bags and laid his coat over both of us, and it had been surprisingly comfortable until, I guess, I started thrashing and kicked them off. I buried my face in the hollow between his shoulder and neck and breathed him in. Cigarette smoke, whatever deodorant he used, the tang of *loup-garou.*

He held me, and it didn't seem awkward at all until he patted my back clumsily. "Dru."

"What?" My whisper cracked in half, fell down his shirt. I breathed out, back in. *Don't move. Just for a second, don't move. Let me pretend I can count on someone.*

The thought was gone as soon as it showed up; I shoved it hastily away. I was doing a lot of that lately. As a coping mechanism, it sucked.

His arms tightened around me. "There's something outside."

I tilted my head a little, trying to listen. My heart was making too much noise for me to really hear. I gulped in another deep breath and tried to calm down. "What does it sound like?"

There was a sharp creak from the door. As if someone leaning against it had shifted his weight. Christophe hadn't said a single word when Graves followed me up the stairs.

Which was probably a good thing.

"Like it's trying to be quiet. But I can hear it. Breathing, kind of." Graves shifted again, a little uncomfortably. I tried to let go of him, but he still kept holding onto me. My heartbeat started to slow down a little. I was sweating. The thin blue lines of warding in the walls glowed soft and reassuring, not sparking or running together in quick distressed lunges.

*Gran would be proud of me. That's quite a few times I've done wards without her rowan wand.* I swallowed the lump of pain in my throat. The dream lingered inside my head, screams and the burning somehow just as real as Graves's arms around me and the sound of my breathing, quick and hoarse. "Shoes."

"What?" He cocked his head.

"Get your shoes on. And give me mine." I squirmed away from him and found my boots right where I'd put them, right against the mattress. A quick double yank had my feet inside them, and I grabbed for my bag, slid the strap over my head. The gun was still inside. The clicks were very loud as I checked the clip, racked it back in, and slid the safety off.

Graves shrugged into his coat. I let out a soft breath and knee-walked over to the window. My back ached, but not as bad as it could have. Maybe I was healing.

The warm-oil feeling of the aspect smoothed down over me, and the locket pulsed reassuringly. The room got brighter. I almost glanced up to see if the light had turned on. I knew it hadn't, though.

I was just seeing better.

I made it to the wall next to the blinds, cautiously inched myself up, and decided I could peer out there. The room was dark, and nobody would see me looking out—or I hoped they wouldn't.

I peered out and realized what was wrong. There was no taste of wax oranges and danger on my tongue. Whatever was out there wasn't suckers.

So it could be something else. Or it could be, you know, all of us in a strange house and nervous.

*Be quiet, Dru.* The silent imperative nailed me in place, my eyes focused on the narrow slice of roof and tree branches I could see—then, something moved, pouring up over the edge of the roof with scary silent grace.

I let out a soft, wondering breath. The shape was long and lean, fluid with hair. A streak of white moved smoothly on its narrow head.

It was Ash.

He paused on the roof, three paws down and one up in an eerie imitation of the way a cat will stop in mid-stride when something catches its attention. The orange gleams of his eyes shuttered themselves for a moment, and his whole body slumped on three legs.

"What is it?" Graves whispered. I didn't look at him, but I could tell he knew I'd seen something. Maybe it was my face. It certainly felt funny, bones under twitching skin as I froze, peeking out between the slats of the blinds.

The hall outside the bedroom door was deathly quiet. If Christophe was moving, I couldn't hear him.

"Dru?" Graves stepped forward. A floorboard groaned under his feet.

Ash's narrow canine head jerked up and swung around. He stared right at me for what seemed like an endless moment, and the sure voice of instinct spoke inside my head. I took two steps to the side and grabbed the cord, yanking the blinds up with a sound that ripped through the sleeping quiet.

"Dru!" This time it was Christophe sweeping the door open, but I already had the window unlatched. I tugged on it, and wonder of wonders, it wasn't painted shut. It hove up with a screech just as Graves yelled and Christophe swore.

Ash tumbled through the window. He left dark prints on the roof and the sash. Blood looks black at night, and he was covered in it. The liquid length of him hit the floor with a wet thud. The same nameless certainty made me kneel down beside him. Chill night air poured through the window.

Ash made a soft canine sound when I touched his furry head. A half-growling yip that went down at the end, like he was too tired to finish it.

"Dru." Christophe, with the careful tone of an adult telling a kid not to pet the nice foaming-rabid pooch. "Dru, *malutka*, little one, move away." There was a click, and I didn't have to look at him to know he had a gun out. Maybe it was even the shotgun he'd driven Ash off with once before.

*What the hell am I doing?* But Ash had saved my life twice. It didn't feel right to let Christophe shoot him. Just like it hadn't felt right to leave Graves behind once he'd been bitten. "He's hurt."

The wulfen made another tired sound, and turned his head slightly toward me. He sighed. And the uncomfortable thought rose up in me—what if I *had* left Graves behind?

How many times had he saved me, too?

Christophe swallowed, audibly. "Dru, *moja księżniczko*, please. Move away from him."

The hair was amazingly silky where it wasn't matted with water and blood and filth. I touched the white streak and Ash made a sharp, quivering noise. "He's hurt. He saved my life the other—"

"He's dangerous, just like any Broken. And he's probably led them straight to you. Move *away*, and I will end his suffering."

I leaned forward over Ash's head. "Goddammit, Christophe, *listen* to me. We've got to help him. He saved my life, and—"

"He could have done that for any *number* of reasons—"

"So could you." I looked up. His eyes were all but glowing, winter sky. Graves had his hands up and stood to one side, staring fixedly at Christophe's profile and the shotgun. It *was* the shotgun, the same one he'd had before.

And it was pointed right at me. A thin river of prickling fear ran down my spine. The end of a gun looks very big and very black when it's staring you in the face.

"Christophe," Graves said, very quietly. A growl rattled under the words. "Put that fucking shotgun down."

"What are you going to do? Jump me?" Christophe snorted. "Shut up, dogboy, and let the adults talk. Dru, *kochana*, please. I beg you, move away from the animal and let me dispatch him." The spaces between his words got odder, and I wondered again, inconsequentially, how goddamn old he was.

"I'm not going to. We're going to help him." I stared at the shotgun's oiled barrel, its deadly snout. My teeth tingled, turning sharply sensitive. "And I think we'd better do it fast."

The thrumming growl in the room wasn't coming from Ash. A crackle of bones shifting their shape and density brushed the air like the soft sound of a bird's wings.

And the taste of wax oranges bloomed on the back of my tongue. Christophe looked up, a quick birdlike movement, and dropped the shotgun's muzzle toward the floor. "Time to go. He's led them here. God and Hell both *damn* it." He turned sharply on one heel. *"Robert! Samuel! Wake up!"*

It was amazing to hear him bellow. Even more amazing was Graves hunching his shoulders, his eyes glittering green. "Dru?" My name came out half-mangled, because his jaw was changing.

"Come over here." I tried not to sound scared half to death, crouching over a broken, bleeding werwulf. "Help me. He's pretty beat up."

Ash made a convulsive movement. Blood spattered on the floor, and a low hurt sound escaped his muzzle. His teeth looked very sharp, and very white. He sighed, and slumped bonelessly into the floor.

"Graves?" *Oh please don't lose your temper now. Please.*

"Time to *go*," Christophe snarled at the door. "Get downstairs, Dru. Now."

"We're taking him with us." I stared at Graves, willing him to help me out.

The crackling went away. He took two long strides, ending up next to me and the streak-headed werwulf. Knelt down carefully, and I could see how pale he was under his ethnic coloring. His hands shook when he reached down, getting a handful of bloody pelt.

It occurred to me then that Ash was the one who'd bitten

Graves. "Help me get him upright." I wanted to apologize, but there wasn't time.

Because the thin blue lines of warding in the wall had begun to sparkle and run together uneasily, sensing the approach of something inimical.

"Jesus Christ," Graves said, breathlessly, and pulled Ash's arm up. "Okay, Dru. Okay. All right."

*Oh, thank God.* Because I didn't know what I would have done if he hadn't backed me up.

Between the two of us, we got the wulfen heaved up. He hung like wet laundry, and he was heavy and bloody. Christophe's hair was slick and dark as the aspect folded over him, his fangs touching his lower lip and his eyes incandescent.

"If you think I'm going to—" he began.

Graves actually snarled in return, a deep thrumming noise. "Shut the fuck *up* if you're not going to help." He took an experimental step, and Ash's weight got easier to handle. "Come on, Dru."

I let out a sobbing breath of relief. We moved forward, Christophe backed up, and I heard a sharp, hateful cry rise in the distance. It scraped against the inside of my head, and it meant that the vampires had found us. And were moving in.

# CHAPTER 28

"**W**hat the hell—**"** Shanks's jaw actually dropped, and Dibs let out a high-pitched squeak that would have been funny if I hadn't been seriously out of breath from hefting an unconscious wulfen down the stairs.

"*Move!*" Christophe barked, and they both lunged into motion. They already had their sleeping bags rolled up and the rest of their stuff together. Dibs shoved everything in Shanks's arms and dug in his bag.

"How are we going to fit that in the car?" Shanks wanted to know, but he was moving. Christophe tossed him the keys. "Shit, I'm driving?"

"Hurry *up.*" Christophe turned on his heel. "Get them in the car. Put her in the back, and pick me up in the front yard." Then he was gone, a shimmer hanging in the air where he had just been. The front door opened, and the smell of early-early morning burst down the hall.

Dawn was a long way off, though.

"Come on, chickadees." Shanks headed for the garage, his arms full of gear. "Let's move out."

Ash's head lolled. I almost tipped over, getting him down the steps into the garage, but Dibs stepped forward with a small spitting sound and subtracted the weight from me. I half-fell aside, catching myself against the wall, and heard a crash upstairs that shook the whole house.

Shanks slammed the trunk. More crashes filled the upstairs. "Get *in*! Backseat, Dru. Get in with them!"

Between Dibs and Graves, they got Ash into the backseat. I piled in on the other side, Shanks slammed the driver's-side door, and the engine roused as I squirmed and yanked my own door shut. Thank God the backseat was big—if we'd been driving an import, someone would have been left behind, and that wouldn't have been pretty.

*Wait a second, how are we going to—*

Shanks dropped the car into reverse, popped the parking brake, and smashed the gas.

The garage door was flimsy plywood, and it exploded out in shivers and splinters. The tires bit gravel, Shanks cut the wheel, and we skidded to a stop in the middle of the road, a hair's breadth from plowing into a parked car. He flicked the headlights on and let out a small *whooo!* sound.

"Jesus!" Dibs yelled, digging in his medical kit. "Hold him down!"

Ash was thrashing. His head snapped back and forth in my lap, white teeth champing, and I reached down and grabbed it. Graves folded down over him in the middle, and the passenger-side front door opened.

"*Go!*" Christophe slammed the door and immediately twisted, bracing his knees against the seat. His eyes skated over me as his shoulder moved, and cold air poured into the car. He was rolling the window down.

Shanks dropped it into gear again and hit the accelerator. The car leapt forward. I shot a glance out my window and saw the house was crawling with dark shapes moving far too quickly and eerily graceful to be human. A gleam of blue-tinged flame sparked high up on the roof and blossomed like a flower.

One of the dark shapes leapt onto the lawn and bounded for the car. Everything was going too slow. Ash's teeth snapped, and Christophe had the shotgun braced against his shoulder, kneeling impossibly in the front seat.

The gun spoke once, a roar that sent Ash into more frantic convulsions. My bag, smushed against my side, dug into my ribs. If I could let go of the werwulf in my lap, I could roll down the window and fire at the things chasing us too.

"Calm down." My voice was lost in the roar of the engine. I bent over Ash's head, repeating myself, trying not to yell. "Calm down, calm down, we're trying to help—*ulp!*" The car jolted over a speed bump, the engine roared, and we slewed into a tire-smoking turn.

"Faster!" The shotgun spoke again. Christophe moved, jamming it down next to the seat and producing a very capable-looking .45 semiautomatic. It was a real cannon, and he checked the clip like an expert, too. "*Goddammit, Bobby, break the speed limit!*"

"I *am!*" Shanks yelled back, but the car took a deep breath and leapt forward again, the engine saying, *Yessir, I'm American heavy metal and we can move this thing, yes we can, just give me a second.*

"Calm *down!*" I yelled, and Ash subsided. His head was heavy, and wet with blood, and he smelled awful. The taste of rotting wax oranges inside my mouth crested, and I longed to retch or spit.

Christophe moved. The window was all the way down, and he pushed his head and shoulders outside.

"What the hell are you *doing?*" Graves's cry was all but lost under the roaring of the wind.

"*Shit!*" Shanks yelled, and I looked up. There were headlights piercing the darkness, and I was confused for a moment before the car started slewing and I realized we were on a one-way street.

In the dark.

Going the wrong way.

And Christophe calmly hooked a leg over the passenger-side headrest, sitting in the window like he'd watched one too many *Dukes of Hazzard* reruns, and started firing behind us.

# CHAPTER 29

"**The freeway! Take** the freeway!" My elbow whapped Ash's face. I leaned forward and screamed. "Right side, right side, on-ramp! ON-RAMP!"

"SHUT UP!" Shanks yanked the wheel. We hit the on-ramp doing at least seventy, and he swore with astonishing creativity. Streetlamps whizzed by. Something hit the trunk and the car fishtailed, righted itself. I choked, the taste of rotten wax oranges filling my mouth again, and wished I could spit. A spot of fierce cold bloomed on my chest, I flinched.

A tremendous weight crashed down on the back of the car. Graves, Dibs, and I all screamed, a three-part chorus of surprised terror. The glass didn't break completely, and Christophe's gun spoke again as his leg loosened almost free of the headrest. His booted foot narrowly missed my face. I threw my head back and got a confused impression of shadows, red eyes glaring down, a flicker of brazen hair and a spot of orange light with a blue center.

It was the Burner. Her hand was full of flame, and she stared down through the crazy-cracked glass, her eyes full of unholy crimson fire. She screamed, a rising crescendo of hate, and Christophe fired again.

The car zigged and the vampire's weight was thrown away. The entire back window was starred with breakage. The blue-threading flame whispered between the cracks and snuffed itself out as I let out a short puffing breath, my skin tingling with the warmth of the aspect.

Christophe's leg moved again. He slithered back down into the car, and the first thing he did was drop his gun, lean over the seat, and grab my shoulders. "Are you all right? Dru? Are you hurt?"

*What the—* "I'm fine!" I had to pitch my squeaking voice over the roaring wind from the window. Shanks wove in and out of thin traffic. Thankfully, we were going the right way—the only thing in front of us was taillights. "Are you okay?"

He nodded. The aspect receded, blond streaks sliding back through his hair as the wind kissed it. He didn't let go of my shoulders. "Slow down, Robert. That was the Burner, and she will burn no more. Not with half her head gone."

"Yeah. Okay." The wildness filling the car slackened a bit. "Jesus. Are you sure we're clear?"

"Sure enough. But don't stop for a while." Christophe gave me a thorough once-over, and his eyes dropped to the wulfen's head in my lap. Splashes of streetlight and reflected headlamp-shine bounced across his face. "You should have left him behind." His lips shaped the words; they were lost in the slipstream.

My fingers were still tangled in Ash's hair. My chin lifted a little, and my face settled against itself. I stared at Christophe, my gaze moving over his perfectly proportioned features. I could draw him, if I ever had the time and the paper. But how could I capture the way he was looking steadily at me, thoughts moving behind the cold blue of his eyes?

My heart hadn't stopped pounding yet. But, thank God, I didn't blush. I was too terrified. One thin pane of automotive glass between me and a flame-slinging sucker. Jesus.

"He's sedated," Dibs said. "I can't give him more, but that should keep him calm. Why isn't he changing back?"

"He *can't* change back, that's what Broken means." Shanks's dark eyes flicked up to the rearview mirror. It had gotten knocked askew sometime in the last scrambled fifteen minutes, and he adjusted it as the car slowed down a little more, achieving a freeway-respectable sixty instead of a wild looping seventy-plus.

"Shit, really?" Dibs actually flinched, as if he expected Ash to wake up and start making trouble. "Why—I mean, um, this is the one? The one you were talking about? The last Silverhead?"

"Yeah." I nodded, but my eyes never left Christophe's face. "This is Ash. We're going to help him. As much as we can. How far are we from the Schola?"

The *djamphir* let go of me. He studied me for another few moments, then slid down in his seat and rolled his window up. The sudden almost-silence was deafening. "Not long now. Keep heading south. We should hit the expressway in an hour or so."

"I don't suppose we'll be stopping for coffee." Shanks yawned, but he was still glancing in the rearview every now and again. Looking at me? Or at Ash, slumped across everyone's lap in the backseat? At Graves, who had straightened and now stared ahead, a muscle in his jaw ticking? Or at Dibs, who was startlingly pale as he dug in his medical bag?

Or maybe just staring at the back window, where the print of a vampire's fist still reverberated in the cracked glass right over my head, bits of it melting together as if a blowtorch had kissed it. What would have happened if that hand had broken through?

I didn't want to think about it.

"I don't know if we can, with him in the car." Christophe let out a chill little laugh. "Just keep moving until the sun's up. One problem at a time."

It was good advice. I looked down. Ash had stopped bleeding. The rips and gouges in his flesh were starting to close up. It's eerie to see a wulfen heal; you get the feeling that if you look away the skin will twitch and the damage unreel itself like in a bad movie.

Silence and uneasy half-light filled the car. I let out a sharp, long breath. My shoulders ached. I stared at the back of Christophe's head. He ran his fingers back through blond-streaked hair, the highlights falling into place. How did he look so perfect all the time? It was goddamn unnatural.

But then, so was I, right?

I peeled my left hand away from Ash's blood-clotted fur and reached over. Graves grabbed my fingers, and when he squeezed, a scalding jolt of relief went straight up my arm and exploded in my heart. "We're almost there," I said to the lean hairy face in my lap, to the silence, to Graves, and to my own heart, palpitating inside my rib cage like a squirrel on a wheel. "Everything will be all right."

Nobody else said anything. I suppose I should have been grateful, but instead I just felt shaky and unsteady, like I might start crying. My tough-girl face was gone for good.

\* \* \*

The city painted the sky above it with orange, rapidly turning to gray as the sun came up. Christophe handed two coffees and the herbal tea back; Graves passed Dibs his tea. I took a Styrofoam cup of coffee and tried not to look at Christophe. My hair was a wild mess, and I felt greasy all over. Being jammed up against the door with a werwulf's heavy head in my lap also made my back really unhappy. I was bruised and aching all over.

"Less than a mile," Christophe said, and dug in the bag. "Egg McMuffin, Dru?"

"Ugh." But my stomach protested. I had to eat *something*. "Yeah, I guess. What are we going to do when we get there?"

"You'll have questions to answer. So will other people"—he started doling out packets of wrapped grease—"since they won't know you exist until you show up at their front door. With a Broken, two wulfen, and a *loup-garou*." He even sounded cheerful. "It will be interesting, that's for sure."

Graves handed me an Egg McMuffin and two searing-hot hash browns. His eyebrows had drawn together. "Wait a second. What are you going to be doing while—"

"I don't want to give them another chance to kill me." Christophe gave him another handful of fast food. "And I have other business."

"So you're sending us in somewhere, again, where you know there's a traitor." Graves kept passing food to Dibs. "Nice."

"This is where I thought you were going in the first place." Christophe's tone was deceptively mild. "You two were whisked away to a back-country reform school satellite instead of the one place I could be reasonably sure you were safe. This time I'm going to make sure you get in the front door, and make such a commotion Dru's presence and survival cannot be hidden. Others on the Council and the Schola will begin to ask questions, especially once you're debriefed." He paused. "I don't know quite what they'll make of the Broken, though."

*The Broken. Not even Ash.* And the way he said it was chill and disdainful.

"I'm betting once he cycles through the sedation, he'll start throwing himself at any wall in his way to get back to Sergej." Christophe sighed. "It will be a mercy if he dies."

I took a huge bite of overprocessed English muffin, sausage that had no relationship to meat, and greasy egg. Said nothing.

"You're not going to stick around to sponsor her?" Shanks accepted a McMuffin and tore through the wrapping with his teeth, spat it aside, and kept one hand on the wheel. Traffic was clumping up, since it was morning. "I mean, that's a one-way ticket to—"

"She'll probably insist on you being kept as her guard. There might be a few others eager for the honor." Christophe shrugged, juggled a hash brown from hand to hand. "If Dylan survived, he's probably gotten a report in somehow."

I swallowed hastily. "He said his contacts weren't responding. Like Augustine. He said Augie's disappeared."

"Don't fear for August. He's canny." Christophe set the crackling paper bag aside. The whole car smelled like salt, blood, fast food, and unwashed teenage bodies. Not to mention sick werwulf. Ash twitched as Shanks slammed on the brakes and hit the horn.

"*Moron!*" he yelled. "*Stay in your own goddamn lane!*"

"City driving." Christophe didn't even sound fazed. "In any case, Dru, my concern is getting you in the Schola's doors. Not worrying for Augustine. Six more blocks and a right, Robert."

"I got it." A light turned green ahead. Shanks eased the car forward. I kept eating, barely tasting the food. My hands trembled, and I didn't think it was from hunger.

Traffic parted like waves. The gray, smoky clouds were shredding, and I saw flashes of blue sky. Sunshine meant we were safe. At least from the vampires.

My mother's locket hid under my sweater. It was comfortingly warm, skin-warm. Like normal metal.

"You know who it was." My voice surprised me. "In the transcript. Christophe, you know."

He shook his head. Took a crunching bite of hash brown. His teeth were as white as Ash's. White as Graves's wide smile now, too. "I *suspect*, Dru. I don't know." A long pause, as another block rolled by. "But I'll find out. And then, God help whoever is playing this game."

*It's not a game. This is my life we're talking about.* I took a scalding gulp of coffee. It didn't help. The same nameless instinct that had made me refuse to leave without Ash told me Christophe knew more than he was telling. Though you didn't have to be a genius to figure that out. He *always* knew more than he was telling. "What are you going to do?"

"I've told you. Do you remember? I have a reason now. Turn here, Bobby."

"I know." The car wallowed to the right.

The engine sounded a little unhappy, and I didn't blame it. "Christophe—" My cheeks were on fire again. Why was I blushing like a . . . like a *girl*, for God's sake?

"Hush, Dru. Two blocks up on the left. Do you see it?"

"I see it." Shanks slowed down. "I take it you don't want a chauffeur?"

The *djamphir* laughed. "Why start now? Take care of her, boys."

Graves glanced at me.

"Wait a second." I had my hands full of breakfast and Ash was stirring in my lap, little gleams showing under his eyelids. "Don't tell me you're going to—"

Too late. The car almost stopped, Christophe's door opened, and by the time I got half my protest out it had slammed. He darted between two parked cars and vanished down an alley between two brownstones.

"I can't *believe* this." But I could. It was pretty much the way everything was going now.

"Don't worry." Shanks actually stuffed the rest of his muffin in his mouth and chewed two or three times, then gulped. "Shit, he took my coffee. Anyway, Dru, we're home free."

"Yeah." Graves gave me an eloquent sidelong look, just as Shanks sped up a little. The two blocks slid underneath the car's tired tires, and just as he turned left through a half-open wrought-iron gate, sunlight burst down the street, dipping everything in gold. "Home free. Until someone else tries to kill us."

"Great." I almost dropped the McMuffin on Ash's face. Then I began chewing. Whatever happened next, I'd probably need a full stomach to handle it.

A wet black driveway unreeled, trees arching on either side. The tips of their fingering branches held delicate green buds. When we came out of the double line of greenery, sunshine splashed across a huge white stone building. The lawns were immaculate. There were a pair of concrete lions standing guard at the end of the driveway, too, and I thought I saw one of them twitch. But it could have been just the blinding, fresh morning light.

It looked familiar, but I realized the other Schola had been a smaller, grayer copy of this place. It had seemed really grand and imposing, but this was the Real Deal. I swallowed sudden dryness, doused with a last gulp of overcooked coffee. I dropped the cup near my feet and hoped my numb legs would hold me up when we finally got out of the car.

"Thank God," Shanks said, softly. "We're safe."

I looked down at my lap. Ash's eyes had shut again, the gleam under the lids gone now. "I hope so." I finished the last bit of my muffin. Dibs sighed, a sound of pure relief.

Shanks pulled up to the steps leading to the front door. He cut the engine, and I sensed that people inside the big pile of white stone were aware of our arrival. Any moment now the door would open, and we'd have questions to answer and things to do and . . .

The huge, iron-bound double door at the top of the gleaming white stairs was already opening, revealing a slice of darkness inside for just a moment before slim teenage forms boiled out. They were all boys, and all *djamphir*.

Which ones were enemies?

"I sure as hell hope so," I repeated, and reached for the door handle.

*finis*